A PROMISE FOR ALL TIME

For All Time, Book 1

by
Paula Quinn

ARE YOU SIGNED UP FOR DRAGONBLADE'S BLOG?

You'll get the latest news and information on exclusive giveaways, exclusive excerpts, coming releases, sales, free books, cover reveals and more.

Check out our complete list of authors, too!

No spam, no junk. That's a promise!

Sign Up Here

www.dragonbladepublishing.com

Dearest Reader;

Thank you for your support of a small press. At Dragonblade Publishing, we strive to bring you the highest quality Historical Romance from some of the best authors in the business. Without your support, there is no 'us', so we sincerely hope you adore these stories and find some new favorite authors along the way.

Happy Reading!

CEO, Dragonblade Publishing

Additional Dragonblade books by Author Paula Quinn

PROLOGUE

Ashmore Castle
Dorchester
Dorset, England 1641

L ADY CATHERINE ASHMORE, Duchess of Dorset, cried out in
her seventh hour of labor, a long time considering it was her
seventh child. It would be another son. Tessa Blagden, the
Ashmore's longtime family nurse, knew it would be. She was
there to end the babe's life and destroy the power of the weapon
the boy, if he lived, would use to kill thousands of people. This
child's lifeblood was all that could cleanse and destroy the nine-
inch ruby dagger hidden somewhere in the duchess's chambers.
Tessa had to drive it into the babe's heart before being discovered. Only when the babe was dead, would everything be set
right, the evil wrought by the dagger rescinded, and its dark
creator destroyed. For Tessa, it was all more personal. If she
succeeded, she would be reunited with her family.

After another four hours, everyone in the birthing room
knew something was wrong. The midwives, experienced as they
were, could do nothing against the curse that was this child. His
mother would suffer for delivering him. But she wasn't innocent.
Indeed, she was an unholy priestess of the demon Raxxix. She
performed ritual sacrifices at night without her husband's
knowledge. To see the duke's gain—which would benefit her, she
used the ruby dagger to slaughter six families, all in a failed

attempt to find a prophesied child who had been destined to kill the babe about to arrive in the world. As payment for her temporary power, the duchess had given up the body of her seventh son, not dead, but given to Raxxix as a vessel of evil to wield the full power of the ruby dagger against hundreds of thousands in his wars.

Tessa prepared more poison tonic for the duchess while she cried out in labor and fed it to her. But the older nurse felt no pity for her mistress. For this was the wretched woman who'd intended to kill a seventh family, or more specifically, Tessa's beloved daughter and granddaughter, the prophesied child. Tessa had learned about the pact between the duchess and the demon eight years ago, and more importantly, she'd learned about the ruby dagger. Like the rest of the women in her family, Tessa was gifted with special powers of the psychic and corporeal. In her case, it was clairvoyance and future time-travel. Her sister Elizabeth could also communicate with animals, a handy gift when a feathered friend could perch outside a window and listen to the duchess's plan to kill Tessa's granddaughter when she was found. Tessa had taken measures to make certain her grand-daughter was never found by taking her and the child's mother to the future.

And now that Tessa had removed the prophesied child able to kill the seventh son, the task fell to her. She only had one chance while the babe was weak for she wasn't the one born to do it. Later she wouldn't be strong enough to kill a man with a dagger that was crafted to obey him, not destroy him.

With another great push and a guttural scream, as if she were using her last breath to tear the babe from her body, Catherine Ashmore bore down and cast him out. Exhausted, she refused to look at him but ordered that he be taken away. "Everyone, get out!" Lady Ashmore commanded. "Bring me clean clothes and my beautician!"

The babe was quickly wrapped and handed over to Tessa, his trusted nurse. While everyone else fled, Tessa, with the babe in her arms, strode to an ash wardrobe and flung open the door. From her bed, Catherine Ashmore struggled to sit up, to breathe.

"Priestess," Tessa said, finding an onyx box. She opened it, and wrapped her hand around the ruby dagger, pulling it from its place. "You'll be dead before you draw ten more breaths." She held up the dagger. "You thought yourself clever? I saw you when you hid it."

Catherine Ashmore's eyes grew black with fury while she struggled to cry out, but her breathless cries were drowned out by her son's crying. "You thought to kill my granddaughter. Now I will kill your son." She watched the babe's mother spit up blood, the poison tonic finally taking its effect, and then stop moving. Without a trace of guilt and with babe in hand, she laid him on the bed and closed her eyes. Could she do it?

She heard someone enter the chambers. She snatched up the baby in her arms, and hurried to see who it was, hoping to persuade them tell them to leave the duchess to rest. When she saw the babe's father, Lord Edmund, she bit her lip and smiled.

"You have another son, my lord," Tessa told him softly when he reached out for him. She watched him coo and kiss his son's tiny face.

"He's more than just another son, Tessa," the duke told her with the hint of a smile very few ever saw. "He's my newest son, Josiah. Important in his own right."

His father had no idea what his son would become if he wasn't stopped. Better he never be told.

"How is my wife?"

"She's resting," Tessa told him calmly. "She wishes to be alone. This was a difficult birth for her." She reached out to take the babe with a pleasant smile. "I must see to him, my lord." She waited for him to leave, eager for this gruesome business to be over.

She returned to the bedroom and set the babe down again. She told herself she wouldn't look at him. She thought of his name. Josiah—*God supports.* Surely his mother hadn't chosen his name. He made a little sound and against her better judgment, Tessa looked down.

He was beautiful with a pale complexion and particularly crimson lips. A spray of black hair and inky lashes stood out in contrast against his skin, casting shadows on his already plump cheeks. Did he...did he smile at her in his slumber? No. She couldn't let him sway her. She had to do it.

She unwrapped him and stared at his tiny, bare chest.

With shaky hands, she held up the dagger and closed her eyes. She had to remember that it was this babe's life or her granddaughter's, including all the others he would be responsible for killing. She tried to steady her hands. Already she could feel the blade's pull to the one for whom it was created. She brought the scarlet dagger down. A strong, unearthly force stopped it before the tip of the blade entered the babe's body. Tessa expected the resistance. If her goal was to kill the boy, evil would try to protect him until he did Raxxix's will.

She pushed. The blade descended. Tessa closed her eyes, not wanting to see. She felt a terrible pressure on her back and looked over her shoulder. The duke stood behind her, his long blade disappearing into her back and breaking through her belly. She stared down in stunned disbelief, then fell to her knees, the ruby dagger slipping from her fingers—dripping with blood that was not her own, and then disappeared with her.

CHAPTER ONE

Manhattan, NY
2022

"**M**Y ALLERGIES ARE all about to kick in." Mercy Blagden fanned away dust motes and traces of cobwebs before her face and was thankful, at least, for the daylight streaming in through the cracks of the boarded up windows. Still, she needed the light from her phone to help her see her way around the abandoned orphanage in Bloomingburg, New York, where she had grown up.

For a moment Mercy let the memories of her childhood in this place wash over her. They were neither good, nor bad memories. They simply were. Just like her. In the columned light she could see Sister Joseph Ann sitting in a chair reading from a book to the twelve children who lived there. Smells that were no longer real filled Mercy's nostrils: fresh bread, old books, Sister Dominique's special mac and cheese, the scent of fresh roses coming from Sister Tess's habit when she returned from one of her visits to her family in England. Mercy could hear the sound of children's laughter running around the spacious old Victorian house as if they were there now.

"I wish I had known some of them better," she told the echoes around her. She didn't imagine anyone could hear her. She was alone, after all. She wasn't daft. "What do the doctors know about me?" she asked. "Nothing is right."

She wasn't sure sometimes if she was speaking to herself or someone who wasn't there, but should be. Like a twin who tragically died at birth, someone she should be sharing her life with. It was a habit that had made her life very difficult since she was four. But, as she had told countless therapists over the years, she'd rather talk to herself than to anyone else.

She remembered herself going up these same stairs to her room to be alone. She didn't like most of the other children. They teased her about the ugly scar marring her face from her temple to under her lower lip, given to her by the thief who had broken into their NYC apartment when she was three and killed her mother and stabbed Mercy in her big-girl bed. Later, she became quiet and secretive around others, untrusting and detached. She became her own best friend, pointing things out out loud, audibly answering questions she'd asked herself in her mind, even giggling on a few occasions as if she heard jokes privy to her ears alone. Her "personality disorder" kept her from getting adopted.

Sister Tess seemed to take a special interest in Mercy's well-being. When she wasn't off visiting other orphanages, she was extra kind to Mercy, giving her extra helpings of food—though Mercy didn't eat it most of the time, and chocolate—when it was forbidden except for one's birthday. When Mercy was twelve, Sister Tess mentioned that she had changed from being an extraverted toddler, even after she lost her mother and was stabbed, to a child who barely spoke and rarely smiled when she was around others. The doctors all blamed the trauma of violence for her disorder. But even though she didn't know about what happened to Mercy in the attic, Sister Tess believed something else had caused the change in her.

Mercy believed it too. Her light had all but died a year *after* the trauma of getting stabbed in the face. Oddly, her first memory was from the age of four, when, after going to the attic alone and discovering a dusty chest of drawers, she'd reached into the third drawer and was bitten hard enough to make her bleed. She'd never investigated what had put a little hole in her. She had never told anyone, and she'd never gone back up to the attic.

Now, twenty years later, she found herself climbing the stairs to that same place, to the same chest of drawers still intact and covered in cobwebs. She was drawn to the third drawer the same way she'd been drawn to it long ago.

She knew that she'd changed when she was four. Why? She'd spent years in therapy trying to figure it out. Did it have to do with a bug? What had drawn her back here?

Cautiously, she opened the drawer and shined her light inside. There was a pile of folded white fabric, silk maybe. "No dead bug." Slowly, she pinched a bit of the silk and gave it a soft shake. Something slipped out.

In the light of her phone, Mercy saw a red shard of glass. Upon closer inspection, she realized it was a jagged dagger. This must be what had cut her finger. How long had it been here, hidden away, untouched for years but for a curious four-year-old finger? The dagger looked ritualistic. She giggled at her mad thought that it had stolen her soul, then stopped smiling when something moved along its surface. "Is that blood? How creepy is this?" She took it closer to a window and held it up to the sunlight. There were facets of crimson and fire that made her blood want to answer some forbidden call. She saw it again. A shadow stained upon the ruby moved, as if it was still made of liquid, from the tip down to the blade. It dripped down onto her fingers as they held the dagger, and seeped into her skin. Mercy let out a little gasp and then her eyes rolled into the back of her head as darkness took her as she sank to the floor. The once silent attic sat empty yet again, but this time it wasn't just its newest occupant that had disappeared, but so had the illustrious dagger that had long called this place its home.

Dorchester, England
1661

MERCY FELT SOMETHING hit her in the shoulder hard enough to make her cry out.

"Get to your feet and explain what you're doing in my barn!" an unfamiliar male voice demanded.

Beneath her face, the scratchy hay made her itch. Behind her chickens clucked and a pig squealed. Wait. Wait.

"Am I dreaming?" she wondered but then quickly dismissed it as she didn't usually feel her heart pounding against her ribs, ready to erupt from her chest. She felt something in her hand. The ruby dagger. She tucked it into her back pocket and pulled her T-shirt down over it. When the owner of the barn tried to kick her again, Mercy slapped his boot away. She'd been bullied in school. She wasn't about to be bullied by some old farmer. "Where am I?" she said out loud. "How did I end up in a barn?" She pushed her hair over the left side of her face, then looked up at the middle aged man and asked him.

"Are we close to the abandoned orphanage?"

Instead of answering her, the oaf pulled her to her feet by the arm. When he set eyes on her T-shirt, shorts and bare legs, he nearly choked on his own breath.

"What happened to your clothes?"

"I'm wearing them," she told him in a scolding voice. He was one of those old fashioned grandpa types.

His gaze was just as offended when it met hers. "Stay here," he commanded. Before she could reply, he turned in his dusty boots and left the barn.

She stared after him, at the door. What should she do? Leave! Leave now! She hurried forward. The door opened and the farmer appeared and stared down at her. "Put these on. I have guests. I won't have you shame me by having them think I would hire someone like you. You better not be a wretched Blagden or I'll skin you alive myself." He shoved a pile of scratchy clothes at her and left her alone again.

"What the heck is wrong with that guy?" She stared at the door again. "Have I been abducted by some serial killer?" Her co-worker, Sandy, had warned her not to go to the abandoned orphanage alone. How much trouble was she in? She looked toward the window. It was beginning to get dark. This was Upstate NY, not the city. There'd be no lights soon except from the stars.

"I have to get out of here and find my car. Breathe, Mercy. Breathe," she told herself as she pulled open the door. Her mind couldn't comprehend that she'd woken up in a barn. She'd been in the attic and the dagger...she felt for it and almost cut her fingers again. "Why isn't there a hilt on this thing?" She stepped out and looked around, hoping to see the orphanage from here so she'd know where she was. She saw nothing but small thatched roofed houses with smoke from their chimneys drifting toward the clouds.

Mercy rubbed her eyes. "What is this? What's going on?" To her left, upon a grassy hill, was a castle straight out of history books. Her stomach flipped and made her feel sick. "Where am I? I need to wake up. How can this be real?" But it looked so real. It felt so real.

Someone grabbed her by the shoulder. "Who are you talking to? Who's hiding?"

Mercy dropped the rough pile of clothes he'd given her and turned to see the farmer who'd kicked her. She slapped his hand away and bolted. His hand shot out and he grabbed her by the hair.

"You must be a Blagden by the way you're trying to escape."

"Let me go! You're hurting me!" she cried out, unable to turn around and glare at him. The dagger in her pocket began to vibrate softly.

"Samuel, do as the lady says," commanded another male voice to her right. His voice was deep and smooth, less gravelly than Samuel's.

"Lord Winterborne!" Samuel sounded surprised to see whoever it was. "My lord, she may be a Blagden. I found her in my
barn, dressed—."

"Let me go!" From over her shoulder Mercy tried to swat his
hand away.

"Let her go," the voice commanded again. "Bring her to the
castle. My father will speak to her."

"Yes, my lord." Samuel released her and gave who Mercy
could now see when she turned to look—a bow.

What? Mercy stared wide-eyed at the horse. "It smells so
real." Like leather and a stable. "Who rides horses up here in
north New York?" she muttered in a low voice. The sun was
going down behind Lord Winterborne when Mercy looked up at
him. He wore a hooded mantle, casting too many shadows over
his face to see it.

He leaned down in his saddle to speak to her. "Do I offend
your nostrils?"

"Yes," she told him truthfully. "Well, it's more your horse
than you."

Beside her Samuel gasped so loudly, Mercy turned to him,
hoping he wasn't about to keel over.

When he remained upright, she returned her attention to the
man on the horse. "He seems like a decent guy," she spoke softly
to herself.

"It depends on the day," he informed her playfully.

When she realized she'd spoken out loud, she said a short
oath, then blushed, thankful he couldn't see it.

"I'm lost," she explained, hoping to change the topic. "Is this
Bloomingburg? Sullivan County," she added when he shook his
head.

"Sullivan County?" The rider repeated, his honeyed voice
falling over her.

"Upstate New York?" she tried, feeling as if her legs were
about to give out. Where was she? What was happening?

"*New* York?"

That was when it occurred to her that this "Lord" and Samuel spoke with British accents. Mercy swayed on her feet and lifted her hand to her head, and before she could take her next breath, the rider leaped from his horse and appeared standing before her. He reached out to her. Mercy closed her eyes and prayed not to pass out in this place, with nothing but two men and a horse between her and civilization. Her head spun but she gritted her teeth and opened her eyes to focus on something else.

His eyes, staring down at her from under his hood, were the color of a storm. His lips, the color of rose petals as they widened into a smile. She couldn't see much else. Of that, she was thankful. What good was a gorgeous man if he was missing his marbles? "Forgive me." His voice fell over her like a favored blanket on a cold, winter night. "I haven't heard of the places you mentioned."

He hadn't heard of them. "How is that possible?"

"Josiah! Come on!" another rider called out angrily. "Father's going to blame the rest of us for being late!"

Mercy looked toward a second shadowy rider as he raced away on his horse; three more riders followed him toward the castle.

Josiah. She had to be dreaming, and if she was, why would she dream of a guy named Josiah? She turned her gaze to him again just as he began to turn to leave. She watched him mount his horse in a single leap. It was a huge stallion and the man—Josiah—didn't even need a stepstool to get on. He raced away calling something to the riders in front of him that was snatched away by the wind. But Mercy was sure she heard his laughter in the breeze.

Right away Samuel grasped her by the arm and pulled her along toward the castle.

"Listen," she told the farmer. "I get that I was trespassing on your property but you can't seriously be this hateful and angry."

"What's your name, girl? What are you doing here?" he asked her angrily.

"Mercy...Smith," she said when she couldn't think of any other names. She was too nervous. She expected him to chide her for choosing such a common name that it was obvious she was lying, but he said nothing for a moment.

"So, you're the daughter of a smith."

"Ooookay."

He yanked her forward and led her up the hill.

She needed to find out what was going on. Had she stumbled upon some weirdo cult?

"What happened to your face," Samuel suddenly asked her. "How did you get such a gruesome scar?"

Mercy frowned at the ground. People always wanted to know. "I don't remember. It happened when I was three." No one knew what really happened, according to the sisters of Angel Lane.

A few minutes later, when Mercy walked into the outer bailey of what Samuel called Ashmore Castle, she thought that if it was a cult, it was an obsession for the middle ages. The men, in the standing torchlight, wore leather and chainmail, which clinked when they walked, and sheathed swords at their sides. It was too real. Her mind denied what her eyes took in. The civilian men walked to and fro and wore short doublets with blousy shirts, lacey cuffs, and full-cut pantaloons and heels. Some wore cravats tied with a red bow. The women dressed in silk jackets, with tightly laced, stayed bodices beneath, showing plenty of cleavage, and full, petticoat skirts. Mercy fanned herself, feeling hot just looking at them. Everyone around her gave her the same interest. The men stopped what they were doing to stare at her bare legs. Women gaped and shook their heads with disapproval. She looked away. So, even here—wherever here was—she was an outcast.

"I've never been inside a castle before," she mumbled. Not one with a high, undamaged roof and solid walls covered in colorful tapestries. This place was impressive. These people took their playtime to the past seriously. Candles burned everywhere in wall sconces and on stands, lighting rooms and corridors in golden hues. There was nothing electrical, no plumbing pipes that Mercy could see when she passed the huge kitchen.

There had to be an explanation. She'd probably been drugged by something on the dagger and then stumbled here to this…this cult. "I'll spend the night outside if I have to and wait until a plane goes by. I'll prove to myself that I haven't been hurled into the past." She might even go to the authorities when this was over about these people threatening to kill any Blagdens. If she lived through it, that is.

She was handed over to a soldier who smelled of leather and sweat. Mercy covered her mouth when she gagged, and then tried to speak.

"Um, Josiah said his father would see me."

The soldier stopped and yanked her back, closer to him. "Wench, who told you you could speak so casually of the Earl of Winterborne?"

"I—he—" how was she supposed to speak of him? "I didn't know he was an earl."

He looked at her the way she probably appeared to Josiah when he didn't recognize New York.

"Have you been drinking? He's the duke's son and you will address him as Lord Winterborne. Do you understand?"

She nodded but she wondered how far these people would go with this made-up world. Were they some super fans of Cos-play or something?

He pulled her down a stone staircase that led to a dimly lit cavern. She heard groaning from somewhere and her blood went cold. "Is…is this a dungeon?" she asked the ruffian in a trembling voice.

"Yes," the soldier answered. He opened a creaking iron cage door and shoved her inside. "You're a possible Blagden. You'll speak to the duke when he calls for you." He slammed the door shut and left Mercy on the cold, dark floor.

She had no one in her life who would even know she was

gone. No one would worry about her. She felt the burning pit in her belly and tried to stop it as it boiled up to her throat, her eyes. If she knew there was someone who would miss her, it would have been her only comfort. But she didn't have it. Sister Tess was the only one of the nuns who'd tried to keep in touch after the orphanage closed down, but after a little while, even she drifted away and out of Mercy's life.

She sat down, leaned her back against the wall, and hugged her knees to her chest. She bit down on her lip, causing it to bleed. "I won't fall apart. I've been through tough times before. I'll get through this."

When she was given a bowl of some kind of brown mush to eat, or not to eat, she knew her death was not just a threat. These lunatics might actually kill her if they found out she was a Blagden!

As the first night passed, Mercy couldn't accept what seemed to be the truth, that she was someone's prisoner in a castle in Upstate NY—or not. There was no way of getting out yet, so she filled the hours with thoughts of escaping and having these people arrested. By the second day, when the smell of the dungeon felt as if it was a part of her, and two other prisoners were taken out and brought back with the flesh on their backs torn from a whip, she had less trouble believing that she woke in a nightmare. It was just beginning, she thought, when she was finally brought before the duke of Dorset, Lord Edmund Ashmore and six of his seven sons, each one bigger and more threatening than the other. In their presence, she learned that it was a Blagden who'd poisoned the duke's wife and attempted to kill his youngest son with a ruby dagger on the day of his birth twenty years ago.

A ruby dagger? Like the one she'd shoved into her back pocket? Mercy was thankful for the two soldiers clasping her under her arms and holding her up, or she was certain she would have crumpled to the floor. What was this about? How much trouble was she in? She couldn't tell anyone how she got here. A Blagden with a ruby dagger? They'd kill her first and question her later. She had to hide the dagger and then worry about getting home.

"What were you doing in Samuel Gunn's barn?"

The duke of Dorset was an imposing man, though his height didn't surpass six feet. His hair was dark, sprinkled with gray beneath his curled periwig. His shoes were polished black leather and his mantle swirled like raven wings around him when he strode into the receiving hall.

Mercy's nose itched. She tried to reach for it to scratch but her arms were being held. Were they going to kill her? She could feel their eyes on her, on her scar. She should be used to it by now, but their stares felt like daggers. "I woke up there, my...my lord." Sure. She'd speak their language while she was a prisoner here. Why antagonize them to kill her? "I...I'm lost and I—"

"How do I know you're not a Blagden?"

The duke's guests who'd come to gape at her all nodded their heads and whispered to the spectator next to them.

Mercy closed her eyes and bit her lip. How was she supposed to prove it? Why did she have to? "Look, I'm sorry a Blagden harmed your family. Truly I am, but I wasn't the one who did it. I don't have my I.D. so I can't prove my name—"

"What is your I.D.?" the duke's sixth son, Lord Nicholas asked.

Mercy bit her lip harder until a droplet of blood flowed from it. "Okay. I really think this has gone far enough. It's not amusing. You had me put into a dungeon. Have you even spent the night there? There are rats! Real rats!"

When the duke rose out of his chair like Poseidon parting the waters and glared at her, Mercy closed her mouth and looked down.

"Bring her back to the dungeon until I decide what to do with her."

What? What? Mercy struggled in the guards' hands. Back to the dungeon? No! She wanted to go home. She'd never complain about her life again. Oh, what was this place? "Mister—my lord, please. I'm begging you. Let me go. I'm not here to hurt anyone. I'm lost, that's all."

He stared at her for a minute and she prayed that he'd show her mercy. "Where are your clothes?"

She looked down at herself while her head spun. "I...I don't remember. I think someone took them."

"You don't remember?" asked one of the duke's sons. He'd been introduced as Lord Dorchester, the duke's first son. "Where do you come from? Fordington?"

"I'm not sure," she told him, continuing to bite her lip. "Do you happen to know where Bloomingburg is?"

Everyone in attendance agreed that they hadn't heard of such a place. "Edward," Lord Dorchester called out to his younger brother, find Bloomingburg."

Yes. Mercy began to smile as a little relief filled her. But really, what was there to be relieved about? They were still all insane.

"Who are your parents?" the duke asked her.

"My mother died when I was three. My father died while my mother carried me."

The duke gave her a long sigh. "Brothers? Uncles? Anyone? What are their names?"

"There's no one, my lord," she admitted quietly. *No one,* she echoed silently. "Hadn't I chosen it to be that way?" she said softly but audibly.

"What?" the duke eyed her from head to toe. "Why? Did your family disregard you because of that unsightly scar?"

Mercy's heart thumped against her ribs. Even the insane were no different. Everyone hated *unsightly.* She mustered up the last ounces of strength she possessed. "Would you disregard your child because he wasn't perfect?"

Instead of answering her question, he called out. "Has anyone checked on Josiah? Has his fever broken?"

"Yes, Father," came the voice of the last of the duke's sons. "I'm here."

He was introduced as the earl of Winterborne as he stepped

forward in the receiving hall, turning every head, bringing almost every lady's hand to her heart as he swept his guileless, jaunty, if not somewhat weak, smile over the crowd. It was the hooded rider from the first night. Josiah. Now, his face and form were clearly visible. He was over six feet tall. His skin was pale, as were his lips. He wore no wig compared to the other men she'd seen so far. His soft, inky black waves brushed against his neck and tendrils fell over his pewter-colored eyes. Instead of the voluminous ruffles on collars, sleeves, pants, anywhere one could put ruffles, he wore a white shirt with ruffled cuffs, but no cravat. His collar was open, giving him a rakish appearance. Despite his practiced greetings, he didn't appear well. When his gaze settled on Mercy, he took a long, slow breath, as if he'd been waiting to inhale for a long time. Seeing him, Mercy knew somehow that nothing in her life would ever be the same.

"Father," he said, coming toward her. She arched her back when he stood over her. What was he doing so close to her, not staring at her scar, but at the drop of blood on her lip from where she'd bitten it? She was too surprised to stop him when he lifted his finger to the droplet and watched it seep into his skin the same way the blood stain had seeped into her back at the orphanage. His gaze settled on hers again and his lips grew more crimson as they widened into a guileless invitation that, for a moment, made her forget where she was. Before her eyes, his health appeared to return to him. "Since I found her," he told his father without taking his smile from her, "can I have her?"

Mercy blinked. And then she laughed in his face. "Who does this guy think he is?" she asked no one in particular. "Excuse me. I'm not available just because you want me."

"Why not?" he asked, unperturbed by her claim. "Do you belong to someone else?"

She shook her head and scoffed. She couldn't believe this guy. "I don't belong to anyone."

His smile deepened. Was he mocking her?

"What year are you people pretending this to be?" she asked

him and anyone else who would answer.

That question earned her some pitiful looks. They thought she was the crazy one.

"The year is 1661," Josiah Ashmore, Earl of Winterborne leaned in and let her know.

Her brain didn't want to hear that, so it felt as if she couldn't keep her eyes off his lips. He had a slight overbite beneath a top lip that flipped upward and made it appear even fuller. His bottom lip was only a little less plump. They were the epitome of lusciousness, the goal of almost everyone she knew. But there were no injections in 1661. They were becoming more red, almost crimson, before her eyes, as if they'd been stained by wine.

She breathed—almost gasped back to reality. Sixteen hundred and sixty-one. Sure. Someone had lost their mind. Mercy didn't know if it was her or everyone else. She was hungry. She was exhausted and frightened. She was close to inner defeat. "I've been fighting the world for a long time," she said to herself under her breath, staring at the ground. "I...I need to go home."

"I'll bring you home," the duke's son told her. "Tell me where it is."

"I don't know," she admitted as a tear escaped the corner of her eye and dripped down her face. She looked up at him. "I can't do this."

His warm smile washed over her, comforting her like a tender caress. "Yes, you can. I'll help you."

He looked up. His tender gaze exchanged for one harder, though no one appeared afraid of him. "Why hasn't anyone brought something to cover her? And prepare a place at my table in the dining hall for her to eat."

The servants happily rushed to do his bidding and brought her skirts and an array of short coats.

"Don't send her back to the dungeon," she heard Josiah tell his father. "If there is anything she hasn't told you, she'll tell me."

Now wait a minute. Mercy tried to step forward but the

servants were told to dress her, and dress her they did, not letting her move. Thankfully, they didn't touch her shorts or T-shirt to remove them. No one saw the dagger. Once they tied layers of petticoats and heavy pale blue skirts around her waist, a good slap on the rump wouldn't reveal the dagger. The royal blue quilted velvet coat they put her into made her sweat. Almost immediately she realized there wasn't an air conditioner. She had to be wearing five pounds of clothes.

"What are you going to do with her?" his father asked. "Why do you want her?"

"Because she makes me stronger," the duke's son told him earnestly. "And because she's alone—and no one should be alone."

"Ah," his father laughed. "You want another adoring female to flutter around you."

Mercy didn't miss the way Josiah looked away from her as if ashamed of what she was hearing.

"And this one makes you feel stronger to prove your stamina, eh?"

"Father," his son looked up at him again, his smile, loving and forgiving, "Please don't deny me."

"Take her then." The duke waved his hand. "Be responsible for her. If she's not a Blagden, send her on her way."

But his son shook his head. "No. I don't want to send her away unless she wants to go."

Well, Mercy thought, at least he wasn't intending on keeping her here by force. But was she sure of that? After all, they *had* dressed her up to look like them. She'd get out of this get-up later, if she didn't pass out from the heat first. She was thankful for all the fluff concealing the dagger.

"Fine. Fine," the duke gave in, rising to his feet. "She's your responsibility."

And just like that she became someone's property? Mercy set her darkest glare at Josiah Ashmore. Umm. No.

"See that she doesn't make any trouble," the duke continued.

She couldn't believe how easily this young man was manipulating his father, and in front of his other sons, his soldiers, the other lords and ladies in the great hall, and the servants. The duke didn't seem to care what anyone thought. Mercy could tell by the warm resignation in his eyes that he wouldn't refuse his youngest. He loved this son, the one who, according to them, was raised without a mother, perhaps earning a special place in the duke's heart.

But she didn't have any special places for anyone in her heart. His charming wiles wouldn't work on her.

"It's Josiah who's the troublemaker!" one of his brothers laughed. "Look at the mischief he's already planning in his eyes!"

"Yes," said another brother, "remember just a few nights ago when he brought thirteen pigs into the castle and set them loose?"

"Jeremy, I didn't set them loose purposely," Josiah defended without raising his voice. "I told you they escaped me. I was trying to save them from Samuel's ax."

"Son," his father said, coming close, "Our table is full because of Samuel's ax."

Josiah leaned into his father and lowered his voice. But Mercy heard him. "Father, did you see their eyes? They were afraid—"

"Josiah," his father said and breathed out a heavy sigh. "Don't let any more animals out of their pens. Do you understand?"

Josiah didn't answer, though it looked as if he wanted to.

Madly, Mercy felt the urge to smile at him.

His father gave in yet again, and left the receiving hall. Two of his brothers drew him in under their arms and tossed him around a little, making him laugh while mussing his hair. Finally, Jeremy, the duke's third son, if Mercy remembered the order correctly, squeezed his face and gave him a kiss on his cheek, leaving him be before they too left.

Without the presence of his family, the Earl of Winterborne turned his attention back to her. Should she thank him for keeping her out of the dungeon, or kick him in the shins for treating her like a stray dog he thought he now owned.

"Please come with me to the dining hall and eat," he said and didn't wait for her to follow him as he left.

Eat? It had to be better food than what they fed the prisoners in the dungeon. She gave up easily and hurried after him, almost tripping over the hems of her skirts twice. How did anyone get around in these kinds of clothes? With a wipe of her brow and scooping up fistfuls of lace, she reached the doors of the dining hall behind him and stepped inside. It was huge but had a warmer atmosphere than where she just left. "It's probably the tapestries," she remarked, looking around.

Her gaze wandered to his and she caught him nod.

"Art makes a place warmer," he agreed softly.

"Hmm?"

He shook his head and smiled.

The grandeur around her pulled her attention away from him for a moment. There wasn't just one table but three long tables, each topped with food. Mercy's stomach rumbled. She rubbed it and gave him a sheepish look.

She wanted to leave when he offered her a seat. She wanted to go home, where she knew it was safe, not sit here and eat with some seriously good-looking screwball. But she knew she wouldn't get far if she was starving. So she sat with a sigh. Without looking at him, she sensed his smile. How did it comfort her and make her anxious at the same time? Her heart thumped. Was it because of him or the ruby dagger sticking out of her back pocket under her skirts?

Her mouth watered from the bowl set before her, and she forgot everything else but her hunger. Including the earl sitting next to her. She picked up a spoon and dipped it into the stew before her. She didn't care how it tasted. The carrots were tender, the meat, gamey, but good, and there was plenty of bread.

She tried to keep her mind on eating and the food but the more she satisfied her hunger, the more her thoughts returned to the duke of Dorset's youngest son. She cut her glance to him just as he turned to her with full cheeks and crumbs around his lips.

She felt her stomach flip—it had to be from all the food she was putting into her mouth. But when he grinned seeing her cheeks just as full, her heart palpitated and she felt a bit lightheaded. Her condition had nothing to do with eating. She covered her smile with her hand and turned away from him.

After two bowls, she swiped her serviette across her lips and stood up. "Thank you for the food," she said, feeling like a stray dog with a voice.

Now what? She thought with a shiver. *Which way is home? How long before I'm starving again? I'm a Blagden with the ruby dagger.* "I can't stay here," she whispered the last out loud.

"Where would you like to go?" he asked her and his soft, sorcerer's baritone went through her like fine whiskey. She was sleepy. She wanted to sleep.

She cleared her throat and pushed her hair closer over her scar to cover it, then pulled at her doublet. She needed air. "I don't know."

His smile didn't falter as he took her hand and led her out of the castle.

CHAPTER TWO

THE INSTANT THEY stepped outside the woman pulled her hand back, breaking their contact. Josiah stopped and looked at her. She was gnawing at her lip again; it seemed to be a nervous habit of hers. When she did, the hint of a dimple appeared in her milky white cheek and snatched his full attention. She reminded Josiah of a bird caught in a cage. One wrong move and her thrashing heart would burst. He'd be careful not to frighten her too much. She was the one whose blood could heal him. He'd been feverish when he tried to paint this morning. He nearly fell faint on his way to his father in the receiving hall. He'd heard her voice and seen the blood on her mouth and he knew she was the woman his dream had told him about. The instant her blood touched his skin, his fever left. All traces of his illness vanished. He was still in awe of it but more than that, he was afraid. If she and her healing blood were real, then so was the ruby dagger. She'd been in contact with it. Did she have it now? If the prophecy was correct, he should feel its presence. But he felt nothing but captivated by Mercy Smith's pretty face and amused by her saucy spirit and cool glare when it came to whether or not she was now his.

He knew about the plot to kill him the night of his birth. But surely this young woman had nothing to do with it. He wouldn't hurt her, and he wouldn't let anyone else do so either.

"We need to get something straight," she said, stopping him.

Josiah swallowed and met her gaze. It was no better. How was he supposed to pay attention to anything but her large blue-green eyes? They were like vast, tumultuous oceans that tempted him closer to peer into their deepest fathoms and discover everything about her.

"I don't belong to you," she continued, folding her arms across her chest, like a shield. He did his best to keep his breath steady while her dulcet, husky voice swept through him. Most of the girls in the castle would fight for the chance to be alone with him, but this girl wasn't impressed by him. It was rather refreshing. "I'm not a sad, helpless little animal that you need to rescue," she continued.

He couldn't help but smile. She was exactly that.

"Why are you smiling?" she asked, sounding frustrated and angry.

"I'm told I do it often."

There was no trace of joy in those big, beautiful eyes of hers. Something terrible had happened to her. He wondered if she would tell him of it.

"You do. What do you have to be so happy about? Wait." she said, holding up her palms. "Don't tell me. The less I know about you and this place, the better." She stomped her foot and sucked her teeth. The green parts in her eyes grew more verdant as they filled with tears. "Why am I not waking up?"

There was fear in her voice, in her eyes. Her hand trembled when she brought it to her head. He'd heard her tell his father that she couldn't remember where she came from. Waking up here from wherever she came and not remembering anything was likely very difficult for her. She didn't want to be here. He understood. She'd been sleeping in a dungeon. He was sorry about that. When he'd spoken to her at Samuel's farm and told her to speak to his father, he thought it would be right away. But then he'd grown ill with a high fever and his father had stayed by his bedside for the first few days, so she'd been held in the dungeon. His heart went out to her for having to sleep in the cold filth.

"Am I the terrible thing that happened to you?"

She turned to stare at him, her soft cheek hidden behind her dark hair. "What are you talking about?"

"Good day, Lord Winterborne!" Josiah turned to see one of Ashmore Village's inhabitants trudging down the hill on his way home, dragging a wagon full of skeins of fabric behind him. "Good day, Harry," he called back happily. "How's your lovely wife, Margaret?"

"She's visiting her sister in Breadwink. Come by when she returns home in a sennight and she'll make you supper."

Josiah lit up. No one cooked like Margaret Lawrence. "I'd like fish stew!"

Harry laughed. "Yes, I know, young lord. Perhaps," he said, growing a bit more serious and curious, "the lady would care to come?"

Josiah turned his bright smile on her. She lowered her face and stared at the ground.

"Good food makes everything a little better." He leaned down so she could see him smiling at her, then returned his attention to Harry. "Let someone from the castle know when your dear wife returns home."

"Margaret will be pleased," Harry told him, looking quite pleased himself.

"Wait until you taste her fish stew," Josiah told Mercy, rubbing his belly and closing his eyes.

"My lord."

He opened his eyes and turned them on Captain Alexander Sherwood, one of his father's most skilled soldiers, approaching. He'd been following them since they left the castle. Josiah waved at him, and then at the other five soldiers, all sent by his father, trying to remain unseen in corners and behind wagons. Josiah didn't mind how protective his father was. Since he could remember it had always been this way. He was the favored, pampered son. Everyone knew it. No one dared to question it.

His father had almost lost him to someone who was willing to murder a babe and his mother for the sake of a prophecy.

"Yes, Captain?"

"You can't just go off to folks' homes and eat supper with them. We've had this discussion hundreds of times."

Josiah stared at him. "Why not?"

The captain had stopped looking frustrated with him a few years ago, after finally concluding that no matter who asked him, Josiah would do as he wished. He still tried. "It's not safe."

"You will all be there with me." Josiah motioned to the five other guards. "And I'm not helpless, you know." His gaze slid to Mercy. She looked up, pretending interest in the sky. Josiah smiled. "I promised Harry I'd come," he said when the captain opened his mouth to warn him again.

"Very well." The captain relented with a sigh then stepped back on the road and moved behind a cart piled high with turnips.

"Excuse me." Her voice made Josiah return his attention to her. "I don't mean to sound ungrateful," she went on, lowering her voice. She took a deep breath—and then four more. "You don't understand what's happened. I've lost everything I know. My entire life disappeared in the blink of an eye. I'm very lost, okay?"

Oh no! Were those tears welling up in her eyes? He pouted and produced a little groan. "Don't cry, Mercy. I'll help you find your way back."

She shook her head. "You don't understand. I'm afraid."

Her eyes were doorways to a million secrets. It must be difficult for one to carry such burdens.

"Whatever it is, I'll protect you—"

"Why? You don't even know me."

"Because you're mine.

The tears in her eyes died up almost instantly, for which he was thankful. But now her eyes widened and darkened on him. "What?"

"You heard my father. He gave you to me, remember?"

She choked out a laugh. "And I told you I don't belong to anyone, *remember*? Goodness," she practically growled at him. "*Now* I believe we're in 1661."

When she spun on her heel and stormed off, he chuckled, looking after her, then hurried to catch up.

"It's a good thing to be mine, you know."

She threw him a mocking smile. "Your shamelessness knows no bounds."

"Being mine means you have privileges others don't enjoy," he continued unfazed by her accusation. "It means I can keep you close to me whenever I want."

"No, thank you," she told him and kept walking. "I'm not an object anyone can own."

"A prize, then?"

She set her hard glare on him again. "No."

He paused his steps. "What do I consider you then?"

"How about a human being?" She didn't stop and kept up her pace.

He smiled behind her.

"Are you thinking of leaving Ashmore?"

She nodded.

"Come with me," he offered, not wanting to lose the one who could not only heal him, but who possibly knew where the dagger was. "I'll bring you beyond the gate and show you what it's like without my protection. I don't know where you came from, but here, you're far too beautiful to be traveling alone."

She looked like she was going to say something but then stopped as her cheeks grew flush. He'd made other girls blush before, but none of them had ever affected him the way this one did. His belly felt as if it had gone up in flames. His heart fluttered and skipped when he thought he saw the hint of her smile. Who was she and why did he want to emblazon her face and every nuance of her features in his mind, never to forget? Why did looking at her, being near her, make him feel as if he could breathe again?

"This isn't right," she resisted. "I shouldn't be going any-where with you. I don't even know you."

"I'm Josiah Ashmore, youngest son of—"

"I know that part already. It doesn't tell me anything about you. If you're a killer, or—

"Do I look like a killer?" He grinned to stop himself from laughing at what she said.

"Your looks don't matter," she argued. "Look at Ted Bun-dy—"

"Who?"

She stopped and drew out a sigh. "He was an infamous serial killer from my time."

"And this Ted Bundy, he was handsome?"

"Yes—"

"Then...you think me handsome?"

"What?" She stiffened in front of him, her eyes opened even wider. "No, no, I didn't say that."

His smile faded into a pout and he lowered his head.

"I mean, yes, you're handsome, but that wasn't what I—you—" She seemed flustered when his smile returned from the darkness and shone brightly on his face. "I...I was saying you could be a killer. And even if you're not, I'd rather continue on by myself." She smiled slightly at herself, exposing not one, but two dimples and nodded, as if finding her courage and letting it lead her. "Thanks for your help. Have a good life."

He bowed, then laughed softly, watching her when she turned to leave. He liked her courage, even if it was a little foolish. It was as if she truly didn't know the dangers awaiting a woman traveling alone beyond the gates. He followed behind her as she walked through the village. Though she didn't turn to him, she had to know he was there since everyone stopped to call their greeting to him.

When she came to the Great Gate, Josiah gave the silent order to the gate guards to open up and let her out. Then he hurried out after her as the gate guards shouted for him to return.

His father didn't permit him to go beyond the gates, but that never stopped him.

At first, Josiah stayed back, watching her scan her surroundings. She looked worried, tempting him to move closer to her. He called out, stopping her when she was about to walk through poison bushes that would make her skin blister and itch for a fortnight. He stayed close behind when she entered Dorchester Forest, southwest of the castle. He hurried forward and pushed her out of the way of a charging boar.

Pinning her between a tree and his body, he watched Captain Sherwood's arrow sink into the animal with a thunk. He closed his eyes and breathed.

"My lord," Captain Sherwood's voice pulled Josiah's attention to him.

"I'm alright," Josiah answered quietly, then looked into Mercy's eyes. "Are you hurt?"

When she shook her head, he stepped away from her and set his gaze to where the boar had fallen. "Please go and make sure it's not suffering."

"My lord, you shouldn't be out here. Let's return."

"Captain, please see to the boar."

"Yes, my lord." The captain bowed his head and then took off.

Mercy pulled herself away from the tree trunk, turned around it, and left.

Josiah didn't hesitate but picked up his steps behind her. Stubborn bird. He thought, then found his smile softening on her. When she heard an animal scurry by her to their right, she turned and looked so relieved to see him, he silently pledged his protection to her right then and there.

"It sounds like a hare," he called out.

She nodded, but took a step toward him nonetheless. He smiled at her and waited until she reached him.

"You don't have to walk behind me," she suggested, trying to conceal her fear behind a stoic expression. "We can walk together and talk a little."

"Very well," he agreed, actually quite pleased to speak with her and get to know her more. Besides her clothes, there was something different about her that had nothing to do with her blood. It was not only her odd dialect, but in her mannerisms. She was bolder than most girls he knew, a bit less refined. And at the same time, she was meek and unschooled in the coy, disingenuous wiles of court ladies. He wanted to smile when he looked at her, not something well-practiced but more authentic. He wanted to keep her close, not just for her blood or the knowledge of the ruby dagger, but because she sparked a light in his withering heart.

"How many guards are following you?"

He closed one eye and counted. "Six. My father is a bit overprotective of me."

"You must be very precious to him."

He turned a grateful smile on her, liking the way she saw it. "Can you remember anything about your home? Anything I might be able to place?"

She started walking again, this time beside him. "I can remember some things. But there's nothing you would be able to place."

His smile turned more playful. "Let's see. Name a few things. What can you remember?"

"Cars. Planes." She looked up at the sky between the canopy of trees and searched the heavens for something. "Skyscrapers, the Empire State Building."

"The Empire State?" he echoed. So, wherever she came from the people there considered it the empire state.

"It's just a nickname for New York," she said as if that explained it all. "Yankee Stadium?"

He shook his head and she cast him a doubtful smile—which, in turn, made his smile grow warm.

"Who has never heard of Yankee Stadium? The Yankees? Baseball?"

He laughed and pointed his finger at his chest. "Judging by your reaction to those things, I am missing much—and you're beginning to remember more."

She let out a little sigh. "The truth is, I haven't forgotten. But how does one admit to a bunch of crazy people that she's just as bonkers, more so because she believes she traveled back in time?"

His laughter had faded into a softer smile. She was telling him she came from the future. This was the second time she spoke of the year and her disbelief that they were living in the seventeenth century. He was certain no one would believe her and it made him feel compassion for her. He would believe her. "When did you travel from?"

He happily noted the trace of a smile curling her pink lips. "2022," she told him, then kept walking.

He was careful not to smile or even look stunned at her claim. He already knew there were things in this life that couldn't be explained—like witches with magic daggers sent to kill cursed babies.

"The word car feels familiar to me," he told her, thinking about it. "I can almost hear it in my head. *Will my car make the trip?*"

She smiled and nodded her head. "I've often thought that."

She'd often thought that? How was it possible that he had heard her thoughts before he knew her? Why did he feel like he missed her—missed her all his life? As if she was always supposed to be there but wasn't. He didn't dwell on it, only that everything about her felt familiar and right.

"What else did you say?" he asked. "Planes? What are those?"

She gave him a look like she didn't believe he didn't know what they were. "Okay, let's say we really are in 1661. You won't believe me if I explain those things to you."

"You're quick to discount my faith in you."

"Why should you have faith in me?" she asked, looking up at him while she walked.

"Faith has to start somewhere."

She smiled, showing off her pretty dimples. "You make everything sound so simple."

"Why shouldn't it be? Why does everything have to be complicated? Having faith in another person is a choice. Until you deceive me, I'll trust you."

She stared at him for a moment and then shook her head and looked away again "All right, well, I'm not deceiving you, even though it's going to sound like it. First, I'll tell you about cars."

When she was done, he knew she was either mad, or he was for believing her tales of the twenty-first century and *electricity* and *toilet bowls*. He was quiet, except for the rumbling of his hungry belly.

"You see?" she said softly. "I told you. You have nothing to say. You don't believe me."

"I'm thinking about how pleasing it would be to have a cell phone."

When she smiled and then laughed a little, Josiah knew he would miss the sight of her by tonight.

"Who would you call?" she asked him.

"Everyone!' he told her exuberantly. "I'd bid everyone a good day. And of course, I'd call you."

"When would you have time to talk to me after you bid everyone you know a good day?"

He thought about it for only a moment. "I'd call you first."

They laughed.

He remembered to breathe when she looked away, still smiling. But it was gone too fast, vanquished by thoughts of something else. He didn't ignore the fact that what she told his father was untrue. She remembered everything. After hearing it, Josiah was glad she hadn't tried to explain it to the duke, or she would have ended up back in the dungeon.

It made him a little uneasy. Not because the tale was so outlandish, but because it made him wonder what else she told him that was untrue.

"We've been walking for a long time and there's still nothing.

Are there cities here?"

He stopped, and after she took a few more steps, she stopped too.

"You don't really believe you've traveled back, do you?" he asked her.

"Do you?" she demanded, looking on the verge of hysteria.

"Your descriptions make it very convincing." He smiled, hoping to set her at ease. "Whether I believe you or not, you're walking on the edge of both worlds. This place and time can't be both."

"I could be in 2022, in a coma, living this in my mind."

He blinked at her. He didn't like the sound of that. She could convince herself that it was true, and that he wasn't real. Was he real? He grasped himself and ran his hands up his arms. He was real.

He heard the sound of her laughter, like the tinkle of light bells, and looked up to find her mirth aimed at him. He smiled, realizing how he must have looked feeling himself like a fool.

"I'm real, Mercy." He held out his hand as an offering to her.

She looked at it and sobered. "Why is your hand blue?" Her smile turned into concern and she snatched up his other hand. "This one's yellow—is that paint?"

"Yes," he answered. "Well, they're stains. I was painting this morning."

"You're a painter?" she asked. Her voice seemed softer than before. "What do you paint?"

"Portraits, mostly. Whatever moves me."

She looked as if she might smile at him again, but then turned away. "How can you be real?"

He didn't withdraw his hand. "Trust me."

She looked around at the vast, sheep-dotted hills and then at him, as if weighing her options: stay in his protection or go on alone. What would she choose? Everyone else was easy to read. They would have chosen survival, but he didn't know what Mercy would choose. No matter, he was patient, and finally, she reached for him.

When she fit her dainty hand into his, his heart flipped in his chest. He cast her a meaningful smile. She responded by tilting her head so that half her face was hidden from him. Was she trying to hide her scar? She'd covered her face in the receiving hall as well.

She was clearly uncomfortable with herself, so he walked on her right side. "Thank you for trusting me not to be a killer," he said, moving in closer to her. He could hear her short breaths while he stood over her. Someday soon, he'd like to kiss her. "We should get back."

Her breath stopped. She stepped back and straightened her spine. "Are you going to get into trouble?"

He nodded his head, laughing a little. I seem to always get into trouble." He pointed the way they had come. "Return to the castle with me. Please." What if she refused? She couldn't live on her own. He couldn't keep her forcibly. He wouldn't. But what about the next time he fell ill and she was gone—or dead, killed by a thief or any of the dozens of dangers outside the wall? Either way, if she left, one of them would likely die. Did he care more because he could die, or because she could?

He breathed a sigh of relief when she nodded. He knew she had nowhere to go.

"Do you remember how you ended up here?" he asked her as they headed back.

"I was holding a—" she closed her mouth and coughed into her hand. "I was in the orphanage where I grew up and then...I...fainted or something. I really don't remember that part."

He offered her a tender smile and started back toward the castle. "You likely fainted from being hungry. Since we're fed, let's go feed some friends."

He led her back through the gates and finally into the Ashmore Castle's kitchen.

After shining his most radiant smile on the helpless cooks, he waited with Mercy while enough food to feed a small army was packed into baskets and sent off with three male servants who were to follow wherever Josiah—and the duke's six guards led.

He led them all to the village down the hill, where she had first appeared in Samuel's barn. Children raced toward him, calling his name. Women looked up from their washing, or preparing food, and with wide smiles hurried toward him. Even the men of the village called out his name, putting down the tools of their labor and moving toward him, as well.

Josiah was as happy to see them as they were him. But really, they were about to feast with him, so they were likely to be more happy.

He introduced everyone to Mercy, and scowled at Samuel when the cranky farmer huffed at her. Soon though, his good mood was restored and he laughed with everyone when they sat on blankets in the grass and passed the food around.

"Where are you from?" Old Philip the tanner asked her, spooning up his stew from his bowl.

Josiah gave her time to answer on her own, and then, realizing she was having difficulty being the center of attention, answered for her. "She doesn't remember. I'm going to help her find her way home."

Everyone cast her a pitying look, which compelled her to cover her face with her hair.

"What happened to your face?" little Miss Anne Harwood, six year old daughter of Amelia and Roger, the butcher, asked.

Amelia scolded her daughter, but Mercy stopped her. "It's all right. But...it's...a bit, um, gruesome. In truth, I don't even remember it."

Anne studied her for another moment and then smiled at her, as did Josiah, but his smile was pained. He'd seen enough scars living in a castle with soldiers to recognize that she'd been cut with a knife. She said she'd been a baby. His blood ran cold when he thought of whoever stabbed a babe in the face.

They remained with the villagers for the rest of the afternoon eating—which Josiah did, unashamed to stuff his cheeks like a chipmunk again, much to the delight of the children. They played, that is, Josiah and the children played. The mothers laughed while the duke's son chased their children around trees and through the tall grass. Mercy chose to watch instead of join the merriment. Josiah didn't force her, but every once in a while, he slowed to take a breath and to look her way. Later, on the way back to the castle, he walked beside her.

"You're a good guy, Josiah," she told him.

He dipped his chin to his chest and smiled at her. "Thank you." He didn't tell her how much it meant to hear it.

CHAPTER THREE

I T WAS THE first night in a bed since Mercy had arrived here, the first night she was going to bed with a full belly. She wiped a tear falling to her pillow. Thanks to Josiah, the villagers would also go to bed tonight on a full belly. They had food, but according to Lillith Crane, there was never enough when it came to feeding little ones. Thanks to Lord Winterborne, he always made sure they were fed well.

The more Mercy thought of him the more she believed this whole thing was a dream. No man alive was that perfect. His sultry gray eyes, easy smiles, and a whipcord tight body she'd stolen a glimpse of while he rolled around in the grass with the children were enough to make her smile just thinking about them. And it wasn't the first time today that he made her smile either. He'd done what others found extremely difficult for her entire life to do. He beckoned tiny butterflies inside her body to find a way out of her and go to him. Her heart fluttered when he was chasing six screaming children around the trees, patient while they tugged at him and his hair while he ate and listened to their stories at first, and then their gripes. He also ate less than everyone else, and even had his own protector, Captain Sherwood and his men, join them in their feast.

She found out that the beloved son of the duke sent the village monthly stocks of grain and seeds and everything else they needed to live.

He was younger than her. "It's only by four years," she said out loud to herself. "He was born and stabbed with the ruby dagger, and across the chasm of time, three days after my fourth birthday, I was pierced in the finger with the same dagger. It's incredible, really." Was it the same dagger? She had a gnawing feeling that it was. She shook her head. Oh, it was too bizarre. Did it mean something? If so, what? But was it more bizarre than her traveling back in time? Why had she been brought here...to him?

She ran her hands down her face and sat up. "I'm never going to get any sleep tonight." She thought about the ruby dagger tucked under her feather mattress. The dagger was the key to everything. But how? "Why had a Blagden tried to kill Josiah with it?" And how did it end up in a chest of drawers in the attic of an orphanage she, a Blagden, happened to live in centuries later?

Even more extraordinary was he hadn't once asked her about her scar. It was as if he didn't see it, didn't care about it. She laughed at herself. "Everyone cares about it. He must be hiding something." But so far, as far as she knew, she was the one doing all the lying. She didn't know him. "What if I tell him I'm a Blagden and he turns me over to his father?" Or if she admitted having the weapon that was used to attempt to assassinate him? No matter what he claimed, he wouldn't trust her once he found out the truth. She hated lying to him but she had to. She was a Blagden with *the* ruby dagger. "You can't lose him right now. If he doesn't protect you, who will? No one."

She'd keep the dagger a secret. She believed she needed it to get home, but she had no idea what to do with it. She'd been carrying it around all day and other than it causing her mental anxiety, she hadn't disappeared into any other eras. Now that it was hidden under her mattress she was afraid to take it out again. If anyone saw it...she was sure the ruby dagger was hated as much as the Blagdens were. Besides, what harm would spending one more night do? It wasn't like anyone was waiting for her or worried about her at home. She didn't belong here and she didn't want to stay, but she wouldn't mind seeing Josiah Ashmore again.

She sighed and flung her legs over the side of the bed. She wondered what time it was and how far the kitchen was from her room.

Helena Ashmore, wife of the *firstborn son*—a title Helena preferred over Earl of Dorchester, or her husband's given name of Thomas—had given her a saffron silk nightdress that was thankfully fashioned with many layers against the drafty castle.

"I wonder where Lord Winterborne's rooms are?" she whispered to herself as she headed for her chamber door. When she swung open her door, she saw him asleep in a chair propped against the opposite wall. At the sound of her creaky door, his eyes shot open and he tried to sit up and almost fell over.

Mercy rushed to help him. He let her take his arm though he caught himself and didn't need her help.

"Do you feel that?" he stopped moving suddenly and asked her, staring at the door to her room. "That vibrating? It feels as if it's in my blood."

She felt for anything, then cast him a closer look. "Are you still asleep?"

"Hmm?" He blinked and seemed to clear his head.

"Why are you sleeping by my door?" she asked him.

"I'm protecting you. Castles can be dangerous places," he said, almost sounding serious about protecting her. But he couldn't be when he'd just nearly fallen out of his chair. That he'd fallen asleep in. Her smirk was meant to mock him, but she felt herself go warm while he stared into her eyes.

She didn't tell him that no one in her life had ever promised to protect her. She'd grown up taking care of herself, and she'd made it to twenty-four before she was sucked up in a time-warp and spit out in the seventeenth century. But now, here in his time, she appreciated his protection. She swallowed and released his arm.

But just an instant later, her gaze returned to him and caught him rubbing his eyes and smiling at her nightdress.

"You look like a sunflower."

She gave in and chuckled behind her hair. "Is that a compliment?"

"Of course, sunflowers are beautiful."

Once again, he put her at ease. But no matter how comfortable he made her feel, she didn't know how to feel much else.

"Do you speak this way to all the girls?"

"You're the only girl I see," he said without bothering to look around.

He had a silver tongue for certain and a very soothing British accent. Did he want something from her? He didn't know she had the dagger, and why would he want it anyway—just to prove her guilty of being there for nefarious reasons? She remembered what he'd told his father in the great hall. He'd guaranteed that whatever she wouldn't tell his father, she'd tell him.

"Are you looking for the garderobe?" he asked her, as she began to walk down the corridor.

She shivered. She'd visited one earlier and decided she'd rather go in the woods. How long could she hold off? "I was looking for the kitchen but now that I think of it, the more I eat, the more I'll have to—" Her gaze shot to him and her mouth snapped shut.

"You can use my private garderobe," he offered with a soft laugh. "It's cleaner and you don't have to concern yourself with eating."

"Wow," she shook her head. "A lot of women would love to hear a man tell them not to concern themselves with eating."

"Why?" he asked with raised eyebrows.

"Well, men can be thought...thoughtless about a girl's weight...and...um...other things." She studied him for a moment with a stoic expression. "Judging by the amusement in your eyes, you're enjoying this right now. I'd guess you're no different."

He laughed again, risking a cold glare from her. "Can you fault a beast for its stupidity?"

"A beast that makes excuses for itself isn't dumb, but cowardly."

His humor faded and he scowled, turning his face to the wall.

Madly, she had the urge to giggle. He was unabashedly adorable without trying, reminding her of a scolded puppy.

"Lord Winterborne."

He set his smoldering, silvery gaze on her and Mercy forgot all about puppies. She felt a warm flush wash over her face and looked down. Heavens, she felt engulfed in flames.

"Come now, Mercy," he said softly, leaning in, forgetting that he was brooding an instant ago. "You don't need to feel uneasy with me."

She closed her eyes behind her chestnut hair, forgetting, for a moment, the flames. "Thank you for making my first day here bearable."

He reached out his hand and tucked her hair behind her ear, exposing her scar to his vision. "Maybe for a little while it won't be so bad."

His smile returned, thankful, friendly...friendly? She blinked. Of course, that's what he thought of her. Well, she sighed inwardly, it was better than being his enemy. No man in the twenty-first century who looked like Josiah would be friends with her. She wouldn't kid herself.

"So, you're not...um...married or—?" she choked out, emboldened only by his encouraging smile.

"I'm not married or anything else," he let her know in a low flirty voice. "How about you? Is there someone special in your time?"

She shook her head and stared at him, feeling a little breathless. "Josiah?"

"Hmmm?"

"Why do you believe any man would be interested in me in my time?"

"Why wouldn't they be?" he asked, appearing genuinely lost.

"Look at me."

"I am."

"No, seriously. Are you looking? Can you see this?" Never in her life would she have believed she'd be uttering words such as the ones she just uttered. But her heart couldn't believe he meant what he said. And she couldn't withstand the pain of being deceived.

"Do you think I'm blind?" He grinned, but the tears pooling in his eyes snatched her breath. "I'm not. I see you. Every part of you. Should you find fault with me because I find you so beautiful?"

What? She swiped tears off her cheeks. She had no idea what to say, and she could have said anything and he'd believe her. But she had to treasure truth. "Why do you believe me so easily? No one would if I told them."

His slow smile curled his lips into something more intimate, more soothing, while it lit her nerve-endings on fire. "I'm on your side, Mercy."

Was he? If she helped him, maybe he'd help her in return. What did he know about the ruby dagger that might help her get home? How would he feel once he found out she had *the* weapon? She wouldn't hurt him with it, but how could she prove it? She believed it best not to talk to him about it. For now, at least.

When they reached a narrow stairway going up, Mercy followed his ascent until they came to a heavy wooden door. Once through the doorway, they climbed another stairwell until the stone walls opened up to the wide battlements, patrolled by a dozen guards.

They bowed to Josiah as he passed them. He greeted them all with a wide, endearing grin and led her to the wall. When she looked out over the countryside bathed in moonlight she breathed out "woooow", then settled her gaze on the dimly-lit village nestled in the hills.

"I live in a city," she told him. "It's completely different. People live in apartment buildings that can reach the clouds. Everything is lit up by elec—artificial lighting. Because of all the light and pollution, it's almost impossible to see the stars, and even if it wasn't, everyone is too busy looking down at their phones to bother to look up." She realized he didn't interrupt her to ask what was pollution, or an apartment building. She was glad. She didn't feel like explaining everything. It was nice to just talk.

"I heard you tell my father that you have no family. There's no one?" he asked when she shook her head.

"No," she told him, breathing in the clean night air. "Just me."

He turned to face her, but he remained silent. She flicked her gaze to him and thought he looked even more torturously handsome in the moonlight. "What?"

"You're alone in that world." He sounded a little shaky, as if he were getting emotional.

"I've learned how to get along there."

"Was your life very difficult?" he asked quietly.

She shrugged her shoulders, trying to shrug off the weight of her past. She felt uncomfortable talking about it but only because no one had ever asked about her life before. She chuckled softly without looking at him. "You're far more dangerous than you look."

His smile widened and deepened, proving that he didn't mind what she said. Indeed, he agreed with it. Yes. His appearance was striking and oozing with virility. He stood out among men whether he was walking, sitting, or just standing around. But no matter how kind-hearted and playful he was, he possessed a darker side revealed in his smoldering diamond gaze and impish grin.

"There's a prophecy about me," he told her, leaning his elbows on the wall and looking out.

"Wow," she said. "You have your own prophecy."

She could see him in the moonlight, his smile curling his lips. "Wow," he echoed with his smile softening when he turned to her. "I like the sound of it. Remind me, what does it mean?"

"It expresses wonder and awe."

"I see." His eyes gleamed on her, his mouth puckered as he formed his words. "So you are in awe of me? Stricken with wonder as you were when you looked out at the view?"

Her eyes opened wide and she was about to deny his charge, but then she saw the spark of playfulness in his eyes. She swatted his arm and laughed. "Not in awe of you, silly. That you have your own prophecy. What is it?" she asked him, growing serious when she found him staring at her, his expression unreadable except for the warm glint that flashed across his eyes.

"Your nose crinkles when you laugh, and...you have dimples."

No one had ever noticed and brought it up to her as if it were the most thoughtful compliment ever to be uttered. She felt her face go flush and hoped he couldn't see it in the torchlight. "What's the prophecy?"

"It has to do with the ruby dagger."

She took a step back, away from him. "What about it?"

He stared at her as if he were trying to read her. Then, hopefully not coming up with anything, "The prophecy says that if I come to possess the dagger, I'll wield its power to kill hundreds of thousands."

Mercy's stomach turned. That was why a Blagden had tried to kill him when he was born. Why did Mercy have the weapon now? Was she supposed to kill him with it?

"To stop it from happening, the ruby dagger must be destroyed by being plunged into my heart."

"What?" Mercy held her hands to her chest, horrified. "Who would make up such a heinous story?"

"I don't necessarily believe the prophecy since I've never seen any proof of anything, but there are those who do believe. They believe a certain way and I must work to prove to them that a dagger won't turn me into something despicable."

She was silent. She wanted to run back to her room, get the dagger and bring it to a place Josiah couldn't go. The future. How could what he was saying become true? Would he truly kill hundreds of thousands? She didn't believe it. Everyone was his friend. Would he kill them all? And who were all the rest?

"What is it?" he asked tenderly, reaching for her.

"I don't believe any of it, Josiah," she told him, moving away from his touch, unused to physical contact. "You're a good man. Don't let a prophecy change you."

"Mercy, do you know where the ruby dagger is?"

She closed her eyes trying to convince herself that he hadn't really just asked her for it. "How would I know?"

"Because on it, your blood was mixed with mine, and now I believe our blood is shared."

What? What? Their blood shared? How did he know her blood was on it? Her heart thumped so hard it made her feel sick to her stomach. "How could that be when...when we were separated by over three hundred years?"

"I don't know," he told her quietly, "But I feel as if I've been waiting for you. From the moment I saw you in the receiving hall, I knew it. When I saw your bleeding lip, I knew your blood would heal me. And it did."

Yes. She remembered how ill he looked when he stepped into the hall, with his gaunt skin, dark circles around his eyes, and pale lips.

"I'm afraid you're not the only one with an outlandish tale to tell." He was quiet for a moment, his smile faint. "I haven't told anyone about the blood. It wouldn't do for the people to think their duke had a mad son. Being cursed is bad enough." He didn't look at her while he spoke.

Mercy wondered how terrible it was to grow up believing you were cursed.

"I've always been sick," he continued. "Our physician says it has to do with this." He pulled up his doublet and shirt and revealed his corded belly and the scar just below his heart. "He says the dagger was tipped with poison. When I was just a few hours old, a fever struck me. I was dying. I'm told my poor father held a vigil for three weeks until the fever broke. But that wasn't the end of it. Every month I fall ill again—up until a few days ago. This time was particularly difficult. I didn't think I would make it. I think it will eventually claim my life."

"That's awful," she lamented with a crestfallen look, which she swore made him look happy. She squeezed the top of his hand, and then after another moment, realizing she still covered it, pulled her hand away as though he were on fire. "There's no cure here?"

"There is now," he told her in a whispered tone that drew her closer to hear. "The blood of the person whose blood is mixed with mine on that dagger is the cure."

She stopped and stared at him. "My blood? You want my blood?" Should she run now? Would it be too late in another second?

"I think you're my cure, Mercy."

How could she have heard him right? This was all crazy. "How am I the cure? And I have to be honest, I don't like the sound of this so far."

His smile widened. He found this amusing.

"Josiah, really, this isn't funny. How am I tied into you?"

"It's mad, I know," he said, shifting his gaze to hers. "I don't have all the answers, but I know I need you to stay well. I once dreamed of a seer who told me that only the one who shared my blood because of the dagger could save me. I know you've seen the dagger. You're the first and only one who has. I can't really live until I get rid of it. It pierced me, and Mercy, at some point, it must have pierced you too and our blood mixed. That's how I was healed."

She closed her eyes, agonized over how much she should tell him. She bit her lip and he reached out to wipe the blood from her mouth. When had he gotten so close? She could feel his breath. She took a step back.

"It was in a drawer in a chest in the attic of the orphanage where I lived when I was a child," she told him, feeling as if she were spilling the secrets of the world—but to her best friend. It was more of a relief, like letting go of a burden. "It was forbidden to go up there. The sisters said it was dangerous and dirty, but I didn't listen." She told him about putting her hand in the drawer and getting cut. "And that's it. That must be how my blood mixed with yours."

"Yes," she thought out loud, "and now we share blood." That's what happened to her when she was four. That's why she had changed so drastically. She had the blood of one who was promised to a demon flowing through her.

"And you never saw the dagger again?" he asked.

She shook her head and turned away. "Why do you want it?"

"I don't. But I also don't want it to come upon me in surprise. I've been expecting it, and truthfully, Mercy, you're the closest I've come to it in twenty years. You've come here from the future, a woman who just happens to share my blood because of that dagger. I'd hoped you had it. If I know where it is, I can get rid of it."

"Would you?"

"Yes. I have no intention of killing anyone."

Should she believe him? Should she tell him that she had the dagger? If he was lying, then she'd be sentencing hundreds to death. If he was telling the truth and he wanted to destroy it, would he also be destroying her chance of going home? Treasure truth. Treasure truth. No. She couldn't tell him. Not now. What if he wanted it to fulfil the prophecy?

"I'm sorry," she said, dipping her gaze. "I haven't seen it."

He nodded, easily accepting her word, which made her feel more guilty about not telling him the truth.

"Come," he said, stepping away, then turning to look at her when she didn't follow. He held out his hand. "It's late. I'll bring you to my chambers and I'll sleep in the sitting room."

She didn't take his hand. "No. Absolutely not. I—"

"Do you truly want to use the garderobe near your room?" His smile brightened on her. "I don't mind. I'd rather have you close by."

She swallowed. Never in her wildest dreams could she have conjured up someone like him, who said these kinds of words to her. If he was trying to get the truth about the dagger from her, she wasn't sure how long she could hold out. Something about him made telling him everything easy. She bit her lip and continued.

"Isn't it forbidden or something to have a commoner alone with you in your rooms?"

"We won't be alone. There are guards—"

She cast him a worried look. "Guards?"

"It's all right." His comforting smile worked like a balm on her nerves. "They won't put a finger near you except to save your life. I'll give them the order and they'll obey it."

"Does your father keep you guarded and protected around the clock?"

He nodded.

"Why?" she pressed. "Are you in danger?"

"As long as the dagger exists, my life is in danger. The closer it is to me the more dangerous I become to everyone else."

Close—as in down the hall in a room and tucked under a mattress? Her heart sank. She had to get it and get away from Ashmore Castle. She couldn't stay here even if she wanted to. She had to find a way to use the dagger to get back to the future. Once back in the twenty-first century, it would be safely out of his hands.

"You know what? I think I'll just sleep in my own bed rather than in a room with seven men."

"There are six rooms." Even when his lips rested in a stoic expression, they were the most excruciatingly full, red lips she'd ever seen in real life or on T.V.

"Still, I think—"

"I'll tell them all to leave."

Sure. Tell the guards who are here to protect you from the ruby dagger, to leave you alone with the Blagden who possesses that same stupid dagger.

"No."

He closed his fingers around her wrist and then slipped them to her hand and held it. "Please, stay with me."

She lifted her stunned gaze from their hands to his eyes. She didn't want their night to end—and she wanted to use a clean toilet. If she were given one wish that's what it would be. A clean toilet. "Okay. But tell the guards to let me out early in the morning, so that I can go to my room and change out of my nightgown."

He nodded and beamed at her in the torchlight when they entered the stairwell. Not like a wolf, hungry to get her into his lair, but more like a human soul who liked spending time with her as much as she liked spending it with him. She'd remain cautious with him—as certain smiles of his warned her to be—but she'd accept his invitation.

His room turned out to be a large apartment-sized space including a sitting area, with painted walls mostly covered in paintings, done with his own brush. With only light from the dying hearthlight, she could barely see the colors or any details. "I have a separate studio where I keep most of my paintings," he told her, and also that he'd like to take her there. His bedroom was enormous with two dressers and various sized tables with ornately carved legs. Chairs with arms made of oak and pine, and the garderobe. Once all the candles were lit in the room, Mercy saw that hanging on the wall opposite the bed was a painting of a raging, tumultuous ocean in hues of blue, gray, purple, and white. There was nothing calm in the painting with its frothy, rolling whitecaps and dark depths, but staring at it quieted her roiling thoughts about where she was.

The men who guarded Josiah's slumber already knew about her, since they were the same men who'd followed after them all day. Josiah's own personal little army. He introduced her to them all. There was Captain Sherwood, Laurence Keast, Gerard Dutton, Rauffe Abbott, Joem Macey, and Henry Hollister. They rotated a duty of two keeping watch while one slept. The other three kept guard outside his door. It was a little awkward but they left her alone, as Josiah said they would.

In his bedroom, Josiah sat in a chair facing her while she climbed into his bed. "No one has ever been here before," he told her, tilting his head to see her from a different angle. "You, my lady, are dangerous as well."

A few minutes later, there came a knock at the bedroom door.

"Come," Josiah called out.

One of the guardsmen entered the room carrying a tray with various fruits and bread with honey and butter.

Mercy and Josiah turned to each other and grinned with glee over the midnight snack.

"You did well, Mr. Macey," Josiah told him, then returned his gaze to Mercy. "I know you were hungry, so I asked Mr. Macey to bring some food."

Mercy didn't know what to say but thank you. She had forgotten she was hungry, but Josiah hadn't. Her stomach rumbled to remind her. They laughed together at the sound.

Before he left them, Mr. Macey smiled.

While she sliced peaches and he peeled her an apple, Josiah told her about himself. He was the seventh son of the duke, inheriting his freedom—at least in his choices, which was far more priceless than riches and power, according to him. If he were the seventh son of any other duke, he would have been betrothed already and be expected to join the military or the clergy, but his father didn't want him to join either.

"I'm sure the church wouldn't approve of me. The military wouldn't be thrilled to have me either."

"Are you bitter about that?" she asked while he cut the peeled fruit and handed a piece over to her.

"How can I be when they're correct about me?" He accepted a slice of peach from her and they both ate. He managed to smile at her the entire time, really tempting her to smile back.

"In what way?" she asked him. "What have you done that's so bad?"

He looked up from the tray between them and settled his gaze on her. "I haven't done anything. They believe I'm cursed, that I'll kill."

"Do you really think they believe it after everything you've done for them?" she asked him, setting the tray aside. "They care about you."

"I made it my life's cause to always smile and never give the villagers any reason for alarm. But they still believe I'm cursed."

"What do they know anyway?"

"Nothing really," he said, smiling at her.

"Nothing is right. Cursed means it's hopeless for you, Josiah. I don't believe that for a second."

His smile deepened. "How is it that I feel so comforted when I speak to you?"

Her heart did a flip that made her feel dizzy. She felt the same way. Had he really captivated her heart like this? It was the first time in her life anyone had ever done so—or even gotten close. He reached in and maybe...even...oh, it was too ridiculous to consider seriously, but...maybe he stepped into the place where someone had been missing.

She almost laughed, but she was too afraid it would turn into tears. She didn't ever let herself fantasize about a healthy relationship. Why torture herself? If a guy showed her any attention, it was to get her into bed and then leave. No, thanks. Even if they didn't have respect for her, she did. Did Josiah's words come from him easily? Did he know what he was doing to her with each one? "I think we're both very tired."

He laughed softly, twisting her insides into knots. Then, in his husky, restrained voice, "As you say."

She leaned over in bed and blew out the candle, then lay her head on the pillow and closed her eyes. She opened them a minute later. She could still see him in the firelight from the hearth. He hadn't left the chair, but was watching her in the light from the hearthfire.

She sat up. "What are you doing?"

"Watching until you fall asleep."

She breathed out a short laugh. "What? Why? No." She shook her head. "Goodnight. Please go."

"Mercy, I—"

"Josiah, get out."

She watched him scowl his darkest scowl yet as he obeyed her command and went to the door. He stopped and turned to her when he reached it. "Mercy, even with a full castle, a brood of brothers, and good men and women around me, I've always felt lonely. Today, for the first time, I didn't." He didn't wait for her response but left her alone to stare at the door.

Had she told him she'd grown up lonely too? She couldn't help but smile. Did she really have to just tear a guy away from her? A beautiful guy? She pinched herself, then threw herself back down onto the pillow and held her hand over the squeal of joy leaving her lips.

No, no, she sobered. She wasn't staying. She had to go home. Didn't she?

CHAPTER FOUR

M ERCY OPENED HER eyes from dreaming of a handsome man of deep compassion and—

The wooden door opened and that same man stepped happily into the bedchamber carrying a tray of food. Josiah Ashmore. He was real then. He looked especially handsome in an untucked cream shirt, hanging open at the neck, with ruffled cuffs and snug-fitting breeches. His feet were bare.

"Good morn, Mercy."

She missed his smile while she slept. Seeing it now made her smile back.

"I wasn't sure if I dreamed yo—yesterday," she quickly amended, trying to ignore his beaming smile.

"I wasn't sure if I dreamed you either," he confessed with a twinkling smile and sat on the bottom of the bed, with the tray between them.

"Wow, breakfast in bed." She offered him her brightest smile before digging in.

"I spoke to the gate guards, he told her, watching her and grinning while she ate. "None of them saw you enter the gates the night you arrived."

"I don't think I entered the gate."

"Right," he said. "But I need something to tell my father. I'm sure he'll ask at supper."

"Maybe I'll be gone by then," she said, chewing on a piece of buttered bread.

She stared at him when he remained quiet. "You're brooding."

"Nonsense," he defended and allowed his smile to return, proving to Mercy that not all his smiles were genuine. "Did you figure out how you got here while you were asleep?"

She shook her head, certain that he was still brooding beneath his mask. "No, and to be honest, I don't know if I should try somehow to return. I've never belonged in my time, the life I was living there. But I don't know if I fit in here either—and being here means learning an entirely new way of living. At least there I can make it on my own. I can't say that here. How many women live alone and independently here?"

"You won't be alone," he promised her in a voice that rumbled through her.

"Josiah, we're friends. What happens when you're told it's time to get betrothed?"

"First," he told her, "I'm free to marry whoever I want, when I want. And I have no objections to being your friend. For now."

She felt her eyes grow rounder and her heart skip a beat. "Would you ever *not* be my friend?"

He grinned and shook his head. "Who else will make me laugh?"

Laugh. Great. She expelled a soft sigh. "I'm glad I make you laugh."

He gave her a doubtful smirk. "You sound disappointed." His voice grew lower, deeper. "Do you want to make me feel something a bit more personal, more intimate?"

She was about to tell him no when he leaned forward on the bed, resting his palms on the mattress as he went close to her. "Something like….desire?" The resonant sound of him sent waves through her that rocked her existence. He moved closer until she could feel his breath on her lips. "Temptation?"

She arched her back. He moved forward with her and then curled his fingers around her nape. He closed his eyes. Mercy's belly flip-flopped and her heart thumped loud enough that she feared he might hear it between them. He was going to kiss her. What should she do? She squeezed her eyes shut. Open her mouth? Close her mouth? She didn't know. She'd never been kissed before.

Someone knocked at the door. At the sound, both Josiah and Mercy sprang out of the bed, forgetting about their almost kiss. Well, Mercy considered, she forgot. Josiah was back to brooding. When he saw his two eldest brothers he managed a smile and stepped away from the bed.

"Josiah," Thomas, the eldest, began, his dark gaze following Josiah as he moved toward the window. "I'm going to tell Father about this." He turned to Mercy. "You slept here?"

She dipped her gaze and hid half her face behind her hair. "I...I was alone."

"She needed a clean garderobe, so I offered her mine, Thomas," Josiah told his brother while a flash of amusement lit his eyes. "If Father scolds me for what I did, it won't matter. I'll be at her side from now on."

Silence resonated through the room as Mercy's eyelids fluttered while she stared at the ground. She felt her fingers tremble as she brought them to her chest.

"Mercy?" Josiah's serene, soothing voice washed over her. "Lift your head, lady."

Both Thomas and second son, Oliver, earl of Weymouth stared at her for a moment or two longer. Thomas spoke first. "You're fortunate that Father went for his morning ride instead of coming to your rooms and finding this mysterious stranger in your bed!"

"Thomas," Josiah said, taking Mercy's hand, "please trust me. She isn't dangerous to me. I'm not going to be parted from her by Father's orders or yours. Now, please go ask your kind-hearted wife if she has any spare clothes for Mercy. I'll be indebted."

Thomas stared at him, looking a bit stunned by his brother. "You're reckless and rash, Josiah. This woman appeared as if from nowhere barely clothed and without her memory. Your enemy knows your weakness is the weakness of others."

"She's not my enemy."

"You don't know that," Oliver chimed in. "You're fortunate to be alive this morning."

Finally, Mercy covered her ears and shouted at them. "I'd never hurt him!"

When two guards rushed in to aid the duke's youngest son, Thomas commanded them in the name of Edmund Ashmore, Duke of Dorset to lay hands on Mercy and bring her to the dungeon.

Mercy looked at the two soldiers Rauffe Abbott and Henry Hollister, who'd followed her and Josiah around all day yesterday. When they took her by the elbows without so much of a glance of recognition, she turned her stricken stare on Josiah.

He let go of her hand and didn't make a move to help her. He simply stared at his brothers first, and then with a dangerous smirk slanting his mouth, at the two guards who'd dared to touch her. "Neither of you will ever guard me again."

"Josiah?" she cried out. Not the dungeon again!

He took a step closer to her, glaring at the men around them. No one made a move to stop him. Leaning in, he spoke into her ear. "I won't be long. Trust me, hmm?"

She felt panic rise up in her. "I don't want to be alone down there."

He looked as if she kicked him in the guts. "I'll always be by your side. I'll always be within your reach. Trust me." He was smiling at her when he stepped back, and silent as they led her away.

She turned to look at him over her shoulder and felt a wave of warmth wash over her. She trusted him. She wasn't sure why she believed him. She didn't have another choice, and if she was ever going to trust anyone in her life—it was going to be him. The one who was kind, compassionate, and good hearted.

A cursed monster who could kill thousands? Never.

JOSIAH WATCHED WITH hooded, gleaming eyes as Abbott and Hollister took her away. As he stood in silence, his brother Thomas reached out to touch his shoulder. "It's for your own—"

Josiah walked away from him while Thomas was speaking. He trembled with fury and for the first time in his life believed he could lose control of himself and do something he would regret. He couldn't. For her sake he couldn't. She would look at him differently, as if he truly *could* become the nightmare everyone else secretly feared. He remembered to breathe and followed Mercy and the soldiers down the hall. His brothers were close behind making sure he didn't try to free her.

Breathe.

He could feel the dagger near, pulling, tempting. He knew it was in her room. He didn't go get it. He didn't want it. He didn't want to turn into some monster that could kill. But even more than that, he didn't want it found in her room. His father would hang her in the morning.

Before they reached the stairs, Josiah stepped in front of the soldiers, stopping them from proceeding. He looked them both in the eye, level with the six foot two inch Abbott. He unclenched his teeth—barely, and spoke. "If just one hair on her head is harmed—" *I'll shred you to pieces with your own swords and toss you to the four winds*—he shook his head to clear it from the whispers of something less civilized within him. "I'll never forgive you, and if that dreadful prophecy is ever fulfilled, I'll look for you two first."

They paled. "My lord, we—"

Josiah held up his palm to silence Hollister when he tried to speak. He set his gaze on Mercy and let the sight of her, the sound of her soothe him. "I'll see you," he promised with a playful wink. He looked over her shoulder at his brothers and at once his gaze darkened.

"Josiah." It was Mercy dragging his attention away from them. "It's all right."

Looking at her comforted and pained him at the same time. Letting her go to be taken to the dungeon, even for a short while, hurt his heart, his belly, his head. He was sure it showed on his face by the way she tried to find a smile for him in the tangle of fear and dread that fought for preeminence on hers.

When his brothers reached them, the soldiers moved on with her, brushing past Josiah. No one else tried to speak to him. He was glad. He had nothing to say to them. The moment he was alone, he leaned his arm against the nearest wall and rested his forehead on it. He had to stay calm. His heart told him they wouldn't hurt her, but his head told him something different. He could feel her fear clinging to him. He had to do something. Vaguely, he thought that he didn't feel like himself. His heart pounded like a war drum in his chest. He closed his eyes, but there was no time to waste, and so, he pushed off the wall and hurried to the east wing of the castle.

His father returned a quarter of an hour later. It took Josiah that amount of time to acquire and prepare what he needed to have Mercy released. He would spend the next sennight making it up to her. Twice, his heart faltered at the thought of her keeping to her plan to find a way back to her home—three hundred years away. If she had the dagger, and he was almost sure she did, she might use it and succeed in leaving. Now, more than ever she'd be eager to go.

With his mind made up about what he was going to do, he headed to the great hall where his father, and most likely his brothers, would be having a drink.

On the way, he thought of Mercy. He had made a promise. He'd keep it.

When he stepped inside the hall, the usual suspects sat at one of the tables. He said nothing while he crossed the hall and reached the table.

"Josiah, we were just speaking of you," said his father.

Josiah didn't reply or sit down.

His father stared at him without a word for a moment, then, "Thomas mentioned you were angry about his suspicions when it comes to Miss Smith and her imprisonment this morning for her dubious behavior."

Josiah smiled to disguise his anger and looked away. "There was no suspicious behavior. I insisted that she sleep in my bed, while I slept with the guards in the next room so she could use my private garderobe. Thomas barged into the room after I brought in a tray of food for her this morning and he found me with her."

"She slept in your bed?" His father's scowl was darker than a winter night.

So, Thomas had kept his word, at least, and hadn't told his father the whole story. It didn't matter. She was still in the dungeon.

"She's mine," Josiah reminded him almost too calmly. "You know this. You agreed to it. Will you punish her because your son was doing his duty?"

"My son, I fear—"

"Father, I don't want to live in the shadow of your fears—or anyone else's—anymore. You must release Mercy. She's the one who will keep the prophecy from happening."

"What? How?" his father demanded, standing to his feet. Thomas stood with him.

"I don't know," Josiah told him. "But I do know that she'll keep me alive—and human."

His father had to remember his dream of the seer. Admitting that her blood was on the blade meant she'd seen the blade, perhaps was in possession of it. Josiah didn't want his father to suspect, but he'd worry about it later.

"How do you know this, Josiah?" the duke asked him. "Are you certain this isn't your young heart believing that her love will save you?"

"You saw me recover the day I met her in the receiving hall."

"You were already up and about, Josiah," his father argued. "You were already almost fully well."

"No. I was still very much fevered, but I was drawn from my studio. When I saw her, there was blood on her lip. Did you not see me touch that droplet? *That* is when I became well." Josiah felt relieved to tell his father the truth.

The duke's blood drained from his face until he appeared about to faint. "She has seen the accursed dagger? You let her into your room alone believing her blood mixed with yours on the dagger? Josiah, your recklessness knows no bounds. This is exactly why I'm relieved your eldest brother locked her from you."

Josiah clenched his jaw hearing his father's words. They were words which he would make certain he never heard the duke utter again.

"She has a hold on you already. You would believe anything to save her. I must refuse your request. But know…"

He continued, but Josiah had stopped listening and produced his dagger from his belt.

"…that I do this for your protection because I love you, Son."

Josiah held up the blade. "I coated the tip with poison— enough to kill a man in a short time. This is the only way I can prove to you that I need her to live by my side." Without another word, he sliced the blade across his forearm.

Everyone rushed to him. The dagger was pulled away from his fingers, but it was too late. The poison was already rushing through his veins.

"Father, release her if you want to save me."

His father stared at him, a mask of horror in answer to the nightmare he just witnessed. "Josiah—" he gasped, then swallowed. "Did you…is there truly poison on the blade?"

"Bring me Mercy," he said, going pale. "Bring her to me."

His father shouted the order to bring her at once! "Thomas! Oliver! Get him in a chair. Oh, my boy! My boy!"

It was a risky move to free her. But if it worked and he lived, then it was worth it.

"My boy, why did you do this?" his father lamented over him.

Josiah tried to focus on him but saw three of him. *Hurry.* "I need her."

His father looked up and bellowed, "Bring her!"

Josiah hoped she'd arrive while he was still awake so he could smile at her. He wasn't fully worried since he wasn't so reckless not to have another plan just in case she didn't get there in time. The castle physician was hidden in the shadows, as ordered by Josiah. In the physician's bag, he had an antidote to administer if Josiah came too close to death. But only then. It was vital that his father knew never to take her from him again—if she didn't return home.

He didn't doubt her blood would save him. By some miracle they'd been brought together. Not only had she been pierced by the dagger, but she'd been brought through time to save him...and save more than just his physical body.

He waited for what felt like an eternity, and just when he was about to admit that he was a reckless fool and give the signal to the doctor for the antidote, he heard her voice. Laden with hysteria, the sound of her broke his heart, along with the sounds of his father and brothers weeping over him.

"Josiah!" she cried, making him turn away. Would he always make her cry? "What do I do?"

"Wipe your blood on my arm," he managed to tell her, but just barely. Pain was beginning to course through him. He trembled in her arms.

Without another moment's hesitation, she turned, yanked a dagger from Oliver's belt and drew the blade across her palm. She bit down and groaned as her blood spilled out. She quickly pressed her palm against his wounded arm and held it there.

Yes. Josiah thought as her blood mixed and then flowed with his, radiating light through every inch of his body. It was working. Her blood was healing him. He knew it would.

"His color is returning!" he heard his father cry out.

The physician knelt beside him and examined him quickly. "He is correct, then. Her blood can cure him."

Silence fell upon the hall as the proof sank in. Josiah opened his eyes, his color still pale, but returning. He stared at Mercy kneeling above him while her teardrops fell on his chest. Her palm was still bleeding all over him. He inhaled, taking in all the strength she gave—strength enough to shout to the physician to see to her wound. She grew blurry to his vision and he soon realized that tears were filling and falling from his eyes. "Forgive me for frightening you," he told her, then spread his loving gaze to his family and sat up, much to everyone's shock and amazement. He pushed the physician's hands away from his arm and pointed to finishing with Mercy's hand. "I had no choice but to show you how much I need her by my side. Now that you all know that, I would have you know, too, that I *want* her there even more desperately."

He hated that his words made her weep even more. It meant one thing.

She still wanted to leave.

CHAPTER FIVE

I NSTEAD OF BEING brought back to the dungeon, Mercy was being brought to new chambers next to Josiah's. She insisted on going back to her room to get her clothes—and the dagger, then was separated from Josiah when they reached her door. He promised to come for her as soon as they were cleaned up and mended properly. He moved in close and whispered for her ears alone. "I'll hurry."

She thought she wasn't in her right mind. That's what all the trauma over the last few days had caused. She wasn't okay because instead of thinking about what he had done, poisoning himself to see her set free, she was thinking about how much she didn't want to go home. Back to a tiny apartment, a job she hated, and no one to go home to or even to talk to on the phone, when the other option was to stay with a guy who "desperately" wanted her by his side. She had to be out of her mind because she'd rather stay in a castle with a filthy dungeon that the Ashmores liked to throw her into just to be close to Josiah Ashmore. Crazy because she didn't want to leave a possible figment of her imagination. A perfect man...as long as she kept him from becoming a demon by keeping the ruby dagger away from him.

"Talk about baggage. Dungeons, daggers, and demons! Sheesh! It sounds like a horror movie," she chuckled at herself, and then shivered and hugged herself.

Her new living quarters almost made her forget the terror of the dungeon. It consisted of a small sitting room with painted walls donned in Josiah's beautiful paintings, which she took her time to admire, two walnut armchairs and two bare tables. A bedroom with a carved walnut four-poster bed and the softest, fluffiest mattress Mercy had ever seen. It made her want to jump on it and test its comfort. She did, right after she tucked the ruby dagger she'd retrieved with her clothes, under the plush mattress. There was a walnut dresser, smaller than the one in Josiah's bedroom but no less ornately carved. The walls were painted white and one was covered with a colorful tapestry like one she'd seen in a museum in New York. She was thrilled and thankful to find a private garderobe. Being his had its privileges.

While she waited for a line of servants to carry a large tub into her bedroom and fill it with water, she thought about what Josiah had done. He'd gotten her out of the dungeon as he said he would. Even though she hated how he'd done it, she had trusted him and he hadn't let her down. Not only did he get her out, but he made her extremely important in his family's eyes. He was a dream come true. A dream. Not real. So, why should she leave? He wouldn't really hurt anyone. The dagger would have no power. How she wished that was true and that she were dreaming.

She knew she wasn't by the stinging in her hand from her wound, and in her heart because she had possibly found someone amazing and he lived three hundred and sixty-two years before she was born.

"My lady," said one of the female servants when the last male servant left. "Undress so we can bathe you and—"

Mercy laughed awkwardly and backed up. "No, no, that's quite all right. I can bathe myself—"

They didn't listen and moved toward her, their hands grabbing and pulling. She couldn't help but giggle as their fingers poked and tugged. They had her undressed quickly enough that steam still rose from the water.

If the bath didn't feel so good she would have died of embarrassment. Three women washed her body and her hair! Three! She'd never get used to it but she would have to. The thought of leaving Josiah Ashmore and his castle brought her mood down. When one of the women, Alison was her name, asked Mercy how she'd received such a scar on her face, Mercy didn't hesitate to answer—after all, they were practically intimate. "When I was three years old, a thief broke into our apa—house and took everything. He killed my mother and tried to kill me next." She didn't stop when she heard Alison gasp, or when the other two—Hester and Emmaline, they had told her while they scrubbed—had covered their mouths to stifle their cries. "He stabbed me in the face, but then ran away before he was caught. I don't remember any of it."

"Oh, my lady," Alison said in a heavy voice, her dark eyes glittering with tears that fell and streaked her golden skin. "How harrowing."

"Yes," Emmaline, the youngest, agreed with a sniff. "I knew you weren't like some of the other ladies who try to come see Lord Josiah. It's because you haven't had an easy life. My mother used to say hardships build character."

"Let's hope the thief was caught and skinned alive," Hester told her, rinsing Mercy's arm and shoulder.

Mercy didn't know. She'd never thought about it.

"Gossip is already running rampant through the castle," Emmaline leaned in conspiratorially, her russet braid falling over her shoulder and dangling over the water. "They're saying your blood healed young Lord Josiah of poison today. Is it true?"

Mercy felt pathetic that these three women, whom she just met, were more like friends than anyone she'd ever known. She nodded hesitantly and then regretted her honesty when they stared at her wide-eyed and open-mouthed.

"How can that be?" asked Hester, who was old enough to be any of their mothers. She had kind gray eyes that matched the color of her loose bun at the back of her head. "How did you discover it?"

"I don't know how it can be." She had to lie to them. They had already taken in much for seventeenth century women. Anymore—like mixed blood—would be too much. "And I didn't discover it. He did."

Hester appeared stunned and a bit paler.

"Well," said Alison, rubbing her fingers through Mercy's wet hair. "We're happy you saved him today."

Emmaline and Hester agreed enthusiastically.

"Is he well-loved here?" Mercy asked and then sighed a little at how relaxing Alison's fingers were.

"Yes." Emmaline told her. "He's nothing like the other Ashmores. He's generous and kind. Though," she added, "all the Ashmores love and adore their brother as much as their father does."

Alison and Hester agreed.

"But…" Alison began and then stopped.

"But?" Mercy opened her eyes and looked up at her. "But what?"

Alison's nervous gaze swept across her friends' faces. She looked as if she was sorry she said anything. When silence reigned long enough for them to feel the weight of it, Alison sighed against the tub. "Some believe he's cursed and that he'll be responsible for killing many—maybe even us here at Ashmore. They're afraid of him. They return his smiles but they're waiting, always cautious of him. We don't believe it, of course." She motioned to herself and her two friends. "No one that handsome and kind-hearted could turn evil."

That damn curse. Mercy clenched her jaw. Josiah was right. The curse prophecy followed him around like a black cloud. "I'm glad you don't believe it because it's nonsense." She would make sure of it by getting that accursed dagger away from him.

After that, they spoke about other things, even sharing laughter as Emmaline and Alison imitated the Ashmore brothers, and the duke himself. Mercy didn't even remember them drying her off and slipping a semi-sheer chemise over her head.

"I heard—" Hester said quietly while she pulled a pair of drawers up Mercy's legs, like soft underwear that reached her knees—"that you've spent many hours with the young lord. It's shocking because he isn't permitted to spend his time alone with women, or anyone, really, unless he's painting."

"Correct!" Emmaline nodded emphatically. "And when he has painted women alone in the past, he has never tried to kiss or touch any of them that we know of."

Hester nodded when Emmaline turned to her, then the older woman added. "Are you in love with him? Is he in love with you?"

Mercy gave her questions the laugh they deserved, but her blood rushed through her body, making her legs feel weak. She fell back and into a chair that Alison had dragged before the roaring hearthfire just moments before. She knew Josiah's father was over-protective, doing his best to isolate him from any other Tessa Blagdens out there. But was it true? Did Josiah hold back his affection with everyone but her? What should she say? She didn't let herself hope.

She peeked up from under her hair, which Alison brushed away from her scarred face at that very moment, leaving her even more bare than when she was naked in the tub.

Hester studied her with knowing eyes while Alison brushed her hair. "I imagine it would be difficult to keep a clear head around all that charm and the light of his playful heart. Hmm?"

Mercy settled her wide gaze on the older woman and nodded slowly. "Yes. That's exactly it." How was she supposed to guard against a perfect delusion? She already missed being with—

Someone rapping on the door shattered her thoughts of him. That is, until Emmaline hurried out of the bedroom to see who it was, and returned less than a minute later behind Mercy's delusion storming into her bedroom.

His arm was bandaged beneath his rolled up ruffled sleeves. He wore a clean linen shirt, open at the throat and free of a cravat. His soft, wet hair caressed the column of his neck and fell over his brows. Dark brown breeches graced the bottom half of him, hugging his thighs and rounded backside.

He was pale when he barged into her bedroom. On his face he wore a panicked expression. "I thought you might have found a way back and left," he breathed, stopping before her chair.

He didn't want her to go, Mercy secretly rejoiced. But was it because he needed her to stay alive? What if he wasn't meant to live?...no. No. She smiled at him and watched him come a little undone. He liked her and it had nothing to do with her blood saving him. She no longer cared how a man like him would want someone like her by his side. She wanted to hold on to this moment.

"I wouldn't go without telling you, Lord Winterborne," she said in front of the women.

He gave her a confused half smile that made Alison giggle behind her. "Lord Winterborne?" he repeated. "Will you speak to me so impersonally now?"

"Josiah," she corrected in a low whisper.

"Hmmm?" He held his hand to his ear. "What was that?"

She sighed and shook her head at him, understanding his family. It was extremely hard to refuse him anything. "Josiah."

His smile widened.

She held her hand to her chest when her heart skipped. Her chest...she felt the fabric barely covering her. She was in her sheer chemise! She crossed her arms over her chest. "You should leave and let me dress."

He gave her a reluctant nod.

Hester, Emmaline, and Alison stared, slack-jawed at him as he left. "I think he answered your question about if he was in love with her," Alison told Hester with a wink. "He definitely is."

Mercy closed her eyes and bit her lip. Did he love her, or were they being dramatic?

"Are you leaving Ashmore Castle, my lady?" Emmaline asked her, looking concerned.

"Eventually I will," she told them. "This isn't my home."

"But you aren't eager to go?" Hester asked her while she measured Mercy with her eyes, then smiled and helped her into her skirts, volumes of them.

"Honestly, no, I'm not. I have no family. I've never had anyone by my side," she replied as they stuffed her into a thin shirt beneath a bodice made of bones that weren't made to be comfortable. "I won't miss these clothes, though."

When Hester smiled and held up a crimson, quilted doublet, Mercy held up her hands. "Enough." She untied the heavy skirts and let them fall in a heap around her feet. She unlaced the bodice, breathed, and then pulled it off. "I'm sorry," she said, wiping her sweaty brow. "Do you have anything thinner and simpler, without so many layers and bones?

The girls thought about their dilemma for a moment and then Emmaline clapped her hands. "I know one! It's more like a nightgown, but ladies are wearing these gowns in public. Most of the ladies here have them for being painted in undress by Lord Winterborne."

"Painted in...undress?" Mercy wasn't sure she wanted to hear anymore.

They stared at her, gauging her reaction. She tried to look unfazed but failed miserably. "Does he paint portraits of women?" Odd, how he hadn't told her.

"He paints everything and everyone," Hester let her know. "I'm surprised he hasn't offered to paint you yet."

She pictured herself sprawled out on a velvet settee in undress while Josiah rolled up his ruffled sleeves and painted her. She wondered how he would see her. "Well, please, let me be free of these cumbersome clothes."

Her plea earned a nod from Hester and a charge from the older woman for Emmaline to go fetch the dress.

"Is it true," Alison asked, resuming her work on Mercy's hair, "that when you were brought to Ashmore Castle, you were dressed in nothing but very small breeches and a single layered shirt without lace or tie of any kind?"

Mercy smiled thinking how she must have appeared to everyone here with her bare legs and arms.

"Yes," she answered. "They were…underwear from my home. My clothes had been robbed."

Both women gasped and shook their heads. "Well, don't you fret," Hester told her. "We'll take good care of you."

Mercy wanted to cry. Why? Why did she have to find friends in a place where she didn't belong? It wasn't fair. She wouldn't cry—no matter how much her eyes burned. If she was in a coma, did she really want to wake up?

"There, there," Alison patted her cheek. "You have the favor of the duke's most beloved son now. Things will be better for you while you're here."

"Better than they are right now?" Mercy asked, then smiled and shook her head. With the *favor* of Josiah Ashmore and three new friends. "I doubt it."

Emmaline returned with the gown, known as undress. He painted women in these things? The one Emmaline had chosen was quite beautiful, Mercy had to admit. The colors of aqua blending into deeper blue, and vivid pink splashed over purple, reminded her of a romance novel she'd read about a guy swimming in a blue lake surrounded by shedding dogwood trees.

She felt Hester's careful, compassionate gaze on her and maintained her smile while they dressed her. The gown was double layered and straight cut, with a dropped neckline from which her breasts threatened to spill. Emmaline and Hester rolled up some blue silk and stuffed it into the neckline, creating a softer look. They also tied a piece of silk around her waist to give her some shape. Mercy stopped them there, not wanting to go too elaborate. Alison tied her hair back loosely with a simple ribbon of dyed blue. They gave her a pair of shoes that were about a half size too small, but Mercy didn't care, she was ready to meet Josiah, who, according to Emmaline, was waiting impatiently in front of the door.

The women giggled behind her when she stepped into the hall and found him there. Her heart beat in her throat.

"I...you..." he stumbled over his words as his gaze took her in from head to toe and his smile widened until it erupted into a short laugh. "Wow."

She laughed with him and his correct use of the word. He held out his arm for her to take. She accepted and let him lead her away, but not before she looked over her shoulder to see the women proudly watching her go off, as if she were their daughter. She waved and Hester held her hand to her mouth and then waved back.

"Are your maids agreeable?"

She turned to him and thought about leaving him but stopped thinking about it before it made her cry.

"Yes. They've quickly become my friends. The first I ever had."

His lower lip jutted out and turned downward. "I thought I was the first friend you ever had."

"You're more than a friend, silly," she chided, giving him a slight slap on the arm.

"I am?"

"Yes." She looked up at him again. "Much more."

That made him happy and his frown almost instantly transformed into a wide grin, which, in turn, changed the look of him from GQ gorgeous to a little kid bent on misbehaving. Did he always have that little dimple at the corner of his lips?

"Will it be more difficult to leave now?" he asked while he led her down the hall to the stairs.

She laughed softly. "Do you always just blurt out whatever you're thinking?"

He mixed laughter with his wide smile for a concoction that made her head spin.

As his laughter faded, his expression changed once again to something more pleading. "The more desperate I become for an answer, the more likely I am to speak from where it counts."

Breathe, Mercy. Breathe.

"Josiah," she said on a slight breath. "Because of you I already don't want to go back."

His gaze on her warmed as they paused at the top of the stairs. He reached out to cup her face in his hand. He looked as if he wanted to say something but then his smile faded and he waited until she grasped the banister before starting down the stairs.

"What is it?" she asked, sensing his suddenly sad mood.

He produced a smile out of his deep stores. "Are you hungry?" he asked, changing the topic.

She nodded and realized they were heading for the kitchen. Not the great hall, where everyone was eating.

"Are we going back to the village?"

"No," he said, accepting a large basket from the cooks. He rested the basket on his shoulder and held it steady with one hand. The other hand grasped hers and pulled her along. "I want to be alone with you."

She slid her gaze to the figure keeping just out of sight but following close behind. There were others. Three to be precise. Mr. Hollister and Mr. Abbott had been removed from guarding Josiah—away from his sight altogether, according to Emmaline, who knew all the castle gossip. And there would be a lot of it if they spent the day alone together. Besides, if he was going to attempt to get the dagger from her, she didn't trust herself not to willingly give him what he wanted.

"I don't think it's a good idea to be alone," she let him know.

He stared into her eyes for a minute that lasted too long and revealed windows for her to look through. When she did, she saw sorrow and curiosity and the mask he'd removed and laid aside in her presence only. She saw a young man afraid of his destiny. Someone somewhat dark, who refused to open up to anyone. Nothing was expected of him, and everything he did was done to convince others that the curse they all believed wasn't true.

Without taking his gaze from her, he stopped a servant about to pass them. "Go bring—what are they called?"

"Hester, Alison, and Emmaline."

"Ah, yes," he said as if remembering them. Had he painted them?

He told the man where to find them and to bring them to the kitchen, then he led Mercy back and asked the cooks to prepare more baskets.

"Are you going to invite the women to come with us?"

He nodded, waving them over when they appeared at the entryway. "Miss Smith seems taken with the three of you and wants you to accompany us to eat outside beneath the trees." While they squealed and nodded, he turned to Mercy to find her smiling at him.

He suddenly turned bashful and, smiling, looked down at his shoes.

"Thank you," she told him, standing on her tiptoes to whisper close to his ear.

CHAPTER SIX

T HE BLANKET JOSIAH packed was made to fit two, not five, so he ended up sitting in the grass while they ate. He didn't mind. The food that the cooks packed was delicious, a mix of everything he loved. Hard boiled partridge eggs, four loaves of fresh black bread, honey, freshly churned butter, slices of roasted rabbit, dried and salted herring, and more.

"Lord Josiah, my lady," Hester was the first to address them. "We've never been invited to eat with our lords or ladies. We don't know what to say to express our gratitude."

Mercy waved her hand. "It's nothing. We're eating together. You don't have to thank anyone for that."

Josiah agreed and added while he picked at fish off the bone, "I feel old, like my brothers when people call me Lord Josiah. Josiah is fine."

"Mercy," Mercy agreed, scooting onto the grass with him. She glanced at him to smile. He caught it and his heart flipped.

What was this he felt for her? Whatever it was, it was strong. Strong enough for him to fill his body with poison to keep her close. He'd told his father that he not only needed her by his side but he wanted her there, as well. He meant it. He liked how he felt when he was with her: peaceful, genuinely happy and hopeful.

He had wanted to tell her how he felt while they ate under the trees and the blue sky, but he was happy that she was enjoying herself now with her new friends. He was satisfied enough to watch her toss back her head to laugh and to learn what made her do so. He was especially pleased that she saved her most radiant smiles for him. She was the beauty of a sunrise after he'd been locked away in a fortress. He was fully aware of the way the ladies sighed and giggled over his constant smiling at Mercy. Even eating didn't stop him, nor did pride, or embarrassment. She made him feel happy. What did he care what others thought?

"What's your favorite food to eat?" Emmaline asked her while she slathered honey on her bread.

"Pasta."

The women shared the same confused look. Josiah watched and listened, amused to hear how Mercy would explain.

They talked about food and laughed over cups of wine. He was sure there were a few moments when Mercy was jealous when she found out he'd painted one of her new friends.

"You painted Alison?"

He nodded and sank his teeth into his buttered black bread with a slice of rabbit on top.

"In undress?"

He nodded again and looked at her curiously while he chewed. "Is something wrong?"

"No, nothing." She spread her gaze over all of them and laughed. "Nothing's wrong. "My goodness, this partridge egg is delicious!"

Josiah laughed, softly watching her look of distaste after popping the whole egg into her mouth.

"Are you going to paint Mercy, my lord?" Emmaline asked.

"If she lived here for the next fifty years, I'd fill the castle with portraits of her alone."

She kicked him softly. He wasn't sure if it was because he brought up her staying, or because he was confessing his feelings for her in front of the women. He laughed, and then she did too.

He didn't sing, but he hummed along when Alison and Hester sang one of the melodies the troubadours played at court lately. They even danced barefoot in the grass. It took her a few moments to allow herself to be so raw and open in front of them, but soon, as she twirled beneath Josiah's arm and danced with him and her friends, she laughed with the abandon of one truly happy. Josiah thought he'd like to make her this happy all the time. He thought of a thousand different reasons why she should stay here with him. He would tell her some of them later when they were alone. For now, they danced and sang and laughed in the filtered light beneath the canopy.

Later, while Hester rested on the blanket, she sang an old English tune about a hero called Beowulf. The melody was slow and haunting and not one for dancing, so he was surprised when Mercy stopped him from sitting.

"Dance with me."

He nodded, but wasn't sure what to do—though he'd already decided to do anything she asked.

When she moved close to him, his smile deepened. He let her take his hand to place around her waist. He wasn't sure he could swallow when she looked up into his eyes and placed her hand on his shoulder.

"Now hold my hand like this." She took his free hand and held it outward.

"Now what?" he whispered close to her ear.

"Lead me."

He was sure she'd hear the beating of his heart when she rested her cheek on his chest.

"Just move."

He closed his eyes and let the melody sink into him. He pulled her in a little closer and swayed, moving his feet instinctually, left—right—left—. She lifted her head to smile at him and he almost tripped over his feet.

He rested his head on hers and closed his eyes, lost in the rapture of holding her. He didn't know when Hester had stopped singing, or when the three women left and headed back to the castle. He held Mercy close with the same desperation with which she held him—as if they were close to parting and losing each other.

"Mercy...I..." Why couldn't he speak? He wanted to promise her that if she stayed with him, he would never change. He would always love being with her, sharing moments with her that would last in their memories for as long as they lived. He wanted to learn what made her happy and then laugh with her every day. What made her cry? He would make certain never to do it. He wanted to kiss her and hold her, make love to her at night and in the morning.

When she moved to leave his embrace, he didn't let her go. He wanted to tell her everything, but he didn't. He knew she had the dagger. He guessed it had been in her first room. She'd returned today to get it and bring it to her new chambers. Perhaps she needed it to return to where she'd come from, but she probably didn't know how to use it. Yet. He worried she'd find a way. He knew he should be pushing her away in order to stay clear of that dagger that had found its way back to him. If she returned to her time with it, it would be out of his life.

But so would Mercy.

That damn blade was always in the back of his mind...and lately, thoughts of it were creeping closer to the forefront.

"It doesn't matter what's said between us now," he told her, fighting to keep his heart where it needed to be, and failing. He took her elbows and put her arms around his neck, then he slipped his arms around her waist and held her close. "Only that if you find a way back, I may get sick and die without you."

Her eyes opened wide with concern, dazzling him senseless by their glory." But I thought you were healed."

"I was, but this is different. This is worse."

"I know," she whispered into his chest, warming it. He believed she knew. "I don't know how, but I think you've been with me my whole life. Or, at least since I was four and my blood mixed with yours. You're the first person I've let into my heart, my mind—you're everywhere in there." She let out a laugh that sounded more like a groan. "And if I find a way back...It isn't fair."

They held each other in silence for a long time. When she finally stepped away, he let her go. He was going to have to let her go if he meant to keep people safe from him.

"Thank you for this perfect day, Josiah."

I would make all your days like this one. He wanted to promise her, but he said nothing as he folded the blanket. The women had taken the baskets, so there wasn't much to carry back.

He took her hand and held it on the way home. "What if you can't go home? Are you prepared for that?"

She was quiet for a moment, then shrugged her shoulders. "I guess I am. It was never my home to begin with."

"I'd like to make a home with you," he said, staring into her eyes. Her smile widened and tears filled her eyes. What did it mean? What was she thinking? Did she really want to stay? Did she know she had to leave? He refused to think of that.

"Would you hate me if my heart rejoices if you can't go back?" he asked, letting her see his heart in his eyes.

She looked into them and then shook her head. "No, I wouldn't hate you. I'll never hate you."

»»»×«««

MERCY FOUND IT extraordinary that this morning she was sitting in a dank, dirty prison cell and tonight she was the center of attention at the Ashmore family table with Josiah. Everyone was nice enough to her while they asked her a thousand questions about her ability to heal Josiah. Could she heal anyone else? Who were her parents? Did they know more about her power? Where did she come from? The questions were endless. Josiah answered many of them but there were times when he kept silent and when Mercy turned to look at him, she found him watching her with a roguish smile, waiting for her answers along with the rest of his family.

"So, you didn't know if you could even save him this morning," Ava, Edward's wife, asked.

"Miss Smith had no idea what I was going to do," Josiah told her, then turned his gaze on Thomas, "because I didn't know. You hadn't foolishly thrown her in the dungeon yet."

"It wasn't fo—" Thomas tried to defend himself.

"You don't call dragging someone down there without a shred of evidence against them foolish?"

"We don't know who she is, Josiah," Edward interjected.

Josiah's mocking smile sharpened. "Do you know how rude it is to speak of her as if she's not sitting right here?"

"It's okay," she said softly beside him.

"Edward, please apologize to her," Josiah said to him. "Let's show her that the Ashmores are courteous."

"What?" his brother put to him. "I don't—"

"Brother," Josiah cut him off and stared at him from under his lids, "apologize to her."

"Forgive me, Miss Smith," Edward said, surrendering easily. "That was rude of me."

Just like that Josiah smiled at his brother and thanked him. For the first time, Mercy wondered if they gave in to him because he was the youngest and they all loved him most, or if they were afraid of him and what he might become.

"I think what you pulled today was the cruelest thing you've ever done to us, Josiah." All eyes shifted to Jeremy, the third son.

Mercy agreed to a point. His family didn't know she could heal him. Heck! She didn't know—and neither did he for sure. They thought he poisoned himself and would die before their eyes. The rest of her was thankful that he was still alive. If her blood had something to do with it, great. As long as he lived. He'd gone to the extreme to keep her with him. Whatever the reason, she didn't care. She liked it.

She looked at him now as he took his brother's blow without

striking back.

"Forgive me, Jeremy, all of you," he told them in a steady voice. "Forgive me for having to show you what could become of me without her. Her blood flows within me, giving me hope, laughter, and life."

Mercy blinked back a flood of emotions that had waited her whole life to come pouring out. Was he speaking of her? How could it be? She'd never dared to dream of anyone so devoted to her. Did he really care for her, or, like his amiable smiles, was his affection feigned and only meant to get his hands on the dagger? But he didn't know she had it for sure. Did he?

"The last thing I wanted to do was frighten all of you—"

"But you did anyway," Gilbert, fifth son said and took a sip of his drink. "You planned it out, and did it. You're clever. Why are you apologizing now for it? Would you do it differently if you could? No? Then stop it."

Josiah looked as if he wanted to answer his brother's accusation, but he remained quiet.

Mercy admired his inner strength to keep quiet. She reached for his hand under the table and held it. When he entwined their fingers together, she felt a streak of warmth flow through her. Her heart thumped hard, making her feel a little lightheaded—or was it simply his touch that made her feel as if she were floating on a cloud?

The conversation turned toward politics and how just ten years ago, Oliver Cromwell had defeated the new king, Charles II at the Battle of Worcester. Mercy remembered learning about the king who brought about the Restoration of England. She tried to remember her history lessons, but it was never her favorite subject. But then, none of the subjects were her favorite. By the time she was in junior high, she was already being teased on a regular basis, not so much about her scar, but more for her odd personality and loner behavior. It carried on into high school and then out into the working world.

But Mercy preferred not to think about those days. Instead,

images of Josiah dancing filled her mind. She never saw anyone dance with such abandon. It was like stumbling upon a beautiful faerie dancing in the glory of a new day. She didn't know when she was more taken with him, when he danced alone, or slowly with her. She liked his arms around her. No, she loved it. She felt safe pressed against his chest. He wouldn't let anything happen to her. He proved it this morning. She didn't feel like everything was happening too quickly. Rather, she felt that everything had been delayed and was now catching up.

"This is tiresome," he said leaning into her. "Let's leave."

Still holding her hand, he rose, taking her with him. "If you will excuse us. I want to show Miss Smith my studio."

"Son, I—"

He pulled her away while she was still bowing to everyone around the table and his father was speaking.

"Hurry," he said close to her ear and began to run, "before he calls us back."

They ran without slowing when they reached the stairs and laughed as they raced up them. His studio was high in the east turret, overlooking the village and the wilderness beyond the gates. When they reached the landing she fell against him, exhausted and out of breath, but exuberant.

She hadn't meant to still him. Was he even breathing heavy? His arms came up and around her slightly, giving her room to breathe. She felt his chin above her head, and then the warmth of his mouth when he pressed a kiss to her forehead. He let her rest against his chest, and she knew she didn't want to leave this spot.

When her breathing slowed, he reached up for the small lit torch on the wall and held it above their heads. "Come."

She followed him through the creaky, wooden door into a dimly lit room with a separate stairway up to another landing. Josiah passed her and reached more torches on the walls and lit them until Mercy could see all the paintings lined up against the walls. There were portraits of men and women, paintings of landscapes and oceans, vases of fruits and flowers. His well-used easel was set almost in the center. A paint stained palette rested on a stool and a small table housed over a dozen small cups of paints and brushes.

When he lit several candles on tables on either side of an olive green settee, he went to her and took her face in his hands. "Yours is the face I've been waiting for. I want to paint you."

Every time he spoke to her, he released thousands of butterflies in her belly. "Now?"

He nodded and sat her down on the settee. "I'll just begin now. It will take a few sittings to finish."

A few sittings, she thought. That meant being with him for just a few days more before she attempted to use the ruby dagger to return.

"Just try to remain still," he instructed, rolling up his sleeves.

She smiled at the way a wavy strand of hair fell over his forehead.

Oh, if she was unconscious somewhere, let her never wake up.

JOSIAH FELT AS if he already knew every nuance of her face while he drew her. Now that he'd seen her, he didn't need to look again to get her angles and lines right—but he did look. He looked until he felt a warm mist fill his eyes as unfamiliar emotions rose to the surface. It was like gazing at the splendor of a summer sunset ablaze in gold and crimson. Too beautiful to look at and not feel moved. He let himself feel what his heart was flooding him with. He cared for her more than he'd been prepared for. When he looked up from his easel, he smiled, realizing when she expelled a little snore, that she'd fallen asleep.

He laid down his brushes and went to sit beside her to watch her sleep, watch her breathe. When she tilted in his direction, he could barely move as she sank across his lap. He sat there for a moment and then laughed quietly and fit his arms under her. He carried her up the narrow stairway leading up to a small bedroom and set her down gently on his bed. It was much smaller than the bed in his main chambers—his bed, where Mercy slept the night before. He'd built this one for when he painted long into the night. It was built for one, and like his bed in his chambers, no one had ever shared it with him.

Setting her down, he covered her with a blanket and sat on the floor for a bit to watch her while she dreamed.

"Mercy," he said from deep in his chest, "I could love you deeply, madly. But I'm afraid of what brought you here and that it has remained. And if it has, that I might find it."

CHAPTER SEVEN

MERCY OPENED HER eyes when Josiah began to snore. She'd woken up when he carried her to the bed, and she'd heard the things he said to her when he thought she was asleep. He suspected she had the dagger. He knew she'd lied to him. How could she face him? But more importantly, she knew now what she had to do. He was afraid of finding it. She couldn't let him. She had to bring it back to her time. Oh, she wanted to cry. She *had* to leave him. There was no other way. "Should I tell him the truth?" she asked herself in a quiet voice while he slept. She stared at him sitting in a chair, sleeping with his head on the bed, resting on his arms.

She was tempted to smile at his parted lips and how they puckered slightly when he blew out air. Poor guy was so afraid of becoming a monster, he could never let down his guard. *I could love you deeply, madly. But...*

Why? Why did there have to be a but?

She reached out her trembling fingers to move the strand of his hair off his cheek. As lightly as she could, she traced the strong angle of his chin and jaw. Then she did the same to her own scar. "He makes me forget it's there." It didn't define her in his eyes— and she could never ever repay him for that. "Will he open his eyes one day and see the real me and run away?"

When she looked at him again, his eyes were open and he was gazing at her wearing a slight smile. She blushed to her roots but he said nothing as he rose and walked around the bed. When he reached the other side, he sat down and gave her a little push to move. When she scooted to the other side of the narrow bed, he laid down beside her.

"You're tired," she said. "I'll go to my room." She moved to sit up and swing her legs over the side, but his fingers shackling her wrist stopped her.

"Don't go." He pulled her closer until they shared breath and he closed his arms around her.

She could feel every part of his body against her, hard like armor, but warm flesh. His eyes shone in the candlelight like silver flashing through a stormy sky. He stared at her, holding her close with one hand and moving her hair away from her face with the other.

"Nothing can happen here, Josiah," she told him softly as his lips came closer. "I don't want to be a single mother in the future."

He said nothing but pressed his lips to her scar. She thought if anyone else had ever done the like, she would have pushed him away, but now, she could do nothing but close her eyes to stop her tears from flowing freely. "You'll always be beautiful to me, Mercy. I'll never run away," he promised. Before she began to cry at the poignancy of what he was doing, he leaned in slowly, keeping his eyes open until the last instant so that he could see her. And then his lips were there, covering hers, curious, cushiony like the lush pillows on his master bed or like clouds, kissing her, tasting her with delectable little strokes of his tongue. Every part of her reacted. Her head felt light, her blood went hot through her veins, her nipples tightened. She wanted to wrap her arms around his neck and hold on to him. She broke away and swiped a tear from her eye instead. This wasn't real, and if it was, it wasn't permanent. She had to keep the dagger away from him. The best place to keep it was 2022.

He didn't back away for a few seconds but perused her with curious, concerned eyes.

He was still close enough to examine his lips while he spoke. She thought of how they felt pressed to hers. Luxuriously soft, moldable, hungry, curious… She closed her eyes to breathe, then heard him chuckle and opened them again.

"What?" she asked. Was this where he told her that she was a fool? Did she want to hear him say it?

"You're shy. It's very sweet." He let his gaze rove over her face. "Mercy?"

"Yes?" she answered, hypnotized by him.

"Tell me why kissing me made you cry."

She felt herself being pulled from his spell. She didn't want to be separated from it. She touched her fingers to her mouth. "I've never felt anything like it," she whispered out, unable to stop herself. "I…I felt like I finally found where I fit." She giggled a little at herself and the tears pooled above the rims of her lids fell to her cheeks, breaking the spell. She wiped her tears and sat up in bed. "I'm sorry. I'm not clingy, I promise."

She wasn't sure he was listening. He was just gazing at her as if she were the oasis he'd been praying for in the wilderness. When he sat up beside her, her heart accelerated and her mouth went dry. She licked her lips. She knew he was coming for her. She could see it in the lightning in his eyes, in the way his lips relaxed and parted slightly, revealing the white tips of his front teeth. The sight of him tempted her to give him whatever he wanted. He reached out for her hand and drew her to him. He leaned in and brushed his lips over hers, then fell back and pulled her with him. She broke their kiss to laugh and blush. He tugged her back and pressed his lips to hers. She let him kiss and tease her, swiping his tongue across hers in a playful dance that made her stop resisting and sink onto him. She exhilarated in the feel of his arms closing around her. She felt a few tears escape her and let them fall. She no longer cared. She felt as if she'd come home. All the searching, all the yearning, here was the answer, with Josiah Ashmore.

He kissed her mouth with a series of short, slow, irresistible kisses that made her head spin and her heart take flight. He took her face in his palms and opened his sultry eyes to look at her, scar and all. "You ravish my soul."

Home. Home, where she belonged. Where she was herself, not a scar-faced orphan with a "personality disorder".

She moved closer until their noses were touching. "You're like a treasure box filled with all the laughter I've lost."

His unblinking eyes were glassy with tears while he stared at her. His smile had vanished, exchanged for a serious, meaningful expression. How? How could he care for her? How could he not see her misshapen face? At the thought, she turned away and closed her eyes.

"Mercy," he whispered. "Don't take your gaze from me."

"Josiah—" how did it hurt just speaking his name? "I've never met anyone like you and I'm afraid you're a figment of my imagination—and my imagination is known for being 'obsessive'—you could disappear at any moment. I don't want to imagine having you and then losing you. If you're real, why would you, the wealthy son of a duke, find any interest in me...unless you think I have the ruby dagger."

He gave a soft push to get her away from him, then left the bed. "Is that what you think?" He turned to watch her leave the bed as well. "That I'm trying to get the dagger?"

"No...I don't know."

"You have it, don't you? Did you use it to get here?

She shook her head. "Why are you making that assumption?" She tried to swallow, but she couldn't.

"Truly, that thing is cursed," he said quietly. "Please, keep it from me."

She moved around the bed to him. He turned to her immediately at the feel of having her near. "It scares me."

"What does?" he asked softly, stepping closer until they shared breath.

"That the dagger can turn you into someone different." She knew it was possible after getting cut by it and becoming a gloomy, frightened, detached child. "You said you wanted to destroy it. How would you do that?"

He closed his arms around her, breathing her in, just as she filled her lungs with him. What was she doing? She couldn't destroy the dagger. She needed it. She was letting her heart get involved.

"I would lock it in a weighted box and hurl it into the sea."

She smiled while he held her close. She was happy he had no desire to wreak havoc on thousands. She let him lead her back to the narrow bed and they got in together and squeezed close. "Josiah?" she asked after a few seconds.

"Yes?"

"What's the curse of the dagger? You told me the prophecy of it. But why or how is it cursed? Do you know?"

He thought about it for a minute, then shook his head. "I don't know, but I think I may know someone who does. We'll visit her in the morning. We'll sneak out before dawn to avoid being followed by the guards."

"Won't you get into trouble?"

"Yes, but do they think I care?"

Mercy thought about how many rules he'd broken since she showed up. He wasn't supposed to be alone with anyone, especially not her. He wasn't supposed to leave the gates. She was sure he wasn't supposed to almost kill himself to prove a point. He obviously didn't care about rules. "No," she whispered into his chest.

"No is right."

They snuggled even closer, loving the familiarity they felt toward each other, but then Mercy withdrew to look at his face in the soft candlelight. "Josiah, do you realize that we speak alike?"

"So?"

"It's as if we've been hearing each other over three hundred years apart. I've always said odd words for my time and you seem to understand and easily use words I have said."

"What does it mean?"

"I don't know, but after I was pricked by the dagger I changed and I began to talk to "myself". But Josiah, I don't think I was speaking to myself. I think I was speaking to you."

His smile widened into a grin of pure delight. "We're destined to be together."

"Yes," she said, knowing she was lost.

When he leaned in to kiss her, she placed her fingers over his lips. "We should get to sleep then."

She felt his lips smile and then pucker against her palm before he kissed it. "Fine," he groaned out without moving. "Sleep well, Mercy."

She should go to her own bed. But she couldn't bear to leave him.

She was in trouble.

JOSIAH HELD HIS horse's reins in one hand and the reins of Mercy's horse in the other. She knew how to ride—a little. He'd wanted her to ride with him in his lap—between his legs—whichever. They were equally dangerous positions for her to be in with him because either way, his arms would be around her while he held the reins. She couldn't tell him she wanted the same—more than anything. It was a new day and she had to keep her head on straight. She didn't belong here. If Josiah really cared for her— well then, it was even more unfamiliar.

He'd brooded over her not riding with him, but not for long. He'd given her her own horse, letting her pick from the available ones in his stable. She chose one of his *unavailable* favorites, a spirited, white mare called Dearest. Thankfully the mare remained docile while Mercy rode her. But just in case, he held her reins. If she did find a way home, Mercy was going to miss him protecting her.

They rode past the village, and half a mile beyond the gate, on their way to the woods to visit Old Lizzie, said to be a seer and healer after her potions healed a boy from a deadly snake bite and a woman who'd gone deaf. Her skills didn't work on everyone though. She hadn't been able to heal the duke's son. Still, she knew every legend, every lore. If anyone could answer their questions it was Old Lizzie. Maybe this seer knew how to get rid of the ruby dagger permanently.

"You can let go of the reins now," Mercy let him know.

Josiah blinked his gaze to her. "Why are you denying me from being close to you?" His usual smile was nowhere to be seen, and its obvious absence brought a smile to Mercy's lips.

"Are you falling for me, Lord Winterborne?" Was she flirting? Was this her, smiling to her dimples' best advantage? He made her forget her ugliness. A small voice in her head was still telling her that he could be winning her over to get the dagger. But she didn't really believe it. He seemed more afraid of it.

He scoffed at her and kept riding. "You think me so easily won, Miss Smith?"

She thought about it and nodded. "Yes, I do." She didn't really, but she liked being playful with him.

"You insult me," he scowled, but she caught his frown easily turning into a smile when he turned away.

They came to Old Lizzie's cottage in the middle of the woods. It looked so much like a cottage from a movie that Mercy almost doubted again that anything was all real.

The stone cottage was overgrown with vines festooned with orange, yellow, and blue flowers. Currant and mulberry bushes grew around it, along with trees almost blocking the chimney. The old seer stood outside the cottage as if waiting for them. Her white hair was tied into a bun at the back of her nape; her skin, as weathered as some of the trees nearby.

"What brings Catherine Ashmore's seventh son to my doorstep?" she asked while studying him with milky irises.

Before he answered, the old woman turned her blind eyes on Mercy. "You should not be here."

Mercy blinked. How did she know? Was she truly a seer? What if she saw that Mercy was hiding her true identity *and* the ruby dagger?

"We've come to ask you about the curse of the ruby dagger," Josiah told her. "Why is it cursed? How did it begin?"

Old Lizzie narrowed her eyes on him. "You ask many questions."

"Don't I have a right to the answers?" he asked in a quiet, steady voice.

"No. You have the right to nothing," the old woman said and turned away from him.

Mercy watched her. Once the initial shock wore off that the seer knew what no one told her, Mercy took a better look at her. She reminded Mercy of someone. But who?

"Come inside," the old woman crooked a bony finger at them. "The birds are listening."

Looking up at the trees, Mercy narrowed her eyes on the birds in the canopy. What? She shook her head and followed Josiah and Lizzie into the cottage.

Inside was almost as green with foliage as the outside, the difference was that the plants inside were in pots. There was a purple and scarlet carpet on the floor and a short, bare table off to the side. Deeper inside, other, higher tables were laden with bottles, jugs, and jars filled with liquid and a myriad of other things. A small stove and a chopping table to the left and to the right, a cozy alcove for sitting.

She cast a disgusted stare to Josiah. "Do you know how to peel onions?"

His eyebrows rose. "What?"

"Onions." She flicked her unseeing gaze to the chopping table. "Do you know how to peel them?"

He opened his mouth and chuckled softly. "What kind of seer are you if you don't already know the answer?"

She scowled. "Anyone can guess that a pampered boy cannot do anything for himself."

"Anyone can be a fool, prone to rash judgment," Josiah countered. He went to the chopping table, picked up an onion from the overflowing sack leaning against the table leg. He plucked the knife off the table and cut both ends off the onion, then peeled it perfectly.

Setting it aside, he looked at Old Lizzie. "Would you like me to chop them as well?"

Mercy concealed her smile behind her fingers. She was glad he proved the old woman wrong.

"Careful, young man," Lizzie said in a low voice, "the darkness in you is stirring."

Mercy scowled at her, but when she set her gaze on Josiah, the glare he was giving Lizzie made her scowl look like a loving smile. The hair on the back of Mercy's neck rose off her flesh. When Josiah glanced her way and saw her disapproving look, his glare immediately shifted into a full-blown pout that banished every misgiving she had of him. It seemed as if one look of rebuff from her could turn the beast into a puppy. Even Old Lizzie couldn't help but notice.

"What's this?" She asked with raised brows, proving she could, in fact, see, even without eyes. She turned to Mercy and stared in silence. Mercy turned away. The last thing she wanted to be was probed with an old woman's 'seer' eyes.

Was the seer about to blow her cover? She cast Josiah a nervous look, waiting, but the seer said nothing. Mercy peeked at her. Lizzie shook her head at her. "It's not enough."

"What?" Mercy whispered. From the corner of her eye she saw Josiah step closer to hear.

"Encouraging words," Lizzie told her. "They are not enough."

Mercy smiled. "We'll see about that." She knew better. When she was in her teens, she would have given anything for just one encouraging word. Just someone to believe in her besides the nuns who raised her. Josiah gave those words freely to her. The very least she could do was give him the same.

Old Lizzie stared at her for another moment and then nodded. "All right. You—" she turned to Josiah—"peel more onions. You—" she turned to Mercy—"what is it you want to know?"

Mercy smiled at Josiah, whose mood lifted seeing her. "Well, as Josiah asked earlier, why is the dagger cursed? When did it begin? *How* did it begin?"

"It's cursed because Catherine Ashmore, his mother, made a bargain with Raxxix of the underworld many years ago."

Josiah laughed without a sound nor did his mirth reach his eyes. "You're lying, and I warn you that you're speaking of my mother, lest you forget and I have to drag you before my father."

"Why do you protect her when she brought this curse upon you?" Old Lizzie demanded. "She murdered six families with the ruby dagger and sold her soul, along with the soul of her own seventh son to an agent of darkness."

Mercy couldn't believe what she was hearing. But the bigger issue right now was Josiah. He was pale. He didn't move. Was he breathing? His lips parted and Mercy could see his teeth ground together. He was angry. Very angry. "Josiah," she breathed out his name. She couldn't let him hurt the old woman. She couldn't let him cross any lines. Was he thinking of crossing them?

The sound of her voice—or his name, seemed to pull him back to her.

"Mercy," he said as the hint of a doubtful smile played around his mouth and he wrinkled his brows, curious about something. When he spoke, she could tell by the heavy cadence of his voice that he was still angry. "What did you think I would do?"

What? How did he know she was afraid he was going to do something—like wring Lizzie's neck. If she was afraid of him, then maybe she believed the whispers about him, just as everyone did. "When?"

"A moment ago."

"Girl," the old seer said, stopping her from answering Josiah and drawing Mercy's gaze to her. "What you already possess will grow stronger."

Josiah didn't respond to the cryptic words, but Mercy shifted her gaze to see him fold his arms over his chest, lean against the table, and cross his boots at the ankles. He was listening.

Was Old Lizzie talking about the ruby dagger? Mercy wanted to ask her why it brought her back to him. Because she was in possession of the dagger, did the task of killing Josiah fall to her? Because if it did, they-whoever they were—could forget it. She wasn't killing anyone. Especially not him.

"You two should go," the seer waved her hand away at them. "There's nothing more to say."

Josiah took a step closer to her. "How do I find it?"

Lizzie sighed and shook her head. "It will find you."

Mercy caught him glancing her way.

"How do I stop it?" he asked the seer.

"You don't. Either you die by it, or it sucks who you are from you and fills your shell with its master."

No. Mercy clutched Josiah's arm. She wouldn't let either one of those terrible things happen. There had to be another way! There was. If she took it to the future with her.

"Let's go," Mercy whispered to him and led him out of the cottage. "There's something I need to tell you."

CHAPTER EIGHT

T HEY DIDN'T RETURN to Ashmore Castle right away, but rode instead to an inlet along the coastal shore. Mercy wanted to speak with him alone and Josiah needed time to take in what the old seer had told him about his mother, so he brought Mercy here, where they could have been the only two people in the world. Josiah knew she would like it here, with its crystalline pools and waterfalls. She ohhh'd and ahhh'd and smiled at him wider than he'd seen yet.

"It's so beautiful, Josiah!" she breathed out more than once. Behind her, he looked around and smiled too. Yes, it was beautiful, he thought, seeing it through her eyes.

"There are many places I'll show you that are even more beautiful than this," he promised.

"I already have the best view."

It took him a moment to understand what she meant, and then when he did, he felt a fiery streak across his face. He smiled and looked away. But only for an instant before his heart pulled his gaze back to her. "I would argue that I hold that position."

"My—" she giggled when he pulled her into his embrace—"what a silver tongue you have, and even while you're blushing."

"It's only the truth I speak." He leaned in to kiss her bottom lip and then slowly down her chin. He dipped his face to her throat and buried his face in her neck, while his arms coiled tighter around her. He wished things were different. But he knew what was coming. He knew what she wanted to say. She had the ruby dagger. It had brought her here and it was likely her way home.

"Josiah?" She trembled in his arms.

"Hmm?" He closed his eyes. He wasn't sure how much more he could take. He didn't know if he dared to believe what Old Lizzie had told him about his mother. It made his head spin and his heart break afresh every time he thought of it. Was his mother truly responsible for the deaths of six families? Had she made a pact with the devil—a devil that was coming to claim him?

"Recently, I went back to the place where I was cut by the ruby dagger when I was four," Mercy told him. "It was still there, in that drawer. When I touched it something dripped down the blade and into my skin. It looked like blood but I don't think it could have been. It wasn't wet. And then I was here."

Josiah didn't breathe. It had drawn her blood when she was a young child and then called her back to it. "It used your blood to heal my body when I was a sick and dying newly born babe. Later, it used you to come to me, didn't it, Mercy?"

She shook her head. But even as she denied it all, her heart told her it was true. "You're suggesting it thinks and acts."

"The one who rules it does," he told her.

"Well, God rules over him and the dagger, so I'm sticking with Him," Mercy huffed, making Josiah want to deepen his smile.

"I want to tell you that I don't care about the dagger," he let her know. "But that it's here forces me to care."

"I...I—"

"It's all right," he told her softly. "I know you have it and I know you're afraid." He went to her and cupped her cheek in his hand, then pressed his forehead against hers. "Don't be afraid of me. You can trust me with this, even if it's about the dagger. Don't ever be afraid to tell me the truth. He hoped this was all she hadn't told him. He wanted to ask her again if she was a

Blagden. He'd defended her to his father and brothers, so her being a Blagden would be devastating for his family's trust in his judgement if she wasn't being truthful. But he trusted her, and trusting her meant not asking again.

"I know you likely need the dagger to go home. Do you know what to do? Are you certain you want to return?" he asked, then let a smile play at the edges of his lips. "You're going to miss me terribly."

"I know."

"I want to tell you not to go," he said.

"But you know I have to take it away."

He clamped down his jaw but nodded. He wanted to hold on to her and refuse to let her go. But the prophecy, which he'd never truly believed, seemed irrefutable now. It was real. The ruby dagger had come back to his time. It was an instrument of evil used to kill six families, and a pact was sealed by a demon to take his body. He knew the unselfish thing was to let Mercy go, but he didn't want to be unselfish and it didn't mean he wouldn't beg.

"The future is the best place to keep the dagger, Josiah," she went on, running her satiny fingers down his temple. How was he supposed to think straight when she was touching him so?

"Mercy, I know what it's all supposed to mean. But there's something about you that gives me hope that those whispers about my future that I hear behind my back are wrong. When I see myself through your eyes, I don't see a monster. If you want to stay here with me, we'll destroy the dagger together."

"What if something happens?" she cried. "What if it washes up somewhere along this coast and ends up right in your hands? Josiah, we can't take the chance."

She was correct, it couldn't stay here. He knew it but he also believed she could change things. She wasn't part of the prophecy. Even Old Lizzie knew she didn't belong here. So, exactly why was she here? Who was she? He liked being with her, looking at her, breathing the same air she breathed. He enjoyed her description of *cars. Cell phones* and *WI-FI* fascinated him. Who wouldn't want to return to that?

"I can't tell you where it is," she told him with reluctance.

He nodded. "When are you going to—"

"Tonight," she finished. "If I wait one more day I won't be able to leave you."

"I must keep you one more day then." His impish grin lit his eyes and made Mercy laugh.

"You're the only person I would stay—"

"—with for the rest of my days."

They spoke the words at the same time and Mercy had to bite her lip to keep from crying.

"Thank you," he said and kissed her eyelids. "I'm hungry."

"You picked a strange time to tell me that."

She laughed when he growled playfully and went in to nibble her neck. Soon though, his playful kisses turned more intimate. His hot breath scorched a path down the column of her throat and moved onto her shoulder.

"Stay with me, Mercy," he said against her skin.

"Josiah." She seemed to pull herself together and stepped away, out of his embrace. "How? Tell me how and I'll do it. I'll do what you want because it's what I want too. But there isn't a way. I have to get it away from you soon. I think every day counts."

They remained at the inlet for a little while longer and then headed back to the castle.

Josiah never wanted for anything in his life besides a happy ending to it. His father made certain to give him whatever he wanted. Nothing was refused him. So he found it especially difficult to lose Mercy, the one person who made him entirely happy. The only one he didn't know he needed to survive. To keep her, he would fight the most fearsome creature, go to any distant land to find her, even to her future if he could. But he couldn't do any of those things. He was a prisoner of the ruby dagger. Nothing had changed.

"Where have you been?" Josiah's brother Nicholas demanded when Josiah stepped into the castle. "Father's been looking everywhere for you. You've been gone all day with no guards."

Nicholas Ashmore gave Mercy a disapproving glance. "You better bring her."

"Where is he?" Josiah asked.

"In his private solar. You should be hearing him shouting for you momentarily."

Josiah's lips curled into an untimely smile and his brother shook his head. "Can you not do anything with sincerity?"

"I'm sincere right now, Nicky. I didn't mean to cause him to worry." He lowered his head and passed him on his way to the great hall.

He turned once to make certain Mercy was following him and smiled at her seeing her there. She appeared unsure and anxious. He reached out his hand and took hers.

How could there be such power in a mere touch? Power enough to buckle his knees and set his heart to racing? *She was leaving. She was leaving.*

Nicholas was correct. Josiah heard his father bellow his name and followed the sound to the solar. When he reached the door and entered, he felt Mercy pull her hand away when she saw his father, Captain Sherwood, and three of his brothers turn to look at her. Josiah turned to her as well, knowing everyone was watching, and smiled his warmest, most radiant smile at her. Expressions froze, along with cups in the process of being lifted to lips, but Josiah never wavered. "Mercy, don't be intimidated. I won't leave you."

She didn't smile back, but he saw the relief in her eyes, her subtle nod. Strengthened by her faith in him, he turned to his father. He knew what was coming. For now, memories flashed through his mind of his father always making time for him to play, teach, and adore. When his father's position called him away, Josiah's brothers watched over him, spoiling him almost as much as their father had. He loved his life here. He loved his father, so when he spoke, his words came from his heart. "Father, forgive me for worrying you yet again. I sometimes fear that I truly am your cursed son, for I do nothing but cause you trouble and vexation."

His immediate confession seemed to diffuse the red-faced duke a bit. He continued. "I went riding, and, being responsible for her, took Miss Smith along. I enjoy her company and I wanted to be alone with her."

His father's dark glare shifted to Mercy. Josiah didn't like it, so he stepped in front of her, cutting off his father's view of her.

"Jos—"

"Father," Josiah cut him off gently, "I'm trying to be as truthful as I can be with you. Please don't make it difficult."

The duke stared at him with a series of quick blinks. "Your defiance knows no boundaries. That's my fault."

"Then punish yourself for it," Josiah told him. "Not me."

As he expected, his father's gaze hardened. "She needs to leave the castle. She can be called upon if you become ill again. But you must end more personal things with her."

"No," Josiah told him with a bow. "I'm not ending anything with her."

"What did you say?" his father demanded.

"Father, I ask that you speak to us in private."

The duke leaned forward in his seat and glared at his son. "Us?"

"Yes."

"No."

Josiah scoffed to himself. He didn't want to bring up his mother in front of everyone, or ever again for that matter, but there were things he wanted to know. "Very well. Let's discuss these matters in front of all."

Mercy tugged on a small piece of his cuff. When he leaned in, she whispered in his ear.

"On second thought," he said, straightening, "let's not. We're going to the dining hall to eat. We'll speak with you later."

"Don't you—" his father began incredulously but Josiah stopped him.

"Father! I'm hungry!" He immediately brooded.

The duke shook his head in disbelief. "Son, please, hear me."

"Of course, I will, Father," Josiah told him. "Right after we eat."

The duke gave in with a grunt and downed the ale in his cup.

Taking her by the hand again, Josiah led her out of the solar and to the dining hall, where he found a table with room for them to sit. When the servers arrived, he offered each of them his most heartfelt thanks. He knew their names, Beth and Louise. It earned him a few extra squeals and slices of beef.

Josiah greeted the people closest to him at the table; Lord Martin Reeve, Baron of Shrewsbury, and his wife Hilary. Gilbert, fifth son of the duke and Dorset's second most eligible bachelor. Lord Edward Hadly, Baron of Lillsburgh and his wife Alysia were also there.

"He seems really angry," Mercy whispered close to him.

Josiah waved his hand away. "He'll recover."

"It's my fault for keeping you away so long," she told him so softly, he almost didn't hear.

"Mercy, I don't remember you telling me to sneak off without my father's guards. None of this is your fault. He's afraid of Blagdens coming here to finish what they started. You're not a Blagden, so stop worrying. I'll speak to him about it later."

He began to eat, but she placed her hand on his wrist and stopped him. "You won't leave my side even if he commands it of you, will you?"

He smiled to reassure her. "I won't leave your side, Mercy."

"Promise?"

His smile deepened and he nodded. "I promise."

He didn't remind her that she was leaving. Mainly because he didn't want to think about it. In fact, the three times it invaded his thoughts while he ate, he had to do everything he could to keep his tears from forming. He didn't care if it was the right thing to do, he didn't want her to leave. He wasn't sure he could let her go.

"You're picking at your food," he noted out loud.

"I'm not in the mood for a pie that had a live bird in it," she told him.

He laughed into his fist then picked up some meat and held it up to her mouth. "Taste this. It's braised venison."

She stared at his offering and shook her head. He didn't back away but urged her all the more. "Here. Try it."

"No, thank you. I don't—"

He popped it into her mouth and smiled at her while he chewed his own. He noticed that she was looking at his lips, so he puckered them a little more while he ate, and then laughed with her when she teased him about showing off his 'sexy lips'. He noticed that others were watching them. His father had arrived with four of his brothers. Josiah didn't care. As far as he was concerned, she was the only other person there. He filled her bowl with food, leaned in to speak to her softly, so that only she could hear, and spread his smiles, the kind he offered to her alone, over every inch of her face.

How had she managed to vanquish his dark thoughts as easily as her blood had vanquished his fever? Even the news that his mother had birthed the terrible prophecy and caused him to live in the shadows of a curse, didn't seem so heart wrenchingly bad when Mercy smiled at him.

"I don't want you to go," he mouthed to her, his appetite gone when he thought of her leaving for the fourth time. He found her hand under the table and covered it with his.

"Miss Smith," his brother Gilbert said, shining his smile on her. Josiah knew his brother was handsome, with his black hair and eyes as blue as the sky. He wore a fitted coat over a matching doublet and a high cravat and made women smile behind their hands almost as much as Josiah did. Josiah didn't think Mercy would be swayed. "I remember that you lost some of your memories. Have any returned to you yet?"

"No, my lord," she answered.

Josiah watched her hide her face behind her hair. He looked around to see if anyone was openly staring at her scar. They weren't, but a few of the younger men were leering at her, as if they just spotted their prey. Josiah cast his murderous glare on them until they nervously spotted him and looked away. His father and brother also saw the dark warning in his eyes from across the hall.

"Stop it," Mercy warned him.

Josiah blinked at her rebuke and then frowned for all he was worth. He didn't like disappointing or displeasing her. And she seemed to dislike his temper the most. He knew it. He understood why. He didn't like it.

And then she moved a bit closer to him and every unwanted thought was beaten back by her sweet voice in his ears. "It's not fair how adorable you are when you pout."

"I'm not pouting." All he had to do was gaze down into her eyes and he was lost and then found again. Smiling at her was easy. She didn't hold a grudge but giggled into his arm. She made him feel lightheaded, as if he drank too much ale. Even knowing he'd lose her tonight, being with her now filled him with too much joy to be in a shadowy place.

When the courses were almost done and many guests left the great hall, too tired or too filled with food to continue eating, Josiah led Mercy to his father's table.

"Father," he said, without sitting, "before we go any further, grant me permission to ask you something."

The duke nodded, though he wore a scowl that said he'd rather ask the questions than answer them.

"Is it true that mother murdered six families and—"

His father sprang up from his seat and stared, wide-eyed at him. "Where did you hear such a thing?"

"—and she entered into a pact with Raxxix of the underworld and sold my soul to him? Is it true that I'm cursed because of her?"

The duke's six other sons came forward, hearing their youngest brother's questions and curious about their father's answers.

"Who spoke of this to you?" his father demanded. His gaze immediately fell to Mercy.

"It wasn't her," Josiah told him softly. "Is it true?"

The duke raked his gaze over the great hall. "Everyone out except my children and their families."

He waited until the last person left and the doors were shut. Then, he appeared to gather himself, pulling the lapels of his coat and loosening his cravat. "I had no idea at the time. I found out recently."

It was true! It was true! Josiah's mind shouted like an alarm. He wanted to run. In fact, his legs ached to go. His mother brought the curse on him.

"Josiah, I didn't know about what she had done. After she was killed, I did my best to get to the bottom of everything and find out the truth. I discovered what she had done with that dagger."

"What about Raxxix?" Josiah asked him, numbly. "Will he take over my soul?"

"No. No, my son—"

"No," Josiah repeated with a hint of a smile, "because Mercy has my heart and she won't let him have anything else." He turned to her. "Will you, Mercy?"

"No," she replied without hesitation. "I won't."

His father's nostrils flared as if the air he was breathing wasn't enough. "You put your trust in a stranger. His dark gaze slipped to Mercy. "I want to know who you are and what brought you here. Your blood can heal my son, but you don't know how or why. I want answers!"

"Father—"

"Silence," the duke shouted at him. He sized her up with a distasteful scowl. "You look as if you've been in a fierce fight. That scar is very unsightly—"

"Father," Josiah's angry warning quieted everyone there.

"Josiah, your foolish heart betrays your youth."

"And what does your heart betray about you, Father? You were married to a woman who was killing people and making deals with devils. And you didn't know. You didn't see the darkness of her heart," Josiah said calmly. "I'm not worried about what you think of me."

Josiah snatched up her hand again and stormed away with her. He wouldn't let anyone insult her in his presence. No matter who it was. His father should have known better than to be so cruel to someone else—anyone else, and especially not Mercy. He could have told his father that she was going to try to leave tonight, but that required much explanation and in the end his father might realize that she had the dagger.

She was leaving. She was leaving. It was all he could think about. He didn't want to let her go.

CHAPTER NINE

"J UST LET ME kiss you one more time." He held her face and moved his lips over her while he spoke. He would have let her go if she told him to. She didn't. He closed his eyes when tears would have escaped them. He kissed her, and then again, and again. He would have done anything, given anything, for her to stay. He didn't question why he felt so strongly, so quickly. He simply accepted it. She was in his heart, perhaps born there, and there was nothing anyone could do to change it. Even if she left, he would continue to need her.

"If there's a way to come back to me without the dagger—"

"I'll find it, Josiah," she promised. "If there's a way to come back to you, I'll find it."

He smiled at her and wiped her tears with his thumb. His heart felt lodged in his throat. He couldn't say anything or else it would tear away from him and go to her.

When she stepped away, out of his embrace, he reached out. But he didn't take hold of her. She had to go. Thousands of lives depended on it.

He stepped out of her chambers and with every reluctant step he took, he had to fight himself not to rush back to her. He knew the dagger was close by. He could feel its vibration in his blood, but he had no interest in the accursed weapon. He hoped Mercy could find a way back to him without the dagger. As he closed the door behind him, he ground his teeth and leaned his back against the cold wood.

He paced outside her door, torn between not wanting it to work and wanting to get the dagger completely out of his life.

It was in the bedroom with her. She would uncover it soon and prick herself in the finger with it. His blood rushed hot through his veins thinking of it. He turned to look at the door and placed his palm on it. He could go in there and stop her and take it from her—no! No, he shouldn't think of it. He felt its power course through him, compelling him to go get the dagger, but he fought it and to do so, he only had to think of Mercy tossing her head back to laugh, or closing her eyes to kiss him, and the desire for anything but her disappeared.

The door opened and her face appeared, delighting him.

"Do you think I should say something?" she asked, staring up at him.

"Did you say something last time?"

"No."

"Then I don't think it matters," he told her, praying it wasn't working.

"I'm holding it up like I did before," she informed him.

He took a step closer to her. How would he get through days of not seeing her? He folded his arms across his chest to keep from reaching for her and stepped back against the doorframe.

After over a quarter of an hour, she returned to look at him, her expression unreadable. "I think you need to get the weighted box."

He gazed at her while his smile widened. When her smile grew into a soft giggle, he knew that even though the dagger would remain in this time, they would be together—and she was happy about it, as he was.

He wanted to push open the door and take her in his arms, but she was holding the dagger and even though, strangely, he couldn't feel its power, he didn't want to get that close. So, he hurried off to his chambers to get the box.

When he returned to her, he brought the heavy box, nails,

and a hammer. After she placed the dagger inside, he nailed the box shut with eighteen nails—just to be safe.

"That should do it," she said, surveying their work.

Without wasting another instant, he went to her and scooped her up into his arms. "Do I get to keep you?" he teased and then grew serious. "I'll pay whatever the cost."

"I wouldn't have you pay anything." She met his loving gaze and lifted her fingers to his lips.

Did she know he was falling in love with her? That he loved her already? There had been many girls who fancied him ever since he could remember. He was always kind to them but he never let any of them touch his heart, or his body. He wasn't sure if he could love at all. Wasn't he the cursed son of the duke of Dorset? The boy who would become a murderer? Murderers didn't deserve to love. He reached his twentieth year never loving a girl. Until now.

"Josiah, we need to dump the dagger. After that your life will be your own and I'll be in it because there's nowhere else I ever want to be."

He looked at the box. It was the closest he'd ever been to the ruby dagger. He felt the pull of it, the faint urge to smash the box open and take what was his—*my life will finally be my own and she'll be in it...*

He let her go and went to the door. "We're going to need to get to the water without my father's guards. We're going to need a carriage. I'll leave now and send a male servant up to carry the box. Don't argue," he said, cutting her off when she opened her mouth. "It's very heavy. Leave the castle through the kitchen. Take the servant with you. Walk toward the western gate. I'll—"

"Wait. Which way is west?"

He gave her a curious look. "You don't know west?"

"No. We had GPS. It's—never mind. What were you saying?"

"Walk west. It's that way." He pointed. "I'll meet you at the gate with a carriage. If anyone stops you on the way, tell them you remembered something about your home and you couldn't find me so you asked one of the servants for help."

She gave him a worried look. "Can't you just order the guards not to follow you?"

He shook his head. "They obey my father."

"It's okay. I can do it. Once this thing is out of your life—"

"Mercy," he went back to her and took her hands in his. "Are you certain you don't want to try again? Once the dagger's gone, it's gone."

"We hope." He noticed she said more to herself than to him. "Yes. I'm sure," she assured. "Go. I'll wait until the muscle gets here."

He quirked his mouth at her. "The muscle?" He shook his head. "Never mind. It's not important." He kissed both her hands, deepened his smile on her, then left.

In the corridor, Josiah stopped and leaned his back against the wall. He rubbed his belly that was beginning to ache. He wasn't hungry, in fact, the thought of eating suddenly made him feel like retching. He wanted to go back to Mercy's room. But this time, it had less to do with her. "No," he growled out and pushed off the wall. He wouldn't see her again until they were hauling the box over the cliff. He searched, stumbling here and there, until he found Oswald Sawyer, a stout servant from Tolpuddle, who'd served the Ashmores for eight years now. He appeared fit and well-able to carry the box.

After giving Oswald his instructions, the servant lingered near Josiah, then finally asked if Josiah was all right.

"I'm well, just tired," Josiah reassured and patted his arm. He smiled as his hand hit a solid log. He walked away and laughed softly. "The muscle."

He felt his own arm. There was muscle there but it was leaner, longer, not thick and seemingly corded like Oswald's, who was shorter by at least six inches. He stopped and turned to look back with a frown. Was he a fool to send *the muscle* to her, when he couldn't even fight off a few rules?

No. Tonight wasn't the night for bravado. They had to get rid of the dagger.

It didn't go unnoticed by him that he'd forgotten all about feeling ill until just an instant ago when he remembered what they had to do. The dagger. Was it possible that something was trying to keep him from getting rid of it? Yes. And it could only be for one reason—the demon his not-so-innocent mother had summoned wanted to use his body to wield the dagger. It was all real. The prophecy was real. He was cursed. The people were all correct to fear him. He reached out for the wall again and missed. Falling to the floor, the terrible truth dawned on him. He was cursed. He should be forcing Mercy to keep trying to go back to her future, because what kind of future did she have with him? Was throwing the dagger into the ocean enough to keep it from returning to him? It didn't matter, as long as Mercy was here with him, even if it returned, she'd help him defeat it.

He pulled himself up to his knees, and then to his feet. He never felt so ill before. He didn't need to see his physician, he knew he was burning up. He tried to take a step. This time he made it to the wall and used it for support as he took each shaky step toward the castle entrance.

He felt his eyes close. His mouth felt as if someone had poured sand into it. He just had to make it outside. The farther away he was from the dagger, the better. Right? "Please. Please, let me make it."

He began to sink to the floor, too weak to even breathe…

"Josiah!"

He dreamed of Mercy's voice rising above the muck and mire.

Mercy, save me.

He felt someone tugging at his belt. Mercy. He opened his eyes as wide as he could and looked at her. Was he dreaming?

His head seemed to clear a bit and she came into his vision again. She was smiling.

"Blood…happened? Are…all right?"

He was coming to. He looked at her bleeding finger and

smiled. She knew to touch her blood to him.

"Is it enough? Josiah, is it enough?" he heard her asking.

He nodded, feeling stronger. "It's trying to stop me from disposing of it," he told her when he was able to sit up again. "We have to move quickly."

She held him back from rising fully and pressed her finger to his hand. "Another moment more."

There was no time to waste, but he liked her concern for him, so he waited as she requested.

By now, it was after midnight and everyone but the guards would be asleep, and only half the guards would be on duty. The trick was getting past them. He prayed Captain Sherwood wasn't at the main gate tonight because nothing would stop Josiah from getting rid of the dagger.

They made it out of the castle together with Oswald staying close. "Hang onto me if you need to, lord."

Josiah thanked him but felt utterly pathetic beside the girl he loved—who just happened to look over and smile at him. He forgot everything else. She made him feel thankful for having people around him like Oswald—who would never think to make himself so familiar with any of the other Ashmores. Maybe not everyone in the castle believed he was cursed.

"My lord?" Oswald looked up at him and then away."

"Yes, Oswald?"

"The box is shaking."

"Hold onto it, Muscle," Josiah told him, stepping away from him.

"Muscle?" the servant asked. Josiah's warm gaze fell on Mercy when she giggled.

"That's what I'm going to call you from now on," Josiah told him. "Unless you don't want me to."

"I wouldn't dare to presume that what I want matters."

"Of course it matters," Josiah let him know and tossed him a smile over Mercy's shoulder.

Muscle didn't ask any questions about the box but waited in

silence until Josiah returned driving the carriage. "Can you get us to the gate?"

"Yes, my lord." Oswald bowed and then climbed into the place where Josiah had been sitting. He set the box down beside him, took the reins, and nodded down at Josiah.

"Where are we going?" Mercy asked him when they started moving.

"Weymouth," he told her. "It's the farthest out in the ocean we can go without a boat."

First, they had to get beyond the main gate.

"Lord Winterborne," called one of the guards, thankfully not Captain Sherwood, when Josiah stepped out of the carriage. "I have orders not to let you out alone."

"Am I a child, Caswell?" Josiah shouted up, brooding at the guard. "Open the gate at once!"

"I have orders from your father. I—"

"And when I complain about you to my father, whose side do you think he will take? Open the gate, or you will find out."

There was a pause that Josiah waited through patiently. And then the gate creaked open.

"To the cliffs," Josiah commanded, disappearing inside the carriage. He smiled when they rode through the gate without opposition. Soon the dagger would be gone...he felt the resistance in his blood, his bones. Some more feral part of himself coming closer to the surface wanted to keep the dagger. He knew it was vibrating though the box was up front with Oswald, who drove the horses faster, eager also to get rid of the strange box.

"You should know," Josiah said quietly, leaning into Mercy, "The longer I'm around the dagger, the more I want to keep it. Don't worry, I'm not so weak-hearted to give in to an evil desire. But—"

"But?" Her eyes opened wider. The look of her made him smile.

He was going to tell her that if anything terrible *should* happen he was going to command Muscle to pierce his heart with the dagger, but why alarm her?

"Nothing," he reassured her in a tender voice. "I'll tell Muscle to toss the box in our sight. But I won't get close enough to help."

"Is it that bad?"

His smile remained. "I don't want it to become that bad, hmm?"

She nodded but didn't look convinced. "I'll go with him to make sure—"

"No. He's carrying an instrument of evil, Mercy. I don't know what that thing is capable of making him do in order to save it. You will stay with me."

"Okay."

His smile widened. "Okay."

He heard a sound he knew well, for he sometimes rode here above the cliffs to look out over the roiling waves, feeling something kindred with them. They had reached their destination.

"Get as close to the cliffs as you can," he advised Muscle. "I don't want you to have to carry it longer than you have to."

"Yes, my lord."

Josiah left the carriage with Mercy but stayed back, watching Muscle walk to the edge. He flung the box over without a moment's hesitation, then turned to hold up his free hands to Josiah. His face paled instantly. "My lord, behind you!"

Josiah counted eight ruffians when he spun around. One of them had just snaked his arm around Mercy's neck! Josiah ground his teeth, yanked his dagger free, and jammed it into the ruffian's arm. He let go of Mercy and Josiah pulled her behind his back. With a series of spins and flips he fought off four of the men. The other four fought Oswald, who looked to be protecting himself well, until one of the miscreants crept up behind him, about to thrust his sword into the beefy servant. Josiah leaped at him and smashed the hilt into the man's side and then his face, but he didn't kill any of them.

"My lord!" Oswald lamented when he saw Josiah's sleeve

turning red. "You've been cut."

"I'm alright," Josiah assured them both when Mercy reached for him. "Let's get back before our absence is noticed." He met Mercy's gaze as he helped her back into the carriage. "It's gone."

She nodded and smiled at him.

"My lord," Oswald stopped before he climbed into the carriage's driver's seat. "You saved my life. I'll always be in your debt."

"Don't mention it, Oswald," Josiah told him and disappeared into the carriage with Mercy.

The guards at the gate let them right in. Josiah was relieved that they were being so agreeable but a few moments later he found out why. Captain Sherwood was waiting for him on the other side.

"Where were you?"

Josiah didn't like the hard look he was giving Mercy, as if she was the one who made Josiah do all these troublesome things. "I took her to the cliffs."

The captain narrowed his eyes on Josiah. "Are you always going to contend with authority?"

"No," Josiah said calmly, despite the accusation. "I wasn't contending with anyone. I was simply spending time with—"

"Josiah," the captain said through a clenched jaw. "You don't have to leave the gate to—what is that? Is that blood?"

Before Josiah answered the captain grabbed him by the wrist. When Josiah grimaced in pain the captain swore. "Were you fighting?"

"They came upon us from behind. What was I supposed to do?"

"They?" The captain asked, growing pale in the moonlight. "How many were there?"

"Eight. But Oswald helped—"

"Eight?!" the captain shouted. "Your father will have my head."

Josiah grinned at him. "Not if we don't tell him."

The captain muttered something unintelligible and pushed him toward the castle. "We aren't going to tell him. You are."

JOSIAH TRULY DIDN'T mean to cause his father so much worry. If the duke didn't try so hard to find out about things, he would have more peace.

After an hour of shouting and pacing, the duke finally fell into his seat.

"May I go, Father?" Josiah asked when his father didn't speak again.

"No. You will stand there all night if I say so."

Josiah didn't want to stand here all night. He barely had a chance to say goodnight to Mercy. He wanted to see her before she fell asleep. He sighed and shifted on his feet.

"You don't understand how I worry, Son."

"You're correct, I don't," Josiah told him. "But I promise I can take care of myself."

"Is that why your arm is sliced open?"

"I put six of them to the ground," Josiah proudly told him.

"All it takes is one stab to kill you, boy," his father growled. "How do you think I or your brothers would feel if you were killed? How Captain Sherwood would feel if he wasn't there to save you because you selfishly left the gates without him?"

Josiah listened but what he heard was how much they all loved him and didn't want to lose him. Not one of them would have used the ruby dagger on him if it had remained here and affected him. He did the right thing getting rid of it quickly and in secret. Now, his life could get back to normal with Mercy in it.

"Please forgive me, Father. I was thoughtless about those things. I want to tell you it won't happen again, but that wouldn't be truthful. Just know that though it doesn't seem to be so, I take everything into consideration before I do something."

"That's not good enough," the duke told him, straightening his back. "If you leave the gates without Captain Sherwood and his men, I will have Miss Smith removed from your—"

"Father!" Josiah didn't mean to shout, more, he didn't mean to sound so commanding to his father, but it was too late. "I won't see her blamed for anything when I'm the one who put her in danger. She's mine," he said through clenched teeth. "How many times do I have to remind you? I won't let her be taken from me."

His father considered him for a moment and then lowered his head. "And if you turn?"

Josiah grinned and leaned forward so that he was eye level with his father. "If I turn?"

"I mean...I—"

"You have no faith in what you raised, Father," Josiah pointed out quietly. He wouldn't tell his father that he had had the dagger in a box in his hands. The power had been close, tempting, and he hadn't let it stop him from disposing of it.

"She gave me strength to see something done that I couldn't have done without her. Leave it at that and don't think to take her from me. Please."

Thankfully, his father nodded and gave in to him—not because Josiah was so beloved, but because he was correct.

He was dismissed without punishment, much, it seemed, to the captain's ire.

"Come with me," Captain Sherwood muttered, walking away. He led Josiah into one of the gardens and looked around to make certain they were alone and then threw a punch straight into Josiah's mouth. His head snapped back and he nearly sailed backward. He felt the blood when he lifted his hand to his mouth.

The captain handed him a handkerchief from his doublet. "Wipe it."

"You're lucky you didn't loosen my teeth, Captain," Josiah low in a low, rumbling voice.

"I wasn't trying to knock your teeth out," the captain told

him. "Just give you a fat lip. If you're deceitful and reckless again, and if he doesn't make you regret it, I will. Understand?"

Josiah gave him his most powerful frown complete with a pout. "I was seeing to something important," he said under his breath.

"And this something made you sneak off, bringing the girl you supposedly care for outside, in the dark, alone?"

Josiah thought about it and a hint of a smile played over his lips. "She wouldn't have stayed behind."

"So you command it of her. She's your servant—"

"She's not my servant."

"What is she then?"

"She's my heart. She's there, helping it beat, spreading light through the deepest chasms. I kept her safe tonight, Captain. I always will. Now, if you don't mind, I'll go to her and ask her if she'll tend to my lip." He walked away and then smiled thinking about how angry she was going to be with the captain when she found out he hit Josiah.

CHAPTER TEN

MERCY OPENED THE door to her chamber. Alison had been right. Josiah was sleeping in a chair outside her door again. When she saw his swollen upper lip, she let out a little gasp. Dried blood colored his lips deeper crimson.

"Josiah?" She gave him a little shake. When he opened his eyes to her he smiled in a way that made her feel like it was the first time he was seeing her. "What happened to your lip? Did someone hit you?"

He nodded. "Captain Sherwood."

"Captain Sherwood? The man who is supposed to be protecting you?" she demanded but didn't wait for an answer. She glared down the hall. "When I see him later I'll be sure to tell him what I think of him putting his hands on you!"

Josiah grinned at her subdued fury and then grimaced and held his hand to his mouth. "Don't let him frighten you, Mercy. Don't hold back with your admonishment."

She pulled him to his feet and brought him inside her chambers to tend to him. "Hester, you and the others can go," she told her friends. "I'll take care of him." After a chorus of giggles the three women hurried out of the chambers.

Alone, Mercy prepared water and rags to clean him up. He sat in a chair in her sitting area, waiting for her ministrations. When she sat in front of him, he stared into her eyes with no awkwardness between them.

"This blood dried all night. I have to rub a little."

He nodded, giving her a slight smile.

The instant she wiped the wet rag across his lip and felt an electric spark, she knew cleaning him was going to be hard. As she ran the rag over him, she took in his full M—shaped upper lip—even fuller now thanks to Captain's fist. Oh, she was spitting mad about it. Thankfully, she had the luscious curve of Josiah's lip to distract her—and his eyes. They moved over her features, taking in every inch of her face. They caressed her, spoke to her, and invited her to dance with him.

"Now that we no longer have to concern ourselves with that pesky dagger, do you feel up to me painting you this morning?"

The dagger was gone and with it, the danger to him and others, and her way home. But did she really care if she lost that door back to the future? Sure, she'd miss things like her blow dryer, Spotify, Kdramas, manicures, nothing she couldn't live without. Josiah wasn't there. She stared into his eyes while she cleaned him. She couldn't look anywhere else. He held her captive in a gray and silver web, compelling her to move closer and closer. She wanted to kiss his bruised lip. She wanted to kiss it tenderly but she wasn't so bold.

His smile deepened, his gaze darkened, and, as if reading her mind, he pulled her out of her chair and over him, and then lifted his head to press his mouth to hers. His kiss was light, cautious of his split lip, but it was clear to Mercy that his restraint was costing him.

Her heart thrashed within her as his tongue parted her lips and stole into her mouth with a slow lick that made her tremble before it withdrew. He kissed her, angling his head, pursing his lips, tempting her to kiss him harder, though she was careful not to hurt him.

She smiled when a knock came at the door and he swore. She hopped off him and hurried to pretend to be busy with something else, while Hester and Emmaline entered her chambers with trays of breakfast. Josiah thanked them for remembering that he was here and bringing him food. Mercy agreed, happy to be eating with him. Funny, she used to go out of her way to avoid sitting with anyone during her meals. It was as if she had always, instinctively known it was the most important time to bond with others, so she always ran off and ate alone.

But not now. She liked watching Josiah fill his mouth and chew, even talk if the desire struck him. Twice, she leaned over the table and wiped the corner of his lips with her serviette, smiling back at him when he seemed to fall into her loving gaze. They found humor and laughed at the most mundane things. When they heard Hester and Emmaline whispering about them, they laughed harder.

When he clamped his fingers around Mercy's wrist and pulled her from her chair, she squealed with delight, feeling, for the first time in her life, like a child playing with her best friend.

He led her out of her chambers and down halls and corridors, giggling behind their hands about this one's wide pantaloons or that one's crooked periwig. When they reached the studio, they fell onto the settee out of breath and holding their bellies. Without waiting until she completely caught her breath, he leaned over her and bent his face to hers. "Mercy, thank you for staying with me," he said over her lips. She leaned up and caught his lips with hers, then smiled with him without breaking their kiss. She lifted her arms and closed them around his neck. She clung to him. She'd never let go. If she had her way, she'd live with him for the rest of her life. She'd be content to look at him, listen to him, laugh with him, and love him and only him until they were parted by death. He kissed her breathless, and then groaned when she pushed him off.

"Josiah, you haven't kissed any of your models, have you?"

He scowled at her and she would have sworn her eyes twinkled at him. Everything about him, every nuance of his face, movement of his body, the way he took her in, it all worked to mesmerize her and lay claim to her heart. She knew her question insulted him. She also knew the insult would be forgotten in an instant.

"If I had kissed any one of them, I wouldn't be kissing you right now," he told her.

She arched her brow at him. "Are you saying if you had kissed someone, you would have remained loyal to them?"

He nodded. "Yes," he said as if the answer was obvious.

"But what if—I mean, you're twenty and…look at you. Haven't you been kissing girls for a long time?"

His smile drew her gaze to his lips. She cleared her throat and looked away. "They were never allowed to spend time with me alone," he told her. "And because I understood why, I stopped trying—and found other ways to cause trouble."

Yes, all she had to do was look at his roguish grin to believe it. "What kind of trouble?"

He laughed shortly. "Once I disturbed a large beehive outside the castle and was consequently chased by the swarm. It was terrifying for a boy of sixteen. I wasn't thinking that I shouldn't run into the castle. I was thinking of escaping, and the castle doors were the closest route to safety."

Her eyes opened wide, and she let out a little laugh. "How many were stung?"

"Thirteen." He scowled and then smiled when he saw that she was. "The more trouble I got into, the more mothers kept their daughters from me."

"The curse."

He left his seat and went around her chair to stand behind her. "Yes," he said softly and then moved his fingers through her hair. Mercy startled but then when she realized he was trying to style her hair for the painting, she closed her eyes and smiled. "You know what?" she asked, relaxing a little. He gathered the mass of it in his hands, smoothing it away from her face, and finally securing it at her left shoulder.

"Everyone's fear saved your heart for me."

He laughed softly to himself. "I like the way you see things in a positive light."

"It's all because of you."

Still behind her, he leaned down and kissed her neck. "You're so beautiful I don't know how I'll capture you."

How did she turn the head and capture the heart of such a man? She was still considering it while she sat in the settee a little while later, dressed in a lacey coral gown of undress fashion. She thought of nasty Virginia and Daphne, two mean girls from her last job. They'd teased her unmercifully about her being a virgin after they found out by befriending her and getting her to confide in them. They would pass out if they saw her now. She smiled slightly to herself, then felt Josiah's gaze on her and looked his way.

He was watching her, his hands with his paintbrush in one, were at rest in his lap, a perfectly happy smile on his face. Mercy bit her lip. He'd changed into a white shirt with ruffles down the center. The ruffles tickled under his chin so he left the first four buttons open. His hair, though he'd pushed it back twice now, fell over the slashes of his brows. Her gaze settled on his lips, deep coral, and yielding...her mouth went dry and fire rushed across her cheeks and nose.

His smile started slow, but he ended up laughing softly, thoroughly enchanting her. "What were you just thinking about?"

He'd noticed her blushing. The thought made her blush more. She lowered her gaze. "You have nice lips."

When he was quiet she looked up and found him gazing at her, wearing a very irresistible smile on that mouth.

"You have nice lips too," he said in a deep baritone that vibrated in her blood. Before she replied, he blinked his gaze to the easel and leaned forward to pick up a different brush. When he dipped it to his pallet and began to paint again, Mercy almost smiled at his unusual ways. But then, he *was* an artist. His focus was sharp. For every two-second stare, he painted for five minutes. When his eyes settled on her for those two seconds, she felt as if he were looking at things others couldn't see. Maybe she couldn't see them either.

Three hours later, he turned his easel to the wall, then went to the door to call for refreshments.

"Are you weary of sitting for so long?" he asked, going to her. "My models always get restless and bored."

"No. In the future there's very little time like this, to just sit and think without all the distractions of the world. It's too easy to tune in to anything you want to know about, be entertained by a million different things. It's always busy."

"Everything is about perspective—in art and in life," he told her sitting next to her. "You appreciate this slower pace because you've been running for so long. But someone who has been locked away under the watchful eye of his father feels the drudgery of this present slowness."

He offered Emmaline a courteous smile when she entered carrying a tray of refreshments and then flashed his frown at her when she tried to peek at the painting of Mercy.

"Is it you, my lady?" Emmaline whispered, handing Mercy her drink.

"Yes," Mercy exchanged a smile with her.

"Yes, it's her," Josiah echoed and whisked Mercy's new friend away. "Please find Captain Sherwood and inform him that we'll be riding to the village this afternoon. Tell the cooks too, and if you and your two other friends wish to come along, you may."

Mercy smiled hearing him. She loved that he took others into consideration, especially her new friends. When he shut the door and returned to her, she offered him her brightest smile. "Thank you."

"For?" He picked up his cup and drank from it.

"Being considerate and kind."

He smiled. "You don't have to thank me for that."

"Yes, I do."

He pressed his lips to her forehead and kissed her there, then returned to her painting without a word. A quiet guy. She smiled.

He picked up his brush and smiled back.

He made her happy for the first time in her life. And she believed he felt the same way.

>>>><<<<

JOSIAH FINISHED HIS mid-day meal with little Anne Harwood in his lap. He shifted his gaze from Anne to Mercy fashioning a *baseball* out of a wooden pall-mall ball and strips of leather tied around it. She searched the surrounding tree line for sticks of the correct size. Lastly, she sprinkled flour around a diamond-shaped space and sprinkled more flour at its four corners. The children found it especially wonderful when they were chosen to be on one of two teams with the grownups. After Mercy explained the game, everyone was excited to get started. The object was to whack the ball and run around the *bases*. But it wasn't so easily done when the other term was stationed at posts around the diamond, ready to catch your ball and *throw you out!* There were things called *strikes* and *balls*, *home runs* and *loaded bases*. Young and old took part and even Samuel hobbled along laughing toward the third base. Little Anne, with Josiah's help, hit the *pitcher's* ball. Josiah didn't wait but picked up Anne and ran with her while the ball flew toward the first base. On the opposite team, Amelia Harwood, Anne's mother, made a slow run for the ball but it rolled past her. Everyone on their team cheered them on, even the pitcher cheered. Josiah smiled at her while Anne's joyful laughter filled his ears. He'd be happy to live this day forever.

When he was almost *home* he set Anne on her feet and walked behind her while she ran for the last base and everyone, including her mother, cheered for her.

He looked across the small field and winked at the beautiful pitcher with the wind blowing her chestnut hair across her face. His Mercy. The more time he spent with her, the more time with her he wanted. He felt as if there were thin tethers—hundreds of them—connecting him to her. He wondered what would happen if they snapped.

She *struck out* the next two *batters*. Josiah felt impressed that she could throw hard enough to cause the batters to miss the ball and swing at the air. His turn came up next. He remembered how he was supposed to stand and hold his stick. When he was ready, he smiled at Mercy. She let the ball fly at him. Without taking his eyes off it, he swung and hit the ball beyond the home run boundary. Once again, his teammates cheered for him as he ran around the bases. When he commanded Captain Sherwood to stand in for Old Philip the Tanner when he swung at the ducks that had come upon the field. At first, the captain voiced his displeasure but once he whacked the ball and started really playing, he laughed with Josiah.

Of course, Mercy found the captain standing with Josiah in between *innings*. After a stiff greeting, she straightened her shoulders and gave the captain a hard look. "I hope you consider the force behind whatever I decide to throw. If you ever put your hands to Josiah again, I'll throw everything in my reach at you."

The captain lowered his head as if he were being admonished by the queen. When she was satisfied, she looked up at Josiah and winked at him, then returned to her teammates.

After the afternoon spent eating and playing *baseball,* they returned to the castle. But Josiah didn't go inside. He took Mercy's hand and led her to a grassy hill, already occupied by sheep, busy grazing. He waited for Mercy to sit first, then followed her beneath a tree and leaned his back against it. "It's breezy," he said quietly and closed his eyes.

"It's a perfect day," he heard the smile in her voice when she spoke and opened his eyes to look at her.

"Mmm," he agreed. "Thank you."

She laughed softly, "What for?"

"Another perfect day." He pulled her closer and closed his eyes. "Mercy."

"Hmm?" She sounded like a purring kitten basking in the sun.

"You heal my soul. I'm never going to leave your side."

"Do you promise?"

"I promise."

CHAPTER ELEVEN

THEY WERE GENTLY awakened by Hester an hour later. Mercy stirred and immediately grimaced at the pain in her shoulder. It had been a while since she'd thrown a ball. She'd overdone it today, but oh, what a glorious day it had been. She opened her eyes to stare at Josiah's chest from her position pressed against him in the circle of his arms.

The air had chilled with the descent of the sun but when Mercy looked at her, Hester's smile was as warm as any mother's. "My lady, forgive me," she said in a soft tone, then smiled at the sleeping earl of Winterborne. "I thought you both might wish to freshen up and dress for the Marquess' ball."

Mercy bolted upright. "The Marquess' what? Ball? You mean where people get dressed up and dance...like in those beautiful regency romance movies?"

The instant Hester's smile warmed on her again, Mercy realized what she said out loud and laughed at herself, then cleared her throat. Soon, rumors would start here just like they had at home that she had mental problems.

Another thought crossed her mind and she turned to Josiah and frowned. "Was this planned? Did he know about it?"

"Yes, but—"

"Josiah! Wake up!" she shook him until he opened his eyes.

His dreamy face broke into a bright smile when he saw her. "I dreamed that everything was a dream. Thank you for waking me."

She blinked her eyes at him and smiled. How did he make her forget everything else except for the instant they were in, with his smile ever on her?

His gaze slipped to Hester and his smile turned purely friendly. "Is it time to eat?"

"No, my lord—"

"No, but it's almost time for your brother's ball," Mercy scolded without an ounce of anger in her voice.

He considered it for a moment, then looking utterly uninterested, leaned back against the tree and closed his eyes again. He opened them when Mercy stood up.

"What? You want to go to the ball?"

She started to nod, but then thought about it more. There were probably going to be a lot of guests and she was new and controversial so their eyes would be on her. Wouldn't it just be nicer to sleep here with him?

Shaking off sleep, he rose up and took her hand. "Let's go."

"Then you'll be attending, my lord?" Hester asked, happily, already touching Mercy's hair as they walked back to the castle.

"Yes," he paused and turned to gaze at her. "I want everyone to meet Mercy."

"Sure," Mercy scoffed and kept walking. She didn't want to meet everyone. Her hair would have to be tied up for a ball. Tongues would wag and she'd been hearing them flap her whole life. She was happy now. She didn't want to start everything over again in 1661. "I'm not attending."

She heard him say something to Hester and an instant later, her friend hurried off.

"Why do you care about what people you don't know think of you? I'm the one who should matter to you."

"It doesn't work that way, Josiah. When they stare in pity or horror, it becomes who I am."

"What if they stare in admiration and even envy?" His grin added something mischievous and playful to the end of his question.

She didn't know why they would, but he made her blush nonetheless. He took the opportunity to step closer to her and dip his lips to her ear. "I want to dance with you again."

He lit her blood on fire. It flowed like lava through her veins. His words vanquished her fears until she felt light enough to take flight.

Still, she'd spent twenty years avoiding people, so she didn't feel ready for another wave. "Josiah, I..."

He waited and then closed his arms around her in a full, deep embrace. "I'll be with you. Trust me."

She breathed him in and smiled, never wanting to leave his arms.

MERCY STOOD AT the entrance of the great hall. The tables, topped with venison and pheasant, all types of fish, fruit, wine, ale and the silver goblets in which to drink them, along with candle centerpieces, were set up in a giant rectangle against the walls with room for dancing in the center. As she expected, every eye inside fell on her as she stood there alone. She didn't think she looked that bad in the clothes Priscillia Ashmore, wife of second son, Oliver, had given her. Mercy had never before worn such fine apparel. A boned-bodice of blue velvet with back laces, lengthened waist, and off-the-shoulder neckline looked too beautiful to let a few pokes and pinches bother her. The full petticoats and gloves of matching velvet and silver gilt were fit for an earl's wife, not her, a woman who couldn't even confess her last name.

The musicians picked up their instruments, including lute, viola, and Baroque guitar. She didn't think she'd like seventeenth century music but the sound of it called to her, and she found it beautiful.

She looked around for Josiah. Would they dance together again? She didn't see him. She'd wait another minute before entering alone. He told her to trust him. She told him she would. He had no idea how difficult it was for her.

Remembering her hair had been swept up into clusters of curls, away from her face, she thought of her scar, bare and in the open for all to see.

She dipped her gaze away from the stares of others, but instead of seeing just her own silk slippers, she saw polished black shoes with short heels and hosed, muscular calves. Her gaze continued upward to snug-fitting pantaloons, and a short, silk, burgundy doublet beneath a tailored long-coat. He'd arrived as promised. Tonight he wore an elegantly knotted cravat, with his glossy obsidian locks falling over his collared nape.

"You look breathtaking," Josiah said, beating her to it. He lifted her hand to his lips and kissed her knuckles. "Forgive me for not being here before you. Did you doubt me?"

She smiled. "No. That's why I was waiting."

His grin widened and made her giggle. He moved in closer and laughed with her as if they shared some secret that made them joyful. When he stood at her side, statuesque and masculine, and held his hand out to her she happily accepted. Her bones felt as if they were melting and she was grateful when he placed her hand into the crook of his elbow and led her into the great hall. She knew people were looking at her, maybe even wondering how she was the one on his arm. At that moment she almost didn't care. She knew every single woman—and some not single women—envied her. While they helped her dress, Emmaline and Alison told her more about the earl of Winterborne. Born as the accursed one, most of the older inhabitants in the vicinity, both lords and vassals, were cautious and distrusting of Josiah. No matter how kind he was to them, they were afraid of him. The younger folks knew of the prophecy, but many didn't believe it, or didn't believe that Josiah would become a monster. Most of the unmarried females wanted to marry him, at least be kissed by him once or twice. But although the handsome seventh son merely had to slant his most aloof smile at a woman to have his way with her, he withheld his affections, barely touching a girl or being alone with her, in case she falsely accused him of something in order to force a marriage.

"Josiah!" his brother Thomas greeted with a stunned smile as he stood from his seat at their family table. "I'm surprised to see you here. You hate balls." As he was speaking, he slipped his gaze to Mercy and eyed her suspiciously. "Whatever you've done to him…" his rare smile spread over her… "keep doing it."

Josiah turned to her, his smile sincere and adoring, making her belly flip.

Thomas' wife, Helena, hurried over with baby Sarah in her arms. They were soon joined by Millicent, Jeremy's wife, who according to Helena, knew how to fight as well as any man and would be glad to teach her, and Priscillia, who doted over Mercy, adjusting a seam here, smoothing a wrinkle there.

"I'm hungry," Josiah told them and pulled her away. He stopped again before his father's chair and bowed.

The duke eyed him and then Mercy. "Why did you come tonight? You've never bothered before."

"I never had a reason to come." Josiah told him, smiling at Mercy. "Now I do. I want to dance with her."

He didn't hold back his delight in her, not even to his father. And watching his son take joy in her made the duke finally smile. "Very well, dance then."

They actually had to wait until the next dance was announced. While they waited, Josiah filled his cheeks with food.

"Whispers are already spreading," Ava, Edward's wife informed them, returning to the table after handing off her son to his nurse, "about the duke's youngest son and the lovely lady on his arm. They wonder who you are."

Lovely lady? She almost laughed out loud but bit her lip. She felt his fingers brush over hers under the table. She looked at him and found him spreading his smile over her. He leaned in and spoke close to her ear. "Did you hear that, my lovely lady?"

He warmed her heart, heated her blood. "Yes," Lady Katherine of Marlboro, youngest daughter of the duke of Marlboro and betrothed to sixth son Nicholas, agreed from her place at the table, "Jealousy is already running rampant among the ladies."

What if they stare in admiration and even envy? She remembered Josiah's question to her. Was this real? Her? The object of envy? Oh, how could it be?

"Have your memories returned yet?" Gilbert asked her.

She nodded. "Some have. I remember being raised in an orphanage after my mother was killed by a thief in the night when I was very young."

Now, Josiah openly covered her hand on the table with his.

"Orphanage?" echoed Lady Katherine distastefully. "That sheds light on everything, doesn't it?"

Josiah angled his head to look at his brother's betrothed. "What do you mean by that?"

Lady Katherine smiled at Josiah, and for a second, Mercy sensed something more in her smile. "Everyone is wondering how she seems to have won your heart when so many have failed. But it's obvious, isn't it? The earl of Winterborne likes taking in strays. That's it, hmm? You have to admit, she isn't as pretty as some of the other well born ladies here."

"Okay. This is more like it," Mercy murmured to herself, but out loud. Maybe it was real, after all.

Josiah's grin hardened, and the imp became something far more dark. Across the table, Nicholas covered his forehead, then looked at his plate rather than his brother.

"The answer to everyone's question is simple," Josiah told her, "Don't be a vicious, prideful shrew, like you and I might have cared if you breathed or not, instead of handing you off to my brother."

Nicholas sighed heavily while his betrothed gasped so deeply, Mercy thought the girl would pass out. Then some of the other wives smiled at Mercy and some hid their smiles by smiling down at their cups. It seemed the wives didn't care for Lady Katherine of Marlboro. It also seemed that Nicholas' betrothed cared for Josiah at some point, perhaps had even been offered to him, but he'd refused her. That probably stung.

"Brother," Nicholas began. He stopped when Josiah stood up, reached for Mercy's hand, and left the table.

"Let's let the scent of each other and the music fill us," he told Mercy as he led her to the center of the hall, "and not her unkind words."

She nodded, already forgetting Lady Katherine and looking forward to Josiah's dancing.

"I don't know the steps of these dances, Josiah," Mercy told him, concerned now that they were standing with other couples.

"Follow my steps, and when we separate—"

"Separating and staying upright might be troublesome."

He smiled as several couples formed columns around the hall. "Take your time. Don't worry about anyone else, just keep your eyes on me."

"That won't be difficult."

They smiled at each other for another whole minute until the music started.

Mercy was thankful for the slow tempo, which meant slower steps. She was surprised to discover many of the movements were similar to ballet with less dramatic bends and lifts. Still, they leaped, and skipped, and rose up on the balls of their feet, while covering the entire floor.

When they did separate, according to the moves of the dance, Mercy counted the moments and movements until they reached each other again, when their eyes met and their hands touched. She giggled at how he frowned when a temporary male partner let his touch linger too long.

He was only two years past being a teen and his passions ran deep. His passions, it seemed, involved her. Mercy didn't mind his minor bouts of jealousy and anger over her. His heart was too big to let him physically hurt anyone, and no man had ever made her feel the way Josiah did. She wasn't about to stop him. But she would speak to him later about Lady Katherine. He'd been cutting and left his future sister-in-law bleeding on the floor. Mercy thought he should apologize.

It didn't take Mercy long to learn the dance, but her favorite part was when, after their steps separated them, watching him move toward her again like a beautiful predator, one arm resting behind his back, his chin dipped and his gaze potent and piercing on her as he neared. Each time he returned, though they'd only been apart for a few moments, he smiled at her as if he hadn't seen her in weeks. He refused to release her twice. It was a good thing his brother Oliver was the dancer behind him and had the boldness to push his way between them to get the line moving. If it had been anyone other than one of his brothers, it would have been far riskier. As it was, all he aimed at Oliver was his pouting frown-which faded quickly enough into a sheepish smile when Mercy tugged on his sleeve.

"Would it be terribly rude if we left the dance?" she whispered as the other dancers swept by them.

"Yes, it would," Josiah said, then took her hand, and led her away. When he didn't return to their table, or pause to bid his family or any of the guests goodnight, Mercy smiled and then laughed softly with him as they left the great hall.

The moment they were away from staring eyes, Josiah turned to face her, closed his arms around her waist, and pulled her closer all in one breath. In the next, he dipped his mouth to hers.

Mercy didn't want to close her eyes. She was afraid of opening them again and all of it being gone. She wanted to look at him and never stop, but soon, as his lips caressed and played over hers, finally parting hers to make way for his curious tongue, she closed her eyes, lost in the rapture of him. She basked in how his hard body fit and felt against her, the tender, yet urgent way he held her in his arms, the way he branded her with his mouth, claiming her for himself and no one else.

He kissed her until she was breathless, but when he withdrew, his breath came as short and as rapidly as hers. He didn't let her go but gazed into her eyes and then smiled softly. "Mercy, I love you."

Mercy didn't wonder or care if it was too soon to love him. She was born to be with him. She felt it in her blood. He vanquished her fears and insecurities with smiles and softly spoken words and made her feel at home in the seventeenth century. All her life she felt as if she didn't matter to anyone. She didn't belong anywhere or to anyone. But in a moment, with one smile, one kiss, he filled all her empty spaces and made her whole. Her life finally had a purpose. To love Josiah Ashmore and to be loved by him.

She raised herself up on the tips of her toes and coiled her arms around his neck. "I love you too," she told him, then pressed her lips to his.

They kissed in the corridor, outside the great hall until a small crowd of smiling people, family and guests alike, gathered to watch them.

"Sorry to interrupt," someone said. Mercy's eyes shot open. She broke away from Josiah's embrace and stared in stunned mortification at the eyes staring back. The man who'd mercifully stopped them was Jeremy, the pleasant-tempered third son. When she moved away, he stepped closer to his brother. "Why don't you bring her to your studio."

Josiah nodded and flashed his loving smile at his older brother, then entwined his fingers with hers. He smiled at the crowd, giving her courage to do the same, despite wanting to hide.

"Enjoy the rest of my brother's ball," he told them all, then deepened his grin over them. "And tell my father to open the good casks of wine he's hiding in his cellar."

The people, including Jeremy, cheered for him. Mercy watched Josiah laugh good-naturedly. Was he trying to win more favor at the expense of his father? It seemed as if he was indeed the hero of their evening as they piled back into the great hall.

He pulled her away toward the stairs, but she tugged him

back. "Why did you give away your father's good wine? Won't he be angry with you?" She wondered if it mattered to him if his father got angry when he knew that anger wouldn't last.

He hurried back to her and cupped her face in his hand. "He has even better wine hidden where I won't tell even you." He laughed and pulled her again. This time she went—running up stairs and more stairs, and even more until he bent with his back to her and pulled her on, giving her a sort of piggy-back the rest of the way.

She marveled at his strength and stamina. When he set her feet back on the ground, he took her in his arms and kissed her as they burst through the door of his studio, locked in each other's arms.

Was this going to be it? Were they going to have sex? She wanted to, but they didn't have birth-control in 1661, did they? And what guarantee did she have that she wasn't going to be zapped back? She didn't want to be an unwed mother in any century. Even if Josiah kept his promise and never left her side, would his father agree and not marry him off?

With more control than she ever knew she had, she broke away from him and twirled happily around until she reached his covered easel. There was only one way to get him to forget kissing her, at least for the moment. She took fistfuls of the covering and was about to pull it away. "Can I see my portrait now?"

"It's not finished." He hurried to her and stopped her from seeing it.

"When do you think it will be done?"

He blinked, looking at her. "Mercy, these things can't be rushed. You have to sit a bit longer for me."

"Should I change?"

He swallowed and nodded.

She gave him an admonishing look. "Turn away. Don't let me catch you peeking."

She had to bite her lip to stop from smiling when he nodded

agreeably and then turned away and glowered for all he was worth.

He didn't peek while she changed into her nightgown. He turned his easel away from her and snapped the covering off. He pulled off his coat and doublet next and rolled up his sleeves.

Mercy smiled to herself thinking how easy it was to distract him when it came to painting. "Is it your favorite thing in the world to do?" she asked, taking her place on his settee.

"Is what may favorite thing?" He barely looked up at her as he mixed his colors on his palette.

"Painting?"

"It used to be." He glanced at her to flash her a smile. "Kissing you is my new favorite thing in the world to do. I haven't finished kissing you."

His words were like a dark promise spoken from the depths of his hungry heart. They awakened thousands of butterflies in her belly and made her doubt her strength to resist him. And she had to, at least, for now.

"Josiah, we should talk."

He gave her a curious look. "Now?"

She nodded and patted the place beside her on the settee. He shook his head but set down his brush and palette. "If it's about keeping my lips off you, I won't be able to make you any promises if I'm that close to you."

He drove away all her insecurities about her face, her scar, her personality. She realized she'd barely spoken to herself since meeting Josiah. She smiled more. She laughed! But although she felt as if she finally found where she was meant to be, the fact was, she didn't belong here.

"My life is too unstable to risk getting pregnant."

"Pregnant?" he echoed, staring at her.

It hadn't crossed his mind? Of course not. Why should it? He was barely out of his teens. She groaned.

"Mercy." He stepped around the easel but took no more steps than that. "Do you fear there's no restraint in me at all? I intend to make you my wife before we—"

"Josiah, I could be zapped into the future in an instant."

He rushed to her and hauled her into his arms. "No!" he breathed raggedly into her ear while holding her close. "I won't let you go. The dagger's gone. I can feel it. You can't return without it."

"Who says? How do we know the dagger had anything to do with me coming here? Josiah, what if—"

"Mercy, I won't let anything separate us." His voice sounded like a menacing growl cooling her blood. She tried to push away to look at him, but he held her still. "I'll find the dagger and destroy time if I must."

CHAPTER TWELVE

JOSIAH SET DOWN his brush two hours later and gazed at Mercy on the settee. She'd fallen asleep but he didn't need her to be awake to paint her. He knew every beguiling nuance of her expressions. He should have carried her to bed sooner, but he selfishly continued painting. Once, he even had to stop to swipe his eyes free of the tears loving her produced. He laughed thinking of all the emotions she made him feel. He'd never felt happy or grateful enough to weep. He'd never experienced jealousy, or the willingness to forgo his needs and meet hers instead. He lived smiling under the weight of a terrible curse, but even knowing now that the tales were true, there really was a ruby dagger, and it apparently possessed enough power to send someone back in time almost four hundred years, he was hopeful that the prophecy would not be fulfilled.

He went to her and fell to his knees before her. She let out a little snore. His gaze on her warmed. The sight of her made his heart thump, resonating like a warning through his body to run. But he didn't have to run from her. She would guard his heart lovingly in her hands, his soul within her needful embrace.

Who was Mercy Smith that she mattered so much to him, that he thought of her night and day, and ached to be with her—just be near her? Why had the force that ruled the dagger chosen her as a link to get to him, and was that all she had to do with the ruby dagger?

He leaned forward until his face was close enough to hers to count her lashes. He loved the shape of her eyes and the color of them, and how they revealed her heart when she looked at him. He let his gaze rove over her brow and the beguiling slope of her nose. He reached out, and, breath held, ran his fingertips over her top, then bottom lip, tracing their shape with a feathery touch. He wanted to kiss the alluring curve of her jaw and whisper in her ear that he loved her. But he didn't want to wake her, so he sat for another hour, admiring her while she slept, until he joined her in slumber.

When he opened his eyes again, the soft light of dawn filled the studio and Mercy was still curled up asleep on the settee. When he stirred she came awake and smiled seeing him. "Good morning, Josiah."

"Good—"

Suddenly, she sat up and her eyes opened wide. "I've spent the night with you again and now I have to sneak off to my chambers before the whole castle sees me!"

"What? Has someone said something to you?"

"No," she reassured him. "But this sort of thing is frowned upon in the seventeenth century."

He furrowed his brow. "Is it not frowned upon in the twenty-first century?"

"No. Not really," she let him know. Then, "Josiah?"

"Hmm?"

"You're brooding."

"No, I'm not."

"I never stayed overnight with any man."

Instantly, his good mood returned and he grinned happily at her.

"Has any other woman—"

He shook his head, gazing at her. "Never."

They laughed together and kissed before he took her hand. "Come on."

"Where?" she asked when he pulled her to her feet and headed for the door.

"There's a rear stairway the servants never use. They're the only ones up at this hour, so we can avoid them and get you to your chambers before anyone sees you."

He opened the studio door and almost knocked Captain Sherwood off his feet. Damnation, how could he forget the guards? "I was painting her. We fell asleep." Why was he explaining?

The captain expelled a sigh. "You should take more care of her reputation, my lord."

Josiah cast him a crestfallen look. He opened his mouth to explain, then closed it again. The captain was correct.

"Lord Winterborne was just bringing me to my chambers by way of the rear stairway," Mercy defended him to the hulking captain.

The captain looked at Josiah, who replied with a smile.

"You can wait here," Josiah told him.

The captain shook his head. Then, after another sigh. "Harry Lawrence, the fabric merchant stopped two of my men who were patrolling the wall. He extended to you and Miss Smith an invitation for supper with him and his wife, who has returned from visiting her sister in Breadwink."

Josiah's belly rumbled. "Will she make fish stew?"

"He didn't say," the captain said, trying to stifle a yawn.

Josiah turned his excited grin on Mercy, and then glanced at the captain. "Go to bed, Captain. You're excused."

He led Mercy around the captain and then past him. But it wasn't long before Josiah heard his footsteps behind him. The captain wouldn't leave his side whether he was starving or exhausted, unless there were at least eight extra men covering his post. Josiah guessed that pretty much meant the captain's mighty arm was equal to that of eight men. He grinned at the captain over his shoulder.

Josiah would thank Mrs. Sherwood for sharing her husband by sending her meat, fish, and grains and perhaps some skeins of fine silk from Harry Lawrence.

Captain Sherwood would try to bring it all back, claiming a soldier shouldn't accept such offerings for doing his duty. But he knew Josiah well enough to know that once the youngest earl set his mind one way, nothing would change it.

They almost made it to the second landing corridor, where their chambers were, without being spotted. But as they approached their rooms, Josiah hit his elbow into a painted pottery vase and knocked it off the table on which it had been resting. The pottery shattered against the wood floor loud enough to rouse everyone in the castle. Josiah turned to Mercy, who was covering her gasp with her hand. He laughed, then grabbed her hand and hurried to her chamber door.

"Meet me outside your door in one hour." He leaned in and pecked her mouth with his and then disappeared into his chambers.

As Josiah washed and dressed in fresh clothes, he thought about the beautiful day outside his window. Mercy might enjoy the spring day under the sun. He wanted to bring her to a place he'd painted once called Daffodil Hills. It was the right time of the year when the daffodils were blooming and scenting the air with sweet fragrance. He thought she'd like to go there.

He'd bring his sketchbooks and charcoal sticks and sketch her in the daffodils. When he was done donning a cream-colored shirt ruffled down the center from collar to hips with bell sleeves, Josiah rolled his sleeves up to his elbows. Doing so had become a habit from his years of painting. He didn't particularly like high cravats and long sleeves, and feeling hot on the outside when he already burned on the inside.

After an hour, he made his way to her chamber door, humming and waving to the servants he passed. With six brothers, he hadn't been a lonely child, but even when he was let out of the castle to travel with his father, other children weren't allowed or were too afraid of him to play with him. So he'd had no friends. As the duke's youngest, most beloved son, he had much. But as the cursed seventh son, he was a danger to everyone. He'd spent his entire life defending and protecting himself from gossip and rumors until he won the hearts of the people. But had it cost him his own heart? It was a question he asked himself more times than he could remember. Now he knew. Thanks to Mercy, he knew he still had a heart and it was beating strong.

He met Hester approaching Mercy's door from the opposite end of the hall. He greeted her with a cheerful smile.

"My lord, are you on your way to visit Miss Smith?"

"Yes, I am."

"May I speak with you?"

"Of course," he allowed. He liked Hester but something within him felt uncomfortable around her. He tried to put his finger on it, but he couldn't find anything about her that should cause him to feel as if he were covered in a prickly blanket.

"If I might speak freely, my lord, you seem to have changed, though not many people would notice."

His smile brightened. "I'm relieved my newfound emotions don't have me playing my lute in front of her door."

"Yes," she agreed with a little smile, "subtlety can be a blessed friend."

He turned to look at her. "What change have you noticed in me?"

"Your happiness is more genuine, my lord."

He laughed softly. "Yes."

Her smile on him warmed. She wasn't afraid of him. Good. He didn't want her to be.

"Every day," she continued, "there seems to be a little more color in your skin."

He nodded and smiled down his nose at her. "You're very astute."

"Can you love her?"

He dipped his brows at her. Why would she say 'can' he, as if he was normally incapable of loving? "Yes," he didn't hesitate to answer. "I can. I do."

She reached for Mercy's door handle and opened it. She stepped inside, leaving the door open for him to follow. Without a word to him, she entered the bedchamber and then stopped, seeing her mistress up and out of bed. "Oh, you're already dressed," Hester said and pulled back the window coverings, spreading bright morning light into the room. "Have you eaten too?"

Josiah stood breathless as Mercy stepped before him and into the light. She was dressed in coral petticoats and a white silk doublet over white stays. She appeared as delicate as a butterfly pausing for a moment in his life. He wanted to reach out and take hold of her, but he only stared at her, breath held, and then smiled as if his soul was starving for her. "You look beautiful."

Her cheeks turned deeper pink and her hand immediately went to her scar, already covered in curls.

"Mercy." He moved closer to her, unable to stay away, and slipped his arms around her waist. "Every inch of the skin that clothes you is perfect." He hooked one side of his mouth into a slight smile. "I intend to prove it to you when we're married by kissing all of you. For now, this will have to do." He bent his head and kissed her chin, then up her jaw and the side of her face to her temple—tracing the path of her scar with his lips. When he came near her ear, he whispered into it, "Perfect."

He heard Hester scurrying around them, so he reluctantly broke away from Mercy. When he did, he saw that her eyes were wet with tears. She caught him looking and deepened her smile on him until she ended up laughing softly at herself.

"I'll make sure she eats," Josiah promised Hester.

The older servant eyed him and then smiled and nodded.

He escaped with Mercy out of the chambers and they hurried down the corridor, picking up their laughter where they left it before. When they reached the main stairs he stopped and took her face in his hands. He stared into her eyes, letting her see what she meant to him in his gaze. He angled his head and pressed his mouth to hers. He'd been waiting all morning to do it. He'd promised to remain chaste with her for a while longer, until she felt more certain she wouldn't disappear. Ah, the thought of it terrified him. He deepened his kiss, then broke away like a tortured prisoner. His breath came hard and heavy. He pulled her back to him and closed his arms around her.

She said nothing and pressed close to his thrashing heart. Hers raced just as hard. They both feared her being pulled back. He was the only one who understood the terror of losing her because she felt the same thing about him. They clung to each other as if doing so enough times or hard enough would meld them together. Then they couldn't be torn apart.

He wondered when his father would approve their marriage. Josiah wouldn't wait long.

He thought—no, he hoped that taking her as his wife would somehow keep her with him. Wasn't it 'til death do us part? He'd promise to be bound to her in the eyes of God.

"Come on." He took her hand and led her down the stairs.

"Where are we going?" she asked, keeping up with him.

He smiled over his shoulder at her. "To the Daffodil Hills."

She repeated the name on a soft breath. "It sounds pretty."

"It is."

He led her to the kitchen, where he had the cooks prepare them food to take along.

"The captain and his men will be following behind so make sure you give them something to eat, as well."

They rode separate horses, with Mercy refusing to ride on her side-saddle and insisting on one like his. He gave her her way, as he suspected he'd do in all things. They raced north, toward Wareham, with six other riders fifty feet behind them at all times.

They reached the Daffodil Hills where the yellow daffodils were in full bloom, spreading across the lush, verdant hills, fragrancing the air. As he'd suspected, Mercy's eyes opened wide. Her smile rivaled the beauty of their surroundings.

"Oh, Josiah, it's so beautiful here!" She leaped from her horse, opened her arms and hurried forth into the daffodils.

He chuckled watching her, then followed her, leading the horses to the shade of an old oak. He sat beneath it and removed his sketchbook and charcoal. He never wanted to forget how she looked at this moment, gloriously free of all her insecurities with her eyes closed and yellow petals in her hair as she tilted her smile up to the sun. Was he dreaming this? He wondered as he sketched her flowing dress and arms outstretched. He'd painted the hills before but hadn't he always dreamed of painting a beautiful woman here? A woman he loved and who meant more to him than anything in his life? And here she was.

She waved to him, laughing when a butterfly fluttered around her face. She swung around and traipsed through the flowers. "Josiah!" she called out, bending to her knees. "It's a baby rabbit!"

He watched her and then gave his attention to his sketch, then watched her again. When he saw a few daffodils sway harder than the rest, he guessed the mother rabbit had spotted her. He was about to call out to her to stand up but she must have seen what was coming at her. With a loud squeak she rose up and ran the other way, leaving her artist laughing against the tree.

Still wearing her joyous smile, she returned to him and sat next to him. "Oh, wow, that's so good!" she complimented peeking at his sketch. He didn't hide it as he did her portrait until it was finished. He beamed at her appraisal, then closed the book and wiped his hands.

"I want to paint you here," he told her, putting his arm around her and drawing her closer.

"Okay!" she said, making his eyes dance on her. "We can come here every day!"

He nodded, happy and willing to travel here every day if she wanted to.

When she reached up and planted a kiss on his mouth, he followed her withdrawal and pressed his lips to hers for something longer and more intimate. When he swept his tongue into her mouth, she received him with eager anticipation. He deepened his kiss, hungry for her, needful of her, holding her closer, it would never be close enough. He slipped one hand over her throat, tracing her pulse with his fingertips and giving her bottom lip a little nibble. The sound it pulled from the back of her throat felt like a whip across his back. He wanted to touch her in places she would allow no other man to touch. He wouldn't do it. Not with Captain Sherwood and his men somewhere close by. Josiah didn't care what others thought of him, but what they thought of Mercy was another matter. He wouldn't disgrace her by having sex with her in the sight of others. So, with great reluctance, he broke their kiss.

He smiled at her because whether he was kissing her, touching her, or just looking at her, she made him happy.

He pressed his palm to his belly. "I'm hungry."

"Josiah!" She stared up at him. "Is that all you think about?"

He was about to smile and say of course, but she no longer looked amused, so he thought better of it. "No." He wasn't sure what else to say, which made him frown. "I promised Hester I'd feed you."

"Oh, good." She sighed dramatically. "Because I'm starving."

He blinked at her and then grinned at her playfulness and reached for the bag the cooks prepared. They passed the afternoon the same as they did for the next month. In the sun, whether at Daffodil Hills or along the shores of Weymouth, in each other's arms, breathless and hopeful in their youth. At night they ate together whether with Harry and Margaret, with the villagers, or in the great hall. Rarely were they apart.

Josiah loved her. He would die for her.

He would kill for her.

CHAPTER THIRTEEN

JOSIAH STEPPED BACK and looked at his portrait of Mercy again. He'd examined it a hundred times this morning. He thought he'd emblazoned it on his mind over the last month while he painted her, but he wanted to make certain he captured the hope in her eyes. It was what she offered him since the day he met her. Hope. It was what had attracted him, and the reason he fell in love with her. She had faith in him instead of fear at what others said he would become. He smiled looking at the exact blue-green color of her eyes, the different hues of rich chestnut in her satiny waves, the delicacy of her fingers. He'd made certain they were all correct.

Today he would reveal it to her. Never had his heart beat so furiously at the thought of showing the model her portrait. His belly flipped and knotted—which it usually did when he saw Mercy, or even thought of seeing her. He exhaled and covered the portrait, then left the studio to go wake her for the day.

He was delighted to find her leaving her chambers, dressed and ready for the day. "Seeing you makes me…" It made him so many things, excited, curious, eager, ridiculously happy.

"I know," she told him on a soft breath. "Me too."

They exchanged a smile, knowing they understood each other better than anyone understood them, and a quick kiss that Josiah was reluctant to end. He tried to hold onto her a little longer and sank his face into her neck.

She broke away and lifted her skirts over her ankles, slipping from his fingers and squealing with laughter. He chased her to the great hall and almost collided with her when she stopped abruptly at the entrance. Every eye looked up. Mercy spun on her heel and tried to leave. Josiah caught her in his arms. He took her hand and led her to his father's table.

"We hardly see you lately, Son," the duke said as Josiah took his seat. "It's nice to hear your laughter filling the halls."

"Yes," Jeremy agreed. "You two seem quite happy together."

Josiah shrugged a shoulder. "Meh," he teased, "she can be irritating."

She scoffed, mocking him, playing along? He wondered. "That's because you get frustrated easily when you don't get your way."

He turned to glare at her but couldn't pull it off and grinned instead when she buried her head in his shoulder and laughed.

"Oh no," Oliver worried, shaking his head. "Now he has an accomplice."

Some at the table laughed, others didn't.

"Mercy," Helena, Thomas' wife said, "you must spend the afternoon with us, embroidering."

The afternoon? Josiah scowled. "She doesn't know how to embroider."

"That's even better!" Helena clapped and the other wives agreed. "We'll teach her."

"No," he insisted. He had plans with her. He wanted to show her the portrait. "Not today."

"So change them, Josiah," Helena whined. "Please, brother."

"Yes, please spare her for one afternoon, brother," pleaded Ava and Millicent.

"Tear yourself away from her, Josiah," said Nicholas' betrothed with a wry smile.

"Son," his father stepped in. "You can't win against them. Let her stay with them today. If you're serious about her, then she should get to know her future sisters.

Josiah was sure he heard Mercy swallow. He turned to look at her. She offered him a reassuring nod. His gaze took in the women around her, like jackals circling a fawn. He wanted to refuse them all, but his father was correct, he shouldn't keep her from finally having a family. But he hated leaving her alone with them. "I—"

"Josiah," Helena slapped her palms on the table. "Do you want her to grow tired and bored of you? Mercy, wouldn't you prefer time to miss him?"

"I won't grow tired and bored of you," Mercy was quick to tell him, then turned to Helena. "No, I wouldn't prefer time to miss him. I've missed him my whole life. But how can I refuse such a gracious invitation to get to know you fine ladies better?"

Helena and the others gleamed at her. Josiah wanted to scowl at his brother's wives, but he was too busy gleaming at Mercy, as well. It seemed he wasn't the only one she enchanted.

Still, he wasn't happy about being separated from her. He found that his appetite had also abandoned him. He smiled when it was expected—a skill long practiced and perfected. He wasn't sure which one of them hooked their pinkies together under the table, him or Mercy, but neither one let go while they spoke with others.

When their meal was over and the ladies broke away from the men, Josiah stood up with her and pulled her closer by the pinkies. He kissed her quickly on the mouth, setting her head spinning and tongues wagging.

He hated letting her go, looking at anything or anyone other than her.

"A new playhouse has opened in London," Gilbert let them all know. "I'll be traveling there for a few days. Josiah, I don't suppose you want to come?"

Josiah tossed him an irritated look.

Beside him, Edward laughed and clapped him on the back. "Have pity on the poor sot. She's his first love."

"He has no idea that his laughter will soon turn to cries for help," Thomas interjected. "Let him enjoy it now." Most agreed.

"I don't know enough about her to approve of marriage," the duke announced, resting his palms on his round belly.

Josiah flicked his gaze to him. "What more do you need to know but that I love her? I told you I won't wait."

"Now, Son, there's no need—"

"Gil," Josiah turned to his brother. "I think I will join you in London. When are you leaving?"

"In an hour," Gilbert told him and then smiled and shook his head at him when Josiah left the great hall and hurried after the women.

WATCHING WILLIAM SHAKESPEARE'S *The Tempest* at the new playhouse without electricity was a very different experience than when Mercy went to see a play on Broadway. The actors, dressed like magical beings, leaped and twirled around dozens of torchlights. They shouted lines and sang in loud, booming voices so that all could hear.

She sat with Josiah and Gilbert and the rest of the gentry in the galleries while the general public stood pushed close to the stage. For the most part, the audience interacted with the characters, either cheering and encouraging Prospero or throwing oranges at him, unable to decide if he was a man or a monster. Mercy thought she understood what made men turn into monsters in many cases. She guessed Josiah felt the same way since he was quiet while the crowd around him shouted for Prospero's demise.

Her heart broke for Josiah. Now that she was staying, she would make sure he knew that she treasured his heart that could never, would never, hurt another living being. He needed someone to have faith in him. She would. She did. She had to wonder though what was the purpose of her being sent back to the seventeenth century? Was this it? To believe in him?

As if sensing she was troubled, Josiah gave her fingers a slight squeeze. When she turned away from the stage and looked at him, she found him gazing at her. It was slightly too dim to see if he was smiling, but she guessed he was.

He leaned in and whispered in her ear, "Don't worry overmuch, Mercy."

She smiled back and nodded; she wouldn't worry over things then. She trusted Josiah. It was hard to believe. She'd never even *considered* trusting anyone before. Who was there to trust? The sisters at the orphanage? She'd left them all without looking back when she went off to college. She never saw any of them again. Some died, some moved away when the orphanage closed. Mercy had no particular reason to trust Josiah. Her heart told her to from the very beginning, She believed what he told her—even when she was in a dungeon—and he hadn't let her down. "No oranges for Prospero?" he asked her.

"No," she replied softly. "We're all just a step behind him. What about you?"

"I don't throw them because I would want someone in the crowd to refrain if it were me huddled in the corner."

"Josiah, it will never be you," she assured him. She wanted to be with him. Not here in a stuffy, crowded theater. She ran her fingertips over his cheek and jaw. "Let's leave and go for a walk."

"Come then," he said almost instantly. Gilbert barely noticed them leaving, lost in the painted smile of a stately lady who'd quietly joined their booth. Mercy and Josiah laughed about them as they slipped away, retrieved their coats, and left the playhouse.

The carriage was waiting to pick them up but they both agreed to walk back to Danbe House. Captain Sherwood and his men followed behind, but Josiah and Mercy barely remembered they were there. It was dark as there were no street lamps, but there was a group of boys who looked to be twelve to fourteen years old. After Josiah hired one and the boy lit his torch and led the way, Josiah explained to her that they were called linkboys.

For a farthing, a linkboy would walk with you and light the way with a pitch and tow torch.

"Danbe House on Fenchurch Place," Josiah told the boy. He held her hand as they strolled along the Thames. Mercy marveled at London Bridge, the original version with its stone foundations, pointed arches and 20 foot wide piers.

"This bridge looks very different in the future," she told Josiah. "It's been rebuilt three times."

"Are you going to miss your time?"

She shook her head. "I have no connections to anything in the future. Only here," she told him, walking closer to him while he entwined his fingers through hers. "Only you."

He kissed the top of her head.

"Josiah?"

"Hmm?"

"I've never loved anyone before. I don't mean I've never been in love. I've never loved *anyone.*"

"Are you telling me that you don't know if you can love me?" he asked into her hair.

"Yes, with you, something's different. It's like, you're the one I've been holding back for."

He liked hearing that and grinned.

"Since you found me," he asked, "there's no longer a need to hold back, hmm?"

She covered her face in his sleeve and giggled. No, she no longer wanted to hold back. "Oh, still," she sighed against his arm. "I worry that things are too quiet."

"What are you expecting?"

"Something. I don't know." Even as she said it, she felt the air go cold against her skin. "Josiah? Where's the nearest church?" she asked, looking around the streets.

Josiah thought about it and then looked northwest. "There's a small church nearby. I think it's called St. Olave's on Hart Street. Why do you ask? Do you want to go to church?"

She nodded. "I want us to pray for you."

He stared at her for a moment and then told the boy where to lead next. "Mercy."

"Yes?"

"Thank you."

"For what?"

"Bringing me to pray."

"Well, if there's a battle coming, I want God to be on our side. And I'll be there too."

Her heart melted when he smiled at her.

They found the church in the middle of a street lined in wooden houses. As they approached, it began to rain. Josiah removed his coat and held it over her head, but it was no use, they were soaked through in seconds, so was the linkboy and torch. They reached the front gate as thunder shook the ground and lightning flashed its silver glow on three stone skulls and crossbones topping the gate. As if they were not chilling enough with their empty eye-sockets and grisly grins, they were impaled on iron spikes.

Mercy watched Josiah pull open the heavy iron gate. A sound pierced her ears. Was it the screech of a cat or the gate hinges? She looked down at the linkboy, who appeared unaffected before he hurried into the church to dry off.

As they walked beneath the skulls, Mercy looked at Josiah as another flash of lightning illuminated him. Sensing her gaze, he turned while hurrying to the church doors and offered her a playful grin.

When they stepped inside, Mercy thought it seemed almost obvious that he would have chosen this church to come to. If one was afraid of getting too close to it they would miss the warmth and feeling of safety on the inside. Dozens of candles in stands and in sconces secured to the wall gave light and more. The oak ceiling and polished, wooden pews added to the church's cozy atmosphere while thunder raged outside the doors. A dozen or so monuments also took up places on the walls and in columns. They read some plaques together and then sat down in a pew to pray.

They remained quiet, either kneeling in prayer or sitting in thoughtful silence for almost an hour. When the rain stopped and they left the church, Mercy stopped to look up at the gate and its spikes and skulls.

A memory suddenly popped up in her mind and cooled her blood. The year was 1661. In five years there would be a great fire here. She scanned her eyes over the church and the surrounding area. Everything was wood—and almost everything burned.

"What is it?" Josiah asked her, noticing her change in mood right away.

"A fire in 1666," she intoned, trying to remember more details. "They waited too long to destroy the wooden structures to prevent the spread of the flames and in four days almost all of London was—or will be destroyed. Oh, but, Josiah, I don't remember the details of how it started or the exact date. And even if I did remember, we can't do anything about it. We can't tamper with the future. And you especially can't do anything about it because what if you change something and thousands are never born in the future? It will be as if the prophecy is fulfilled."

He swallowed and nodded. They both heard a man's footsteps pick up, as if he'd paused in the shadows to eavesdrop. They let him pass and watched as the man met a friend of his on the street just before he entered the church gate.

"Good evening Mr. Pepys. Welcome back."

Mercy paused. Pepys? Where had she heard the name before? She thought about going back to ask who he was, but Josiah's good mood had returned and he pulled her along.

The linkboy, with his torch already lit, waited to be told their next destination.

They walked along the wet, cobbled alleys, and despite the loud, mewling stray cats, men sleeping off their drunkenness in dark corners, and the smells that were almost as bad as the dungeon at Ashmore Castle, Mercy felt happier than she'd ever felt in her life. She stopped wondering if it was all real and decided to simply enjoy every second of being here with Josiah at her side.

"What did you pray for?" she asked him as they walked back to Danbe House.

"I prayed for you to stay with me until my last breath," he told her.

"Me too," she let him know.

He lifted their entwined fingers to his lips and kissed her knuckles. When he lowered their hands, he smiled at her in the torchlight. "Then, you'll be my wife?"

CHAPTER FOURTEEN

RAXXIX RECLINED ON his rocky throne, with his hand over his eyes. He didn't think he'd get over seeing Josiah enter a church. None of the head demon's horde could enter the sanctuary, so he had no way of knowing if his vessel had prayed to Him. It was enough to cause Raxxix to want to kill the woman for bringing him there. She shouldn't be alive anyway. She was the child he'd been warned about. The one who'd escaped Catherine Ashmore and the ruby dagger. Raxxix guessed Tessa Blagden had whisked the girl away and hidden her granddaughter in the future. When he finally picked up a trace of her, he'd sent one of his soldiers across time to kill her and end her line. But his demons had returned without proof of the job done. He'd been told she was dead, along with her mother, and when he tried to sense her, he couldn't. Everything seemed to be going as planned up until the seventh son was born. Then Blagden turned up again and escaped with the dagger after almost succeeding in killing his vessel. For that, the Blagden name would be cursed by men for centuries.

He hadn't known or expected the prophesied child to pierce her flesh on the dagger and transfer her healing power to her enemy across time. At first, Raxxix was going to kill her right away when she showed up in the seventh son's life. She had the dagger. She could kill him. But then she'd proven that she wasn't here to kill but to heal him. After the dagger was no longer in her hands, Raxxix had decided that if she could keep him alive until he took over, he'd let her live. He just had to claim the dagger.

But things were changing. The vessel was quickly losing his heart to her. Raxxix knew what had to be done. A grin made more macabre by its utter sincerity and thirst for evil curled his lips. There was a way to perhaps catapult the son into giving up his soul sooner. But Raxxix had to use caution. Tessa Blagden still lived. She, along with her sister, still possessed their powers and were able to retrieve the dagger from the depths of the ocean. Fools they were to think that throwing the dagger into the sea would be the end of it. This time though, the Blagdens would fail. He would destroy love's work and take back the dagger when it fell from Mercy Blagden's dead fingers.

He couldn't wait to wield it through Josiah Ashmore's body.

But first, he had to stop the girl from stabbing his vessel in the heart. There was only one way of ensuring that even if the dagger ended up back in her hands, the vessel would have no heart left to destroy. Raxxix had to hurry. The prophesied child could heal the vessel, and while she could, Raxxix couldn't take him over. Enraged, Raxxix uttered blasphemous things. It was time to rip out Josiah Ashmore's heart.

He called his horde to gather around him and commanded them to go out and harvest a small army.

He stood from his throne and looked around at the flames and dry darkness beyond. "Soon. Soon I will wreak havoc on that lowly species once again. I won't kill hundreds. I will destroy thousands here...and in the future."

>>><<<

"I'M NERVOUS ABOUT seeing it," Mercy told Josiah, standing outside his studio.

"Why?" Josiah asked her.

She loved how he didn't find her foolish or frustrating. He

always smiled at her and gazed at her with affection and amusement.

"It's how you see me, Josiah."

He nodded. "That's correct. Trust me, you have nothing to feel anxious about."

She finally smiled and moved to follow him into the studio. A sound stopped her. She wasn't sure she heard anything at all. As high up as they were, it could be the screech of wind. But Josiah went still.

"Did you hear that?" she asked him.

"Yes," he said, listening for more.

The sound pierced the air again. Men below were shouting but the ominous crashing sound rising upward, as if the castle doors were being smashed down, drowned the men's shouts out.

"Father!"

"What is it?" she asked Josiah, her heart pounding.

"Stay here!" he commanded and then was gone, rushing down the stairs.

Stay here? Was he nuts? She looked after him. She wanted to call out, but he was already gone. The booming sound continued, echoing up to the tower where the studio was, sending tremors through her blood. The next sound froze her blood in her veins. It sounded like a battering ram! Was the castle under attack? It couldn't be. How had men gotten past the gates and all the guards patrolling the walls?

"Josiah?" she called out meekly, then closed her eyes. Was she supposed to wait here not knowing if he was in danger? Impossible. Images of him lying bloody in the halls set her to running.

When she reached the main part of the castle, she ran straight into pandemonium as the castle doors splintered. Anyone who wasn't an Ashmore resident or a guardsmen ran this way and that, covering their ears and crying out in terror. She searched the faces but couldn't find Josiah.

The thunderous crash sounded again, as a great battering ram smashed into the doors, the sound so much louder now that she was closer to it. The wood cracked and splintered more. It wouldn't hold up to another hit. Someone pushed her back up the stairs then rushed to the door. It was Captain Sherwood! She had to ask him if he'd seen Josiah. She had to find him. While she ran back down the stairs after the captain, the ram struck again and slivers of wood flew everywhere and stopped Mercy in her tracks.

Finally, she saw Josiah with his brothers Edward and Oliver running toward the doors. They meant to fight whoever was trying to get in. She had to stop him. But when she took a step, the doors came crashing down and a swarm of armed men rushed inside. Josiah was swallowed up and disappeared.

"Josiah!" Mercy screamed. Someone took her wrist and pulled, trying to lead her back up the stairs. She turned to see Hester. "I have to help Josiah!"

"No!" Hester yanked with surprising strength. "Your duty isn't to help him. Come with me!"

"Hester, what are you saying? Let me go! I have to find him. Don't you understand? I can't live without him!" she cried, struggling to be free. "Let me go!"

"Child! Child, you must live without him. Now that he's an adult—"

Mercy fought to be free of Hester's surprisingly strong grasp. She *had* to live without him? No! Her tear and terror-filled eyes scanned the men around her. Everyone was either fighting or screaming. A terrible smell wafted through the halls. The metallic smell of blood mixed with something else, not as strong as sulfur, but it still made Mercy gag. "Josiah!" She screamed out. "Josiah!"

"Mercy, listen to me," Hester took her by the shoulders and shook her. "You know what will happen if he gets the dagger. Now that he's an adult, you're the only one who can do it."

"Do what? I don't understand."

"You must kill him, Child."

Mercy stared at her, stunned and horrified. "What? No! Never! Who are you?" She broke free of Hester's vise-like fingers and turned to run the other way. Just then, she caught sight of Josiah breaking through the crowd, bloodied and staggering. Her heart rejoiced. In the middle of death and battle, she wanted to run to him and leap into his arms.

"Josiah!" Kill him? What kind of madness was going on? Did Hester have something to do with the prophecy? Mercy didn't care about her or anyone else right now, except for Josiah. She had to reach him and get him away from here. She tried to enter the melee but Josiah was emphatically shaking his head at her.

"Don't come!" he shouted as Jeremy appeared beside him, one arm bloodied and limp at his side.

Hester stopped her again. "Listen to him, Child."

"Stop calling me that!" Mercy shouted, whirling around to face her. "Let me go! I have to help him!"

From the corner of her eyes, she saw a movement of emerald silk rushing past her.

"Jeremy!" It was Millicent, his wife. She carried a short-sword and rushed down the stairs and entered the fighting, swinging and slashing and trying to duck and reach her husband. But one of the marauders swung his heavy sword at her and struck her down before their eyes.

Mercy wanted to scream but Jeremy's wails stilled her blood and broke her heart. She wasn't going to be able to reach Josiah without putting him through the same torture his brother was suffering.

"Josiah! Son!"

Mercy turned to see the duke being dragged toward his youngest son's feet and deposited there by men with gleaming amber eyes—red in the torchlight, and laughter on their lips. Behind them, Thomas, Oliver, and Edward were bound, gagged, and dragged forward. The fighting stopped for a moment when the attackers moved in formation to stand around the duke and his sons and their captors.

"Let them go!" Jeremy screamed. Josiah remained silent, grinding his teeth together.

In response to Jeremy's command, one of the men held a knife to Oliver's throat and without another word, drew the blade across it. Mercy screamed and felt as if she was going to faint. This couldn't be happening. Josiah broke his silence with a cry that sounded as if it had been issued by an animal rather than a man. The duke cried and begged for mercy, and for them to spare the rest of his sons. He was stabbed in the throat for his request. Josiah leaped upon them and killed two of them while Jeremy collapsed to his knees and beat his chest. Still bound, Thomas and Edward threw themselves into the men, trying to inflict some injury on them. Edward fell easily with his wrists tied. Thomas fell over his brother's body, trying to protect him while he could and that's where he too took his last breath. Captain Sherwood and two of his men, Gerard Dutton and Joem Macey, killed six of the men, including one that killed Millicent and another who sliced Oliver's throat. The captain shouted at Josiah and Nicholas to run into the castle but the brothers didn't listen to his command to retreat. When he saw his father and brothers dead, Nicholas wielded his blade and killed a dozen men by himself. But in the end, he too, fell, his belly split open. It seemed as if they kept coming, charging through the castle, swords raised, shouts on their lips.

"This is Raxxix's doing," Hester said beside Mercy.

"Why?" Mercy asked, sobbing and heedlessly wiping her eyes.

"Look at Josiah, Child. He's watching his entire family fall before him. It's likely there won't be much left of him when this is over. You have no choice. You must see your task done."

Mercy shook her head. "I don't know who you are or what you want but I'll never hurt him."

Mercy spotted Gilbert rushing into the fray. He was able to hold off the men for another twenty minutes with the help of Captain Sherwood and even Josiah, who was beginning to look too exhausted to lift his sword. Without knowing why, Mercy turned to Hester for help.

The older woman gave her a soothing look. "His body will

not die here, unless it's by your hand. Raxxix needs it. The evil will use Josiah like a puppet. His will, as well as his soul, will be lost. He'll be a shell. You will be showing him mercy by killing him."

Mercy felt her blood boil. How many times did she have to tell this woman, who obviously wasn't a servant, that she wasn't going to harm a hair on Josiah's head? "I'm not the merciful kind," she told Hester and turned her back on her. When she did, she saw one of the enemy soldiers thrust his blade at Josiah. Mercy screamed his name. Hearing her, Gilbert leaped in front of his little brother and took the blade through the belly.

As he slipped to the floor, Mercy was faced with the utter horror on Josiah's face as he watched his brother fall. Color drained from her face, as well. Her eyes widened and immediately filled with tears.

"Gil!!" Josiah pitifully cried out, falling to the floor and lifting him into his lap. "Gil, hold on! Hold on! Please, don't go!"

The men around him laughed, sneering down at them and Mercy knew they weren't human. They couldn't be.

Now Jeremy stood up and with a cry and his sword raised over his head, he attacked the men. But he too, fell to the blade.

"Find the women," someone called out.

Josiah set his brother down gently, then rose from the floor. He moved toward Mercy, knocking men over as he went.

As if they all shared one thought, the men turned to Mercy and Hester, then started toward them. Mercy's heart pounded hard enough to make her ill. She prayed she would faint in Josiah's arms before the men reached them and cut them down. With a second to spare, she set her gaze on Josiah from over the horde's heads. There was so much she wanted to say—

"Here, take this." Hester shoved a rag—no, something wrapped in a rag, into her hand. "Remember you're a Blagden. Do what you were sent to do," she commanded and then ran. "You must kill him!"

The men reached her. And then passed her without a single

touch. When Hester stopped running and disappeared, they returned their attention to Mercy, but instead of cutting her to pieces, one of them held up her hand holding the ruby dagger while their comrades took hold of Josiah.

"Mercy! Mercy! Long live Mercy Blagden, who showed us the way in so we could cut down our enemy! Today's victory belongs to her!" the man shouted, and the rest cheered.

What? Mercy looked up at the oaf and then turned her gaze back to Josiah. He was staring at her, looking even more defeated than he had when they killed his last brother.

"Josiah!" she shouted to him. "It's a lie!"

"It's all right, Lady Blagden, we've got him now. You no longer have to pretend. You have the ruby dagger. We'll hold him down while you stab him in the heart."

Her brokenhearted gaze met Josiah's. Tears streamed down his blood-stained face. He heard it all. "Josiah." Saying his name felt like an arrow in her heart. She wanted to say it a hundred more times until she poured out her blood to him. If giving every drop of her blood was what it took to heal him of this day, she'd gladly give it. "Don't believe any of it. Believe in me."

She yanked her wrist free and swung the ruby dagger over her shoulder ready to fling it into the future if she had to. "I'm not stabbing anyone," she cried and hurled the dagger. Before it left her hand, it disappeared the same way it had the first time—taking her with it.

JOSIAH STOOD STILL. He didn't feel his heart beating. He didn't care. He didn't care if he stopped breathing. In fact, why wasn't he dead along with the rest of his family? His family. He didn't want to move or look around his feet. His brothers were there. Dead. All of them. His father—no! "No." A sob escaped him. He closed his eyes.

Someone was shaking him.

"My lord! My lord!" It was Oswald. "Come! We must be away. Everyone is falling. You will be next!" The hefty servant yanked on his arm.

"Where's Captain Sherwood?" Josiah asked him.

"He went to save the women and children."

The women and children, Josiah thought. Yes. He wanted to go help. But he didn't move his feet. The assailants were Blagdens. They'd been sent to finish what Tessa Blagden couldn't finish. And Mercy was one of them. In possession of the ruby dagger. With an army at her back. No. No.

Don't believe any of it. Believe in me.

He remembered all the warnings from his father and brothers about trusting her.

He covered his eyes with his hands and let his tears come. And they came hard and heavy, even after Oswald hefted him up on his back and ran toward the tower stairs.

No. He didn't want to leave them! He reached out his hand. Gil, who gave up his life for him. He wanted to throw back his head and howl and wail. His father, who pampered and spoiled him to the point that if Josiah didn't have a curse to battle he most likely would have let himself become rotten. Poor Jeremy, who had to watch his beloved wife die. Nicholas, who hadn't even had a chance to wed the girl he loved. All of them. All of them. Everyone he loved. And Mercy, gone, most likely taken back to the twenty-first century. Taken from him like everyone else. He didn't want to breathe, to think, to live.

Oswald carried him up to the high tower, a feat that went unappreciated by his tormented master. The muscular servant bolted the door of the studio and brought him to his narrow bed in the highest point of the tower.

"Rest now, my lord. I'll stay with you and take care of you," Oswald told him, pulling off his shoes and covering him with a blanket.

Josiah was mildly aware of him sitting at the top of the stairs, guarding him with nothing but his brute strength.

"There's a sword on the wall," Josiah told him. He didn't want to sleep. He would dream of every horror over and over. But his body was weary from fighting. His mind was too terrorized to take a step on his own. His heart was numb, as if every shred of hope in it had poured out over his family's dead bodies, at Mercy's feet.

She was a Blagden. He'd heard Hester remind her. Hester. He scoffed at himself alone in his bed. No one was who they said they were—and anyone who was, was dead. He groaned out loud and clutched his belly, though he knew the pain came from his fractured heart. He felt guilty for doubting her. She hadn't lied about having the dagger—well, she had at first, but it was understandable. She was frightened, especially knowing how the Ashmores hated the Blagdens.

It was understandable until his father and his brothers were all slaughtered before his eyes.

Do what you were sent to do.

He closed his eyes to stop the rush of tears fighting for release. They broke through and soaked his hair, his pillow. She'd let him argue with his father when the duke questioned who she was. She'd let him believe she was completely harmless when it appeared now that she wasn't.

After an hour of sobbing into his hands, he finally fell asleep.

He didn't dream, but fell into a deep, fevered sleep that compelled Oswald out of the studio to search for help.

When he finally did open his eyes, four days had passed. Oswald sat by the bed, patting his head with a lukewarm rag. For a blessed moment, Josiah forgot. But the moment vanished too quickly and sorrow took the place of peace.

"Has Miss Smith returned?" was the first thing he asked.

"No, my lord."

Josiah tried to rise. He couldn't think of her now. His family needed to be buried. But Oswald informed him that the villagers, not knowing if he would live or die, had already buried them. He knew he should feel grateful, but it had been all he had left to do for them. Now there was nothing.

"My lord."

Josiah gave him an impatient look when the servant didn't speak right away. "Out with it, Oswald."

"My lord, your brothers were buried with their wives and children. Your father's guard, including Captain Sherwood, have all perished."

Josiah covered his face with his hands while he wept again for his family and friends. He lived. They could have killed him a thousand times, but no iron had been put to him. Him or Mercy. Was it truly because it was her duty to kill him with the ruby blade? It had to be, he told himself. It had to be why she came here with it and didn't tell him about it. But why not just kill him? Why his entire family? How had she gotten it back in the first place? It should be at the bottom of the ocean. If she was innocent, where was she? Had she taken the dagger out of his time to protect him? Her shy, hesitant smiles, half-hidden behind a curtain of chestnut tresses flashed across his thoughts. Was her innocence used to trap him? He would forgive her if only she came back. He waited, alone in his castle while rage and loneliness fought for rule in his life. Finally, he gave in to both.

Still, he waited for her to come back.

But she never did.

CHAPTER FIFTEEN

2022
Upstate, New York

MERCY OPENED HER eyes. Darkness surrounded her. She sat still, letting her vision adjust to the absence of light. Her heart thrashed wildly in her chest, so fast she couldn't count the beats. Had she moved through time again? *No,* she prayed. She was taken from him with him believing...a sob escaped her. *Please.*

She searched her surroundings. She was inside. She could make out the silhouette of the four-drawer chest that was in the orphanage, where she'd been pricked by the ruby dagger. Her heart sank. No! No! Oh, no please! She'd been sucked back! Almost four hundred years away from Josiah. Through a seemingly unending well of tears, she saw her phone on the floor. She needed light to find the dagger. It had to be here. She'd slice it across her hand and draw her blood. It had been with her when she woke up in Samuel's barn the first time. It had to be here. The battery on her phone was dead. There was no light from the windows. She was going to have to stay here until the morning and the sunlight came. She had to find the dagger. She leaped up and checked all the drawers of the chest, shoving her hands inside, not caring about getting cut. The dagger wasn't there. She had to go back. If she had to stay here, it meant being alone for the rest of her life. She hoped that as long as Josiah lived, Hester needed her to kill him, so they would send her back.

She sank to the dusty floor and pulled her knees up and hugged them to her chest. "Josiah," she cried. "I don't want to be here without you. How am I supposed to live without your eyes on me, as if my beauty stilled your heart. Please, don't believe what your head is telling you. I'd never do anything to hurt you. Please trust me."

She wept, trying to cling to a tether of hope. "Hester? Hester, can you hear me?"

She rubbed her eyes. Had her personality disorder grown into full-blown schizophrenia? She cast the shadows a fearful look, then continued to call out to Hester. Let people think what they want. They always had. She didn't care. "Hester, whoever you are. Bring me back. Please. I can't kill him, but I can prevent him from turning into what you fear. Please!" Her voice rose to a hysterical pitch. "Do you hear me?"

She didn't sleep at all. Not with her thoughts haunting her. Thoughts of him always smiling, images of him lost to painting her portrait that she never got to see, sitting with him under a tree surrounded by daffodils, running in the rain. And never once had he made her feel self-conscious about her scar. He hadn't just told her he loved her, he lived as if he did. She knew she meant everything to him. She prayed he trusted her enough not to believe what those men said.

"You knew who they were and who sent them, didn't you, Hester? All you cared about was me killing Josiah."

When a peal of thunder shook the walls of the old orphanage and lightning lit the floor enough for her to see that the dagger wasn't there, she remembered going to St. Olave Church and praying with him. She prayed now, asking God to send her back to Josiah.

As dawn approached, casting light into the dusty attic, she searched every nook and cranny of the orphanage. The ruby dagger wasn't there. She tried to think calmly. Where could it be? With Hester. She grabbed her purse. Thankfully, her car keys were still in it. She left the orphanage and thought about buying a plane ticket to England and searching there. That was where he'd lived.

Her car was where she'd left it—parked in the grass outside the orphanage. How long had she been in the seventeenth century? A day? A little over a month? She got into the car and started it up. She remembered explaining cars to Josiah and she almost smiled thinking of his facial expressions and how he believed everything she told him. How could he be so unconditional in his belief on whatever she told him? In the way he saw her, the way he loved her? She wiped her eyes and her nose. There was no time to fall apart. She had to find a way back to him. That was all that mattered. Most likely she needed the ruby dagger. To find it, it looked as if she was going to have to find Hester. There was comfort in one thing though; if her beloved was still alive, Hester would find her. If he was already dead and Hester never came for her, it was just as well because Mercy didn't want to be anywhere without him. How long would she wait? That was why she had to find the dagger on her own.

She drove to a small convenience store about half a mile away and checked the balance on her debit card. A little over five thousand dollars. She'd saved almost every penny she'd earned that didn't go on her rent every month. She didn't eat much and she hadn't gone out after work. There hadn't been any men in her life, and for the most part, she'd shopped at thrift stores to save. For what? She didn't know. Maybe for today, so she'd have the money to buy a plane ticket to the UK. She picked up some snacks and went to the counter to pay. The young woman ringing up her items looked out the window and then at Mercy.

"Nice car."

Mercy blinked. "What?" She looked over her shoulder to see which car the girl had mistaken for being hers. Her 2009 little Accord had seen better days. It was the only car outside. "*That?*"

The girl, who was about Mercy's age, smirked. "When you have very little, you appreciate what others take for granted."

"Yes, that's true." Mercy dipped her head and squeezed her eyes shut to stop her tears.

"Would you sell it?"

Mercy looked up. "What? Oh, I don't know. Actually, if you could let me charge my phone and direct me to a bus to the city or the airport, you can have the car. I need to get a flight to the UK."

"I can have the car for free?"

"For free," Mercy repeated and then watched the woman disappear into a room in the back.

After a minute or two, she reappeared, accompanied by a gray-haired woman wearing dark glasses and walking with a cane that looked like a polished branch. "You the one giving away your car?"

"Yes, if you can tell me how—"

"You're not from here."

Mercy stared at her, feeling, for an instant, transported back. "What?"

"Manhattan?" the old woman guessed. "We don't get many lowstaters here."

"Oh, right," Mercy said. She didn't want to hang around, but it was because she had someplace else she needed to be, not because she was so shy and insecure she didn't want to be around others. He had changed her. Love saw past her imperfections and if someone's eyes couldn't, then she didn't need to know them. "Is there a bus?"

The older woman shook her head. "Bernadette will call a taxi from town to pick you up and bring you to the airport. I'll pay for it since we're getting a car for nothing."

"Thank you," Mercy told her. "But I'll pay for—"

"Forget it then." The older woman turned to head inside the back room.

Mercy couldn't help but smile at her spunk. "Okay, fine. You can pay the carfare."

The older woman nodded and crooked her finger at her,

signaling Mercy to follow her into the back room. They called the DMV and made arrangements for the registration to be signed over. The whole time Mercy was on the phone, the older woman, whose name was Elizabeth Black, studied her as if she was going to be tested when Mercy left.

"So," she said when Mercy hung up. "What are you going to the UK for?"

Mercy smiled a little. Older people were forgiven for being brash and intrusive, weren't they? "I'm searching for someone."

"A man from the looks of you."

"Pardon?"

Mrs. Black stared at her. "You look like your heart's been broken and you're off to try to mend it."

Mercy prayed that she could hold back her tears. "Hmm." She slipped out of the chair and headed for the door to the store.

"Sometimes love isn't enough," Mrs. Black called out to her.

Mercy paused and shook her head without turning around. "Love is always enough."

She was about to leave when she stopped in her tracks. Elizabeth Black reminded her of someone. She turned on her heel and blinked. Old Lizzie. How? How could it be? She didn't care about that now.

"How do I get back to him, Seer?"

The older woman smiled and then chuckled softly. "Clever girl. You know the answer to that."

Mercy's heart raced. She'd found someone. She reached for the nearest chair to sit. "Hester," she said softly, though she felt about to burst into tears. "You know where she is. Where the dagger is." Please. Please help me. I'll do anything to get back to him."

"Only Hester knows where the ruby dagger is. But she won't put it into your hands unless you promise to destroy him."

Mercy clenched her teeth. "I'll deal with her when I have to, please just tell me where she is. Please."

"You're on the right path."

"But where—"

"I won't tell you anything else," Mrs. Black said and turned her back on her.

Mercy blew out a frustrated, shaky breath. "You told me something when we met before."

"What was that?" the older woman asked.

"You said that what I already possess will grow stronger. If you were speaking of the power of my love for Josiah Ashmore, then you were correct."

Old Lizzie turned and watched her when Mercy left. She shook her head. "No," she muttered softly, "that wasn't what I meant."

Mercy stepped out of the convenience store and waited. Finally, she turned to the woman who rang up her snacks and called her a cab. She was sitting alone on a porch swing built for two.

"The car service will be here in twenty minutes," she told Mercy.

Mercy bit her lip and realized she hadn't bitten it in a month.

"Are you going to stand there until he comes? Why don't you sit?"

Mercy also realized she wasn't as anxious at being alone with someone as she had been a month ago. She nodded and sat on the bench with the girl.

"Are you her granddaughter?" Mercy asked.

"Yes. Don't pity me. She isn't that bad." Bernadette smiled, proving that she was joking.

"I know," Mercy gave in and smiled back. "She would have paid for the car if she had to."

Bernadette nodded, then sighed. "If not for her crazy cryptic ways, we'd probably have more customers. Thankfully, I have three other jobs or I'd pull my hair out from boredom."

"Oh, listen," Mercy said sincerely. "Let me pay for the cab."

"Granny wouldn't let me forget it. No. We can afford it. Gran saved money over the years."

I'll bet. She probably has a nice little nest egg after at least three hundred years.

Mercy smiled at her and then had another thought. This one, she asked out loud. "Have you ever met Hester?"

Bernadette shook her head. "Who is she?"

"I don't know. Your grandmother mentioned her living in the UK."

"Oh, don't mind Gran. She's older than she looks. She's actually my great grandmother. She gets things mixed up," she said the last in a whisper, turning to Mercy's ear. "Where did you get that scar?"

Mercy had almost forgotten she had it. "I was stabbed when I was a baby."

"Ohh," Bernadette said, staring at her as if she was seeing her for the first time. "Are you her?"

Mercy's eyes opened wider. "Who?"

"I heard my great aunt, Tessa, talking about you to her sister." She motioned into the store.

Tessa? Mercy lifted her palms to her head. What? Tessa? It was too much of a coincidence. Mercy had a thousand questions. She started with the most important. "What did she say?"

"She said she lost her daughter because of what she did. Gran reminded her that she'd saved her granddaughter and she lived, despite being stabbed in the face."

Mercy felt sick to her stomach. Was Tessa Blagden, the woman who killed Josiah's mother and tried to kill him when he was baby, her grandmother? Was Tessa Blagden the same as Sister Tess, who favored her, at the orphanage? The same as Hester, a servant at the castle? It was too much to take in. She stood up, ready to march back inside and demand answers from Elizabeth Black.

"Was your great Aunt Tessa a nun at an orphanage?"

Bernadette shook her head slowly. "A nun? No, but she did have a job at an orphanage not far from here." Her smile widened. "You *are* her, then. My family."

Mercy covered her mouth while tears spilled over the rims of her eyes. In all the truths she'd just learned, this one hurt the most. She had a family this whole time? And they kept the truth from her, letting her grow up alone her whole life? Okay, she got it. From what she'd learned from Hester and now this, she realized they were probably trying to hide her. If she was the only one who could kill Josiah, then whatever wanted him alive would want her dead. So her grandmother, who was obviously able to travel through time, hid her in the future. She got it. She was thankful. But letting her grow up alone still hurt. Still, she'd never really been alone, had she?

"They said something about the child—you—being part of the weapon, the hilt," Bernadette continued. "I thought it was part of this fantasy world they sometimes lived in. I mean, what kind of kid is a weapon? And a hilt of all things. Whatever that means. Do you know?"

"It doesn't have a hilt." Mercy said out loud.

"What doesn't?"

"The dagger." Oh, it was just too much and she was tired. So tired. "I'm the handle used to kill him."

Bernadette stood up, her eyes wide and suddenly fearful. "What are you saying? Kill who?"

"Mercy Blagden!"

Mercy turned to Mrs. Black standing at the door. She held out Mercy's charged phone. "Take it and go."

"How can you be so cold to me, your great niece?" Mercy asked her, stepping up to her. "How could you and Sister Tess lie to me as if it was nothing? Do you know what I lost? What I just lost again?"

"Do you mean the cursed earl of Winterborne?" her great aunt asked. "He was never yours to lose."

"He became mine," Mercy told her. *You're mine.* She remembered how he infuriated her when he claimed that she was his. She understood now. Yes, she was his and he was hers. "I even share his blood."

"What am I missing?" Bernadette asked in a worried tone. "Is it genetic?"

"You were never supposed to find the dagger at such a young age," Mrs. Black said, as if to herself. "She should have known that accursed thing would draw you to it. The babe was dying. Mixing your blood with his saved him and nearly destroyed you, you disobedient child."

"I already know all that," Mercy told her curtly. "Tell me something I don't know. Like how do I get back to him?"

"We already talked about this," her great aunt reminded her with a stern scowl.

Having been scowled at her whole life, Mercy learned well how to ignore it. "Is Tessa Hester?"

"You can ask her yourself when you see her again."

Mercy scoffed. "I'll take that as a yes."

The cab pulled up and waited for her.

"Did it ever occur to you or my grandmother that my poor mother named me Mercy for a reason?"

"Not for him, girl."

Mercy gave her a hard look. "You and Hester are so quick to tell me how he needs to die, but he doesn't have a shred of the arrogance you possess. You think because you call yourself a seer, you know all things. But only God knows all things and last I read, He desires mercy over judgment. So that's what Josiah will get from me when I see him again. I pray it's not too late because by taking me away from him, especially after he watched his family die, you've taken away his defense against Raxxix. Why didn't you see that?"

Old Lizzie blinked, and to Mercy's surprise, it appeared that the old woman was more affected by her words than she would admit.

"It's going to be either you or him, niece."

"What?" Mercy didn't understand but her heart skipped nonetheless.

"Send the car away," her great aunt commanded. "Then

come inside. You can't get to the UK today. You don't have a passport."

What could Mercy do but frown? The old woman was right. Before she could say anything, her aunt walked back inside and shut the door. Bernadette sent the cab away and urged Mercy to follow her inside.

"This isn't real, right?" she asked Mercy as they went. "You're all part of some secret society that maybe partakes of some hallucinatory drugs and—"

"They...I... don't live in a fantasy world," Mercy assured her. "It's all real."

"I was afraid you were going to say that."

Old Lizzie made them tea while Bernadette showed her the upstairs rooms. But Mercy was eager to get back to her great aunt and find out what she meant about it having to be her or Josiah.

"Did you mean one of us has to die?" she asked her aunt when she returned to her.

"Yes. You are the child prophesied to be born with the power to kill him. Catherine Ashmore slaughtered six trying to find you. But you had a grandmother who could travel through time and hid you away in the twenty-first century. After her attempt on Josiah Ashmore's life, Raxxix found you and sent one of his minions to destroy you. Your mother died and you know the rest." She stopped to sip her tea.

Mercy wiped the tears she shed for her mother and for the six children killed in an effort to find her. "What's the power I have that set a monster after me? Is it hereditary?"

Her aunt shrugged her shoulders. "It's been in our family for generations. Some have multiple abilities. Some have one. Tessa and I are clairvoyant. She can travel through time and I can communicate with animals. Your mother possessed the power of dream telepathy, but she wasn't clairvoyant. And you—"

"Yes?"

"You can't be possessed or persuaded by Raxxix," Old Lizzie told her. "You can't be influenced by him or by anything that serves him. That's why when the dagger was in your possession it didn't affect the seventh son. As long as it is touching you in some way, you hold power over it. It's why only you can kill the seventh son with it. Tessa wasn't ever the person meant to do it. Perhaps that's why she failed. He was a babe, and as horrible as it sounds, he was helpless to fight back."

Mercy closed her eyes in disgust.

"Gran," Bernadette cried, covering her mouth. "What has Aunt Tessa done? What baby?"

But Lizzie didn't answer her. Her gaze was fixed on Mercy. "Your grandmother tried to do it because she knew that as long as the seventh son was alive, your life was in danger. It was only a matter of time before Raxxix found you. The dagger will resist an attempt against him and now that Josiah is a man, he will resist as well. Your grandmother can't fight him.

"I didn't see that your blood could heal him until you arrived in his time and did it. We didn't expect that the babe wouldn't die when Tessa wounded him with the ruby dagger. It didn't pierce his heart. But we didn't realize that you had pierced your skin and bled on the dagger or that it healed him of the fever brought on by the poison. I'll be quite frank, I don't know what it means. I still don't see the end of this. But I know that Raxxix won't let you live when you're the only one who can kill the one promised to him. The only way for you to live is to kill the cursed one."

"He's no more cursed than you would be if Raxxix took you over," Mercy told her. She knew it was no use. Old Lizzie wouldn't spare Josiah an ounce of pity. To her, he was already evil.

Pushing away from the small table where she sat, she turned to a pale Bernadette. "Can you take me to the post office so I can rush my passport?

"Umm, sure."

The poor girl looked completely shell-shocked by what she heard.

"I know it's a lot," Mercy told her while they got into the car.

PAULA QUINN

"It was a lot for me when I woke up in 1661."

"Did you really?" Bernadette asked breathlessly. "How is any of it possible?" She shook her head when Mercy didn't answer. "To be honest, I want to laugh and say you're as off your rocker as the two old ladies, but I've been hearing about this kind of stuff my whole life. So, as much as I don't want to believe it, I guess I do. Mercy shook her head. They were quiet while Bernadette drove, but finally she asked Mercy about the man she'd been referring to as Josiah.

"Josiah Ashmore. He came to mean more to me than anything in my life. More than the breath I don't want to breathe if it isn't laced with him."

"So what happened? How did you end up back here?"

Mercy told her about the attack and the death of the Ashmore men, all besides Josiah. And the lies those monsters said about her.

They ended up spending the day together, spending lunch on their phones, trying to find any information on Josiah Ashmore. Bernadette pulled up something on Ashmore Castle in Dorchester. "It says it's being repaired after the last master of the castle, the duke of Dorset's youngest son, the earl of Winterborne..."

Mercy's teeth chattered, but she wasn't cold. She was afraid to hear what came next. Was he known for being a murderer?

"...let it fall to ruin."

So, he lived long enough to let the castle fall apart? But where was he while it was crumbling?

"He's the earl of Winterborne," she said. "Let's try that."

They keyed in the title and a few things came up. When Mercy read the first article she clicked on, she stopped breathing. "The earl of Winterborne caused the death of his entire family after a vicious betrayal from which he never recovered. He lived as a recluse, painting in his castle while it fell to disrepair around him. His paintings will be on display in the castle when it's repaired in...three years."

"Oh, Mercy," Bernadette said, covering her hand with her

own. "Don't cry. You'll find a way back and change this."

"He didn't do it," Mercy whispered.

"Do it?"

"What he was prophesied to do. What everyone expected him to do." She couldn't contain her smile. It probably seemed macabre to Bernadette. He went through hell but he held onto his soul. "He didn't kill all those people."

CHAPTER SIXTEEN

MERCY WORKED DURING the day in a small bakery upstate and went to school at night at the local college. The first year passed slowly. She spent most of it in England. She visited Ashmore Castle but couldn't get in. Still, she hoped, prayed that she'd somehow be transported. Her grandmother hadn't needed the dagger to skip across time. But nothing ever happened besides a breeze out of nowhere a few times. Her grandmother didn't show up that year.

"Why did you save me, Tessa?" she cried out more times than she could remember. "You ignore me when I need you. You've left me alone in this cruel world. And then I found Josiah and he wasn't cruel at all. He saw me with hearts in his eyes and accepted everything about me. He made me feel things no one's ever made me feel in twenty-five years! Do you hear me? Tessa! Tessa!!"

She always ended up shouting and crying at nothing. How could anyone think she could kill him?

At night she began to dream about a pretty woman with clear blue-green eyes, like hers. Her mother, standing over the open third drawer of the chest. She dropped the pearly silk cloth she was holding into it and smiled at Mercy. *I put this here for you.*

When Mercy returned to the States, she lived with Great Aunt Lizzie and Bernadette. They were the first real family she had. She told her aunt about the dream of her mother and asked her what it meant.

"Claire couldn't have put the dagger in the attic. She died when you were three. Tessa didn't have the dagger yet."

They knew Claire Blagden had been gifted with dream telepathy, but she was dead.

"Could it be," Old Lizzie said, "before she died, she sent a dream into the future?"

"I don't know," Mercy told her with a sigh.

"I would venture to say," Old Lizzie said holding up her bony finger, "that Claire Blagden was also clairvoyant and not only that. She was able to send dreams into the future. If your mother had anything to do with the dagger being in that attic, it was for you to share your blood with his. Why she wanted that, I don't know."

Mercy knew why. To keep her from killing him. "Thank you, Mom," she said quietly.

Though she pined for Josiah, if she had to be separated from him for a little while, she'd choose to spend her days with her family.

Bernadette's cheery personality helped Mercy smile, and Aunt Lizzie acted more like her mother than her grandmother did. Mercy didn't even mind when the old seer barged into her room one night while she was sobbing over him. After she scolded Mercy, she sat next to her on the bed and closed her arms around her.

"I miss him, Aunt Lizzie. I miss him so much."

"I know, girl," she comforted.

"Every day feels like my skin has been peeled off and I've been left in a windy desert. But it's worse for him. He has suffered. He's been blamed for everything, and he did nothing wrong." She wept and wailed and spoke of him for another hour. Surprisingly, her aunt sat with her and tried to soothe her.

The days didn't get easier. Each one away from him reminded her, like an arrow in her heart, that she was helpless. Helpless to stop time while she tried to find the dagger. Helpless to ease his terrible pain.

She didn't go on blind dates with Bernadette, nor did she date anyone from her classes or her job. Not that she had offers. They smiled at her until they saw her scar and then they stopped smiling. No, thank you. She had no interest in lesser men.

She saved enough after two years to be able to travel wherever any leads on the dagger led her. But she didn't find it. The constant disappointments were difficult for her to bear, but she bore them. She didn't lose hope. She spoke to him every day, in silence and out loud, whether he could hear her or not. She didn't care. She spoke of him almost all the time to Bernadette and Aunt Lizzie. Bernadette especially enjoyed hearing Mercy's descriptions of his eyes, his lips, his storehouse of various smiles. Mercy's cousin began comparing the men who tried to date her with Josiah's thoughtfulness and single-minded purpose to pursue her. To give up his own desires to please her. To gaze deeper than her physical appearance and to take a good look at her heart, and then vanquish all the demons of hidden depression, insecurity, fear, and a host of others that clung to her. And to make her happy while he did it. If he lost the ability to speak, his gaze alone would reveal his heart.

Mercy would never stop searching. She'd scratch and claw her way to Tessa, Raxxix, whatever it took. But she'd never ever give up on getting back to him. She needed to be loved by him again.

In her third, tortuous year back, she moved to Dorchester, England. It was nice to be able to take a short bus ride to the site of Ashmore Castle. She couldn't see it yet through all the scaffolding and boards from the repairs still going on after three years, and the fog that cloaked it most mornings, but it was there. She tilted her neck backward to see the tower, where his studio should be. The scaffolding did nothing to thwart the magnificence of the castle. She could imagine it in its full glory, with square and pointed towers piercing the clouds like strong, battle-scarred arms, crenelated fingers reaching toward heaven. It still made her cry knowing that in this century, he'd been dead almost four hundred years.

"Josiah, I miss you," she whispered every morning. "I can't let you go. I promise, I'm coming back."

She found a job at a publishing company on the weekdays and at a clothing store on the weekends. At night, she attended classes in self-defense. She never missed a morning though to go to the castle and speak to Josiah.

"Mercy, right? Mercy Blagden?"

She turned around fully to face the man behind her. It was dark out, but the street lights lit his face enough for Mercy to recognize him. He recently joined her self-defense class, and the women in the class all became flirty dolts around him. That was all Mercy knew. All she cared to know.

"What are you doing following me?" she asked with suspicion gleaming in her cerulean eyes.

He chuckled. "I'm not following you. I mean, I guess I am, but I'm going this way to catch the bus."

"Oh." Hmm, Mercy sighed in her head. The bus.

"Mind if I walk with you?"

"To tell you the truth, I—"

"I'm Zack, by the way. I just joined the class but I hear you've been at it for a year. You seem like you're quite good. You can protect me if something happens." He grinned playfully.

She broke eye contact and pivoted around to continue walking. She walked briskly, uninterested in sharing a conversation with him.

"Do I make you feel insecure?" he asked, then continued, missing her incredulous glare. "Is that why you don't like me? You're the only one in the class who hasn't—"

She sighed and rolled her eyes. "Are you serious right now?"

"What?" He paused his footsteps, but then hurried to catch up when she kept her pace.

"Why would you make me feel insecure? Explain that."

"You seem shy, and I'm not."

She stopped and stared at him, at his eyes. They shifted for an instant to her scar. She scoffed and kept walking. "I'm not shy. I only speak to people I like. So goodbye."

He chuckled again as they came to the bus stop. "What do I have to do to get you to like me?"

"Nothing. I'm madly in love with my boyfriend. Here's the bus."

They waited for the bus to stop. When the doors opened, Mercy stepped back to let Zack get on first. When he turned to see where she was, she looked off in the distance for the next bus.

"Aren't you getting on?"

"No. I take the 12."

He smiled ruefully, knowing he'd been fooled. "The 12 doesn't stop here," he said quickly as the door closed in his face.

Mercy shook her head at herself. Now, she had to wait at least twenty minutes for the next bus. It served her right for being anti-social. Maybe she should feel bad for any man who thought to get to know her for any reason. It was probably impossible for them to live up to Josiah's standards. But then again, did they really try?

Twice, early in the morning while she stared up at the castle, covered by a gossamer fog and a web of metal and wood, she felt as if someone was watching her. It made her hair stand on end. She'd looked around, heart pounding both times, even checking around corners and in doorways, but no one was there.

Two months later, in the winter of the fourth year, Ashmore Castle's repairs were finally finished and the castle was ready to be revealed. Mercy took the day off from work, and everything else, and was one of the first in line for the tour. She thought she might faint at the sight of the castle looking very much the way it had in the seventeenth century. Tears pooled at the rims of her eyes. If only he were inside. Her heart felt as if it were dripping out of her. Soon, there would be nothing left. "I waited four years," she mumbled, her breath turning white from the cold and rising above the others on line. "I'm running out of hope, Josiah."

She swiped her tears from her cheeks and didn't look up again until the line started moving. Excitement and anxiety shared a place in whatever was left of her.

As she walked closer to the place she dreamed about—had it all been a dream?—she remembered the horse-drawn carriages that had taken her and Josiah to the sea. She could hear the metal ting of the blacksmith as he hammered his forged steel into glorious swords that would flash against the sun when wielded by the fierce warriors who lived here. But they all died because what they fought against wasn't human. Ghostly echoes of the cries of the unprepared drifted on wind swirling her hair around her face.

She wasn't sure she could go inside. But she didn't stop and she wouldn't turn back. She'd waited too long. So she bit her lip, shoved her hands in the pockets of her coat, and followed the tour guide inside. Surprisingly, she didn't see the bodies of the fallen all around her, blood all over everything, the floor, the walls. She saw instead, the image of her beautiful beloved Josiah standing at the foot of the stairs wearing a smile as wide as the sea when he saw her.

"Ashmore Castle was built in 1583 by Philip Avensey, Duke of Dorset," the tour guide began right away. "The name was changed in 1629 to Ashmore Castle when Edmund Ashmore took residence after gaining the title of Duke of Dorset. On the walls are some of the beautiful paintings done by the infamous earl of Winterborne, Lord Josiah Ashmore, seventh son of the duke. The Ashmores have a colorful history. They—"

Excuse me," Mercy held up her hand. Something was terribly wrong. When she and Bernadette had checked history, it hadn't said anything about Josiah being infamous. Granted it was years ago. What could have changed? "You said the *infamous* earl of Winterborne. What happened that made him infamous?"

"I was coming to that," the guide said with a practiced smile. "The spot in which you're all standing was once covered in the blood of the entire Ashmore family and their staff, after the Blagdens attacked and slaughtered everyone, except for the earl of Winterborne. He was the only one who was spared, sentenced to live with the burden of his betrayal."

"Pardon me again," Mercy smiled shyly. "Sorry, but he didn't betray anyone."

The tour guide offered her a mocking smile and continued. "He was foolish enough to fall in love with one of the Blagdens and against his father's wishes, let her into the castle. His family suffered for his foolishness when the girl told her family where the gate was least patrolled."

Mercy stared at her, her eyes glistening. She wanted to shout. *No, that's not how it was!* "What makes you an expert?" the tour guide asked her in a low voice. "Were you here?"

Mercy bit her lip until she tasted blood. "Just don't bastardize a man you know nothing about as fact."

"Ma'am, if you continue to disturb the tour we'll have to ask you to leave."

"Sorry," Mercy said and sealed her lips shut.

They continued on to the great hall, which looked almost as it had in the past, except the tables and benches were more worn—and it had never been empty. Josiah's paintings hung throughout. There were many from the studio that she'd seen leaning in piles against the walls. She wanted to get closer, touch the canvas where his brushes touched. When they moved on up the stairs, she wondered if they'd be taken to the studio.

"The next room we'll see is the earl of Winterborne's private bed chambers."

Mercy's heart bashed against her ribs. His room where he let her sleep so she could use his private garderobe, his bed, where he kissed her.

"This is the only room in the castle that the earl didn't completely let fall to ruin, and where many of his later paintings were kept. Nothing has been changed. The placement of everything is the same as it's been for almost four hundred years."

The instant Mercy entered the room, her eyes went to the painting on the wall opposite his bed. It was the portrait of ...her?

It couldn't be. The girl in the painting was beautiful.

"We believe this is the girl the young earl fell in love with," the tour guide told them. "As you can see, she's very pretty and he could look at her every night from his bed."

Mercy stared at the portrait. Her hair was up and falling down one shoulder. There were yellow spots—were they flower petals—sprinkled in her hair? Yellow daffodils. She swiped tears away from her eyes remembering. Not that she'd forgotten the smallest detail of every day she'd spent with him. Her skin practically glowed with youth and innocence, without a scar or blemish. Her eyes—a little wider than normal, a bit more vividly colored in person, were set on the painter.

Oh, how Mercy missed him. She felt like falling to her knees and wailing.

"The girl in the painting looks like her," someone called out, pointing to her.

The tour guide and everyone else turned to look at her.

"No, it doesn't look like her," someone else said. "Look at that terrible scar. The girl in the painting is prettier. No offense, Miss."

Finally, after the tour guide examined her for a minute or two, she continued on with her incorrect information and then led them to the solar.

When the guide wasn't watching, Mercy lagged behind and then crept back into his bedchamber. Alone, she moved closer to the painting and stared up at it. This had been how he saw her. Her heart ached for him, knowing how he must have longed for her also. He hung her portrait where he could see it to remember her. Her heart swelled with love for him. She wished he would have done a self-portrait so she could look at him again. "Your face is fading from my memory," she cried quietly.

She turned to his bed and was startled to see a woman standing in the doorway. "Sorry I'm in here alone. I just—"

"I don't care what you're doing here, Child."

Mercy took a closer look at her. She knew her voice—

"Hester, Sister Tess, Tessa, whatever your name is, you finally decided to show up."

"You forgot *grandmother*."

Mercy glared at her. "I have no grandmother. You made me wait four years. FOUR YEARS!" She hadn't meant to scream. She bit her lip again and began to cry. It was too much. She couldn't stand anymore and went down to her knees. "How could you take me away from him? How could you ignore me all this time? Why now? Did you sense that I'm at the end of my rope and you came here to put the dagger in my hand in the hopes that I'll kill him now, right?"

"Raxxix has found you," Tessa told her. "We have to go." She grabbed Mercy's elbow and tugged her away. "I can disguise a scent and keep the demons off your tail for a little while but—"

"Wait!" Mercy dug her heels in. "Unless you're sending me back to the seventeenth century take your hands off me."

"Mercy, listen to me. I have no choice but to send you back, but before you rejoice, remember you were born for this purpose. It's your destiny. Once you kill the seventh son with the dagger, everything that's been wrought in evil will be put right. Raxxix will be destroyed."

"And so will Josiah. Don't you understand?" Mercy pleaded, not bothering to wipe her tears. "Why did you keep the dagger around me? Didn't your seer sister see what I'd become because it cut me?"

Her grandmother shook her head. "Neither one of us did. I don't know why. It's what's causing this reluctance in you."

"Love is causing this reluctance in me," Mercy corrected her. "I love him. I won't kill him."

"Mercy, Raxxix will kill you."

"Then let him kill me."

"No! I won't!" her grandmother insisted. "I'll never let him touch you. Do you think it was easy for me to leave you here mostly on your own, now or when you were growing up? I had no choice. He watches me in the hopes that I'll lead him to you. If

I stay around you too long, he can zero in."

To Mercy, it sounded like a punishment on her grandmother. She didn't say so. Maybe it was. Mercy was too hurt by her and too exhausted and angry to feel sorry for her.

"You could have told me who you were instead of being Hester. You could have helped."

Her grandmother shook her head. "You would never have been able to handle it. Also, it was too dangerous. If anyone found out who I was…" she scoffed softly, leaving the rest unsaid. "As far as helping you, the best way to do that was to get you away from Josiah Ashmore."

"And you did it—" Mercy told her miserably.

"You were never supposed to fall in love with him. I wanted to save you from having to kill him, but I failed. It wasn't my duty to destroy him and the ruby dagger. It's yours."

Mercy shook her head and swiped her tears away with her fingers.

"Then," Tessa continued, "are you prepared to accept the deaths of however many people Raxxix kills using him? Will you be able to withstand the guilt of seeing him as a shell of what he was? Of seeing him used to kill and destroy—this young man who, at one time, couldn't bear to take the life of anything? I thought the decision to take his life would be more difficult if you loved him, but I think it should be easier, knowing the one you love so much will suffer immeasurably, never able to return to humanity again."

Mercy brought her hands to her mouth. She couldn't bear that. Oh, there had to be a way to save him without killing him. How could his mother have sworn his body and soul over to a demon?

"*Grandmother*," Mercy said now to the woman standing with her, "that dresser in the attic of the orphanage was mine when I lived with my mother, wasn't it."

The dresser with the ruby dagger wrapped in silk that would prick her flesh and exchange her blood with the blood of

Ashmore's seventh son. The blood left there by her grandmother's failed attempt to kill him. "You know who left the dagger there for me to find one day."

"I did after numerous dreams of my daughter begging me to."

Mercy nodded. "My mother, Claire, who gave me a name one wouldn't expect for an assassin. She created a path for me to live out a different duty. One of mercy, even on a monster. Isn't it what we are taught on Sundays? Grandmother, let me go back. Please, oh please, give me a chance to destroy Raxxix. Without Raxxix the dagger loses its power and can be destroyed."

Tessa smiled indulgently. "You think you can destroy the demon?"

"Not me," Mercy said without hesitation. "The love I carry. I believe my purpose is to show Josiah mercy and forgiveness, not fear and the threat of death."

"Maybe so, dear one, but that's even more of a reason for Raxxix to come after you. I can't let you—"

"I'm asking you to trust me, Grandmother. Trust that your daughter, Claire, knew that this path is the right one. Bring me back to Josiah. Give me a chance to save him."

CHAPTER SEVENTEEN

Dorchester, England
1665

J OSIAH ASHMORE TUGGED at his unkempt hair. With an oath on his clenched teeth, he pulled the painting off the easel and flung it across the studio. Tonight he'd collect it and the others like it and burn them. He'd burned at least a hundred already, and there were already another hundred or so to go. They were all the same. All her. Damn her! "Damn you!" he groaned almost pitifully, like a bear caught in a trap. No matter what he painted of her, he could never capture the lies behind her eyes. In his mind, her smiles were well-practiced—like his were before he met her. But no matter how hard he tried, he couldn't get it right on the canvas. There, she always looked happy, innocent, and in love. But there was nothing innocent about her. There were no accidents. Everything had been planned, and like Samson, he'd fallen to the wiles of a woman.

Don't believe in them. Believe in me.

He tried. It was what kept him alive. He'd believed her from the beginning when she told him she came from the future. He tried to believe her until the end. But he couldn't. With each year that passed, he realized she wasn't coming back. He'd been wrong to trust her. She'd left him here in the ruins—of what she'd done.

He wanted to pull his hair from his head and shout at the

191

heavens. To scream from the depths of his soul, hoping, praying God would hear him and help. Each day was like walking through a house of glass, and all the glass was broken. On some days or nights, when he couldn't bear it, he stood outside on his terrace and emptied his heart of the sorrow weighing him down. But the darkness remained just beyond the veil, waiting for him to give up—to become a murderer. But as long as Mercy Blagden was alive he would never give up his soul to Raxxix. First, he would kill her. She'd taken everyone from him. "How? How could you do it?" he found himself crying out often in the last four years. He held on, waiting for the last thing to change him. If anything was going to do it, it would be strangling the life from Mercy Blagden.

He gave his studio a look of disgust and left it. He descended the stairs without falling, though most of the torches on the walls were cold. He kept them unlit, preferring the darkness over the light. Despair ruled him. He'd tried to fight it at first, but his efforts were weak and it wasn't difficult to let hopelessness, grief, and despair overtake him. He had one reason, and one reason alone to press on. He waited with his only friends: hatred, fury, loneliness, regret, and guilt for the day when he could exact revenge on the one who betrayed him and caused the death of everyone he knew and loved.

When he reached the bottom of the stairs, he barely looked at the spacious foyer where they died four years ago. He heard the swords clashing around him, the screams of his brother Jeremy as the Blagdens killed his father... Oliver, Thomas, Edward, Nicholas, Gilbert. They all called to him, reaching for him as he stormed past them, ignoring their ghostly cries. He left the castle and strode to the stable to get his horse. He needed food. He'd hunt for it.

He rode out, passing Oswald on the way. One of the only people of Ashmore besides Josiah to live through the attack was his devoted friend, Oswald Sawyer. "Muscle" chose to remain with Josiah, and some days Josiah was grateful. Some days he wasn't.

He rode into the forest north of the castle and shot his arrow at two hares. He retrieved their carcasses without any regret and leaped back onto his horse. A little while later, he spotted a grazing roebuck. He dismounted as slowly as he could and without making a sound, crept closer in the bramble, arrow ready to be released.

He pulled back. The buck looked up from the ground. Josiah stared at it. The buck stared back, seeing or sensing him. Their eyes met and Josiah thought about how every life he took brought him closer to being able to kill Mercy.

He knew she'd return. She had a duty to fulfill. She had to kill him. Let her try. He clenched his teeth and let his arrow fly with a loud whack. The buck went down.

He was waiting.

MERCY SCRATCHED HER nose, but something was sticking in her nostril. What was that awful smell? She scratched again and then her eyes shot open and she sat bolt upright. It was dark with thin columns of moonlight breaking through the cracks in the walls and shuddered windows. The barn! "Am I back?" Oh, it was too good to be true! She had to be back! There weren't any barns near the castle in 2026. "Oh, I'm back. I'm back. Thank you, God. Thank you, Grandmother. Hello hay!" she greeted gleefully. "Hello barn cat!" She wondered vaguely if it was the same cat as the one in 1661. She'd returned. But when was it? She rose to her feet, ready to go out and find out. She remembered the ruby dagger and checked around in the hay for it. This time it didn't come with her. Her grandmother must have held on to it. "Grandmother? Are you here?"

Silence. Mercy suddenly wondered why the barn was empty. Where was the pig, the ducks and chickens that had been here the first time?

She went to the doors and pushed them open slightly to creep out. If Samuel was still here, she didn't think he'd appreciate the one who betrayed the Ashmores.

What she saw was confusing. It looked as if nine or ten of the fifteen cottages belonging to Ashmore's villagers had been abandoned. Smoke only billowed from five chimneys despite the cold weather. Samuel's house was dark, as was the home of the butcher, Roger Harwood, and his wife and his daughter, Anne. Old Philip's cottage looked cold and empty.

Mercy pulled her coat tighter, and turned slowly to look up the hill.

Ashmore Castle stood like an imposing force, rather than a protective sentry on top of the hill. It appeared as abandoned as the cottages beneath it, but smoke rose to the charcoal clouds. Someone was inside. Josiah was inside. Her beloved.

With her heart thrashing against her ribs, she took a step. And then she ran. He was there, inside. She was in his time, *her* time. Yes, she belonged here. And after all the longing and praying to be with him, and missing him more than she could understand, she was about to—

One of the heavy wooden doors creaked open as she reached them. Mercy leaped back, hands clenched to her mouth. She felt sick and thrilled at the same time. It was Jo—"Oswald?" She rubbed her eyes and then smiled and latched onto his arm. "Oswald! Oh, it's so good to see you!"

"Miss Smi—"

He dipped his gaze as if remembering something unpleasant. Of course, she knew what it was. Smith wasn't her name and he knew it. Did he believe the lies and hate her? She wanted to tell him the truth. "Oswald—"

"You shouldn't be here, Miss. You should go. Hurry." He stepped back inside and closed the door in her face.

"Okay, so it's worse than you thought, Mercy," she said to herself and stared at the door. She realized that she may have to face down a very angry man but she didn't care if Josiah hated her. She'd win him back. He wouldn't hate her for long. Would he? She'd tell him everything she'd learned from Tess and explain what her mother had done. She'd explain to him that she'd had nothing to do with the attacking army that killed his family. It was all Raxxix's doing. She knew it must have destroyed him. She would never, no never do anything to hu—

The door opened again, this time with such force, it didn't creak. He stood under the lintel. His broad shoulders, encased in black velvet, rose and fell with his heavy breath. Gray eyes that once took her in the way the earth takes in water after a long drought now glittered with fury in the moonlight.

"Josiah," she barely breathed.

His lips tightened around his teeth and without a word, his hand shot out and closed around her throat. He murmured something through his clenched jaw while she struggled to breathe. She couldn't think, but...this couldn't be happening. Had Raxxix taken him over? Was she too late? No! No, she didn't care. Even if the demon had possession of him, she would heal him. She remembered Tessa's words. *One of you must die.* Was he going to kill her? Just when she almost stopped fighting, he released her throat and clutched his head.

Mercy gasped and then sucked in a huge gulp of air that hurt her throat. Before she could stop herself she glared at him, and then took a step back when he made a move.

"Do you dare to glare at me, Blagden witch?" he growled like a lion about to pounce.

"You almost choked me to death," she coughed and clutched her throat, "and I'm not a—"

"Silence!" He shouted. "Oswald!"

"I'm here," Oswald answered from behind him.

"Get rid of her. Don't let me see her again or I'll kill her."

"Yes, my lord."

Mercy watched Oswald coming for her. If there was one thing she learned in the four years trying to find a way back, it was to stop being a doormat. And as much as she wanted to throw herself at Josiah's feet, she wouldn't.

"That's quite all right, Oswald," she said, shaking off his hand when he reached for her. "I won't stand here being treated like this."

"Like..." Josiah mouthed, giving her a dangerous stare beneath his lashes. "Were you always this bold, or did I foolishly choose to see a delicate flower when I looked at you?"

If her heart could have torn through her chest and leaped to him, it would have. She would give anything for him to look at her that way again. She reached out and touched his wrist, but he pulled his arm away as if her touch burned him.

"I know you think you have every right to hate me and try to squeeze the life out of me, Josiah. But you don't."

While she was still speaking, he gaped at her, then turned on his heel and slammed the door in her and Oswald's face.

"My," Oswald said in a quiet voice, "that went much better than I expected."

"Oswald! He almost killed me!"

"Miss, if you knew how badly he has wanted you dead, you'd see it my way."

All at once, tears rose to her eyes, stinging, burning. Her throat closed to contain her sobs. How badly he wanted her dead. She would never forget those words or how terrible they made her feel.

"But, Miss," the burly servant said quietly. "He didn't do it. When the time came, he didn't do it."

Right, true, she thought, but he did *almost* strangle her.

"Still, I don't think you should return. He may not kill you but I can assure you that seeing you is painful for him."

"But Oswald, I had nothing to do with what happened. It was Raxxix."

The door flung open again and Josiah stood there once again, brooding and breathing fire. "Oswald, get in here!"

He didn't wait for Oswald to move on his own but grabbed

his sleeve and pulled him in, then slammed the door again.

Mercy didn't know what to do. Bang on the door? What if he opened it and choked her again? She hadn't expected things to be good or to receive a warm welcome, but to try to kill her? To want her dead for these past four years? But even worse was that the sight of her that used to bring a smile to his face every time now pained him. She still couldn't take it in. His hands that wouldn't hurt a fly had just tried to kill her. She'd had no idea what four years of loneliness and vengeance could do to a man. She'd underestimated the dark power of what he'd gone through—of the thing desperate to have him. She wiped her eyes and rubbed her neck. She wanted to bang on the door until he opened it and then she wanted to take him in her arms and kiss his face, his tears. But even if he never let her, she was going to help him.

She headed back down the hill. Maybe she could squat in one of the abandoned cottages, though she still might freeze to death without a fire. Knocking on doors was too dangerous. If Oswald knew about her being a Blagden, then so did everyone else.

She saw the silhouette of a horse-drawn cart. It lightened her heart a little, bringing her back to when she and Josiah were walking together and met up with Harry Lawrence, one of the village merchants. Her smile widened when she heard the man's voice as they met on the way down.

"Why, Miss Smith! Never thought I'd see you again."

"Harry Lawrence?" She was surprised. "I was just remembering you."

He chuckled, then tilted his head toward the castle proving that he either knew about the gossip or that he remembered her being a part of Josiah's life. Or both. "Where are you off too?"

She looked down at the darkened village, then smiled at him. "I'll find a place."

"You just did," he told her. "Margaret would love to see you again. It's cold and dark in the abandoned houses and the barn smells." He scrunched his nose. "You've already been there, then."

She closed her eyes. Oh, great. She smelled like the barn when she was standing near Josiah…when he was choking her.

"Come on, then, Miss," the merchant urged. "You'll have some stew and sleep in a warm bed."

"Thank you, Harry." She needed to stay strong to find Josiah beneath all the rubble of his heart. It couldn't be too late. Her grandmother would know, but she hadn't shown up yet. And if Raxxix was waiting to get his hands on the dagger and her grandmother had it, then Mercy hoped she stayed away.

"Why did you return now?" Margaret Lawrence asked her candidly, setting down a bowl in front of her. "He's not the same man. He lives alone up there in that castle with just Oswald Sawyer still by his side. Before they left the village, the mothers who lived here asked their children if they wanted to end up like the devil of Ashmore, alone in his castle, accursed and condemned. That's what he's considered. Accursed and condemned."

"That's what he's always been considered," Mercy told her. "Imagine growing up with that stupid prophecy hanging over your head and *still* managing not to turn into a madman?"

"But, Miss," Margaret patted her hand. "He *is* a madman."

That night, in the warm bed the Lawrences provided for her, Mercy thought of poor Josiah hearing the villagers tell their children, the same children he used to play with when he visited, that he was the devil, condemned and cursed. No wonder he lived alone in the castle. No wonder he let it fall to ruin. She cried, soaking her pillow. She finally rose up out of the bed and went to stand by the cottage window. The wind howled from the top of the hill. Mercy pulled a step stool closer and looked out the window. Had it been the wind? It sounded a little like a sorrowful wail.

She heard it again and this time her blood ran cold. It *was* a sorrowful wail. And it was coming from the castle. She felt as if her heart was being wrenched from her body. She stepped off the stool but still stared at the window. She wanted to go to him, but she was afraid, for the sound she heard couldn't come from a man with a human heart. She wanted to fight Raxxix for him but if the demon already possessed him, or if he surrendered to it while in her presence, she wouldn't be able to fight Josiah's body. She'd lose because looking at him would make her forget Raxxix—even for an instant—and remind her how much she loved Josiah, too much to ram a dagger into his heart.

She covered her face in her hands and wept over her helplessness, and his.

She finally slept for a few hours, but her sleep was riddled with Josiah. They were sitting in the great hall about to eat after Josiah had words with his father about him being gone with her all day.

You won't leave my side even if he commands it of you, will you? she asked him in her dreams.

He smiled to reassure her. I won't leave your side, Mercy.

Promise?

His smile deepened and he nodded. I promise.

She woke feeling refreshed even with so little sleep. In fact, she didn't only feel refreshed, but hopeful. She smiled at no one. "You promised."

CHAPTER EIGHTEEN

MERCY WASHED AND dressed in the clothes Margaret gave her. The dark blue skirts were a little short and a few sizes too big, but with a proper belt and some extra pins, they fit fine over her borrowed petticoat. Above her waist she wore a large shirt under uncomfortable stays pulled tight around her waist. She let Margaret feed her some bread the merchant's wife had baked before dawn. When she would have bolted from the table and hurried back up to the castle, Margaret stopped her.

"You heard him last night?"

Mercy nodded her head. "Does he cry out like that often?"

"Less often than he used to," Margaret told her.

Mercy bit her lip. In this case, him crying out less often was not a good thing. Once he stopped completely, did it mean his heart was dried up and ready to accept Raxxix?

"He's suffering," Mercy heard herself say.

"He must have indeed been in love with you," the older woman remarked, smiling pitifully.

He loved her. He loved her more than anyone in her life loved her. "He isn't crying for me anymore, Margaret. He's crying for what he's afraid of losing."

"What remains for him to lose?"

Mercy opened the door and looked out. "His soul."

"Are you going to help him hold on to it?"

"I'm going to try."

She stepped out into the sun and smiled at Harry.

"Ah, good, you're awake. I could use your help rolling some skeins, folding some others." He gave her a wide smile and she wondered if he was trying to keep her from going to the castle. "It shouldn't take too long. An hour at most."

She couldn't say no after he gave her a place to sleep and food for her belly. She gave the castle a longing look, then followed Harry to his cart.

"You can start by folding those."

Mercy looked at them. There were about one hundred sheets of different colored fabric all needing to be folded. "Okay. Just begin," she told herself.

Thirty minutes in, Mercy folded the last sheet and rubbed her arms. She looked up at the castle and saw a snorting black stallion galloping toward her. Upon the beast's back Josiah sat in his saddle controlling the horse's movements using the reins and his powerful thighs. As he grew closer, he seemed to bring the cold with him. She sensed Harry moving closer to her and Margaret coming out of the cottage.

He stopped his mount a few feet from Mercy and stared at her. There was nothing warm in his steely gaze, no smile to soften the hard angles of his face.

He was older. Only by four years but he looked like more time had passed. His black hair fell to his shoulders but was tied at the back of his head with a strip of leather. In his usual fashion, he wore no cravat. His long black coat fell over his thighs, encased in snug fitting pants.

"No one is permitted to help this woman," he shouted for all who were listening to hear. He raked his gaze over her, and then over the folded fabric.

"And she is not allowed to help any of you," he said, turning his powerful gaze on Harry.

"Just a minute, Josiah," she said. "Without their help, I'll freeze to death."

"Leave here," he warned.

The arrows he shot at her with his hard gaze tore at her body. She had the urge to shield herself with her arms. She folded them across her chest. It would have to do.

"Where shall I go?"

He took no pity on her, though Harry and Margaret came closer to her. Josiah moved his snorting beast of a horse between her and them. "What do I care where you go?" he demanded. "I'm showing you the mercy you never showed me. But the longer you dare try to bewitch me, the more I want you gone." He let the horse bump her forward. "Don't tempt me." She lost her balance and fell on her back.

Instead of trying to move away when his horse continued to come forward. She remained on her back and stared up at him. "Go ahead. Let your horse trample me, Josiah. But one day when you understand that I was innocent, you'll have to live with this."

She heard his boots hit the ground. She took a breath and then she felt him clutch her under her arms and lift her to her feet. He gave her a shake before he let her go, almost causing her to lose her balance again.

"Leave my sight."

She watched him leap back up into his saddle. "I have no intention of doing that."

"What?" He offered her a slight, twisted smile that was more frighteningly empty than his darkest scowl.

"I could never have done what you think I did. I didn't tell you my last name because Samuel and the others made it clear—"

"Enough!" Josiah held up his hand, then turned back for his horse. "I've heard enough of your words. Get out of the village or I'll hunt you down and make sure you never return."

"You haven't heard any of my words!" she argued, following after him. "If you had, you would have trusted me."

"I did trust you!" he shouted. His throat sounded sore.

She had to call upon every ounce of strength she possessed to remain still and not go to him. "You shouldn't have stopped when all fingers were pointed to me, Josiah!"

"Until when should I continue trusting someone who lied to me about who she was and that she had the ruby dagger. You told me, but not at first."

He was right. She had lied to him. "I'm sorry for that."

"I don't want your apology," he ground out, brooding over her. "I want you out of my sight."

"I'm going to follow you to the castle."

He took hold of his horse's reins. "Then I'll put you in the dungeon and let Oswald see to you."

"Josiah!" she hurried to him before he leaped into the saddle and took him by the arm. "Let's talk, please."

He untangled his arm from hers and widened the stretch between them. "That won't happen."

"Why not?"

"I'm not taking any chances of being beguiled by you again."

"I…" What does one say to that? She didn't know. "I don't even know how to beguile a man."

He sprang up into his saddle, gave the reins a yank and turned the horse to leave.

Mercy watched him, with the Lawrences standing behind her, and the other villagers staring disapprovingly at her and walking back into their cottages.

She thought about the seventh son, more handsome than the six before him.

Of course, Raxxix wanted Josiah's body. She would find out tonight just how much was the demon hanging around Josiah. She'd put a stop to it. He wouldn't get Josiah.

"Well, I think you should forget about going to the castle today," Harry told her in a comforting voice.

"I'm still going. I've waited four years to get to him," she said. "It's better that I leave anyway. I don't want you to get into trouble because of me. Thank you both for all your help." She took off before they could convince her not to go yet. She wouldn't let them stop her. She ran up the hill, shaking her fist at the castle more than once.

When she reached the castle doors, she pulled back the knocker and hit it on the door. Once. Twice. Three times. She waited, prepared to wait all day. But someone pulled open the door and growled like a bear.

"Josiah." She had to speak quickly, before he slammed the door in her face again. "I searched for a way to get back to you for four years. Please, please don't tell me to leave you alone."

He looked away from her, his stoic expression unchanged. "Searching for a way back to me was your choice. Telling you to leave me alone is mine."

He couldn't mean it. "Josiah, no. Don't tell me to go," she shamelessly pleaded.

"Go, woman."

She gazed up at him until he set his eyes on her again. But she saw nothing there for her but anger and disdain. They were like daggers piercing her heart. She couldn't bear to look another second. Almost instinctively, she lifted her fingers to her scar, then turned, shoulders slumped and left.

The entire way down the hill she hoped he'd call out after her. As each silent second passed, her heartbeat grew faster. He didn't call.

Harry Lawrence insisted she come back in, but Mercy refused to stay with them for the night. Doing so was blatantly disobeying their lord. She wouldn't forgive him if he hurt them. She agreed to help Margaret prepare lunch for the other villagers who still lived there. It turned out, the Lawrences fed them often. Thanks to the horrifying plague that hit London and some of the neighboring cities, food was scarce, money was scarcer. Harry, being a traveling merchant, picked up food from village to village. She admired Harry and Margaret for sharing their bounty, but the Great Fire of London was still to come.

Like their lord and his castle, Ashmore village was crumbling, soon to be no more.

She was happy to see some old faces when they arrived, even if they weren't all happy to see her. As they sat around the two tables set up outside, Harry told them who she was and let her speak to them directly. She defended herself mostly, swearing to them that she had nothing to do with the attack on Ashmore Castle.

Joem Macey, one of the guards who used to protect Josiah, held no animosity for her. "I was there, lingering close by all the time," he told her and the others. "I witnessed the two of you together and I can honestly say you both seemed very happy and very much in love."

"I still love him." Mercy told them. "I would never betray him. He has a bigger enemy than me."

"Yes," they agreed, knowing full well about the prophecy.

"But that being cannot break a young man's heart the way Lord Josiah's was." Louise, one of Ashmore's former servants, said.

Mercy gave her a steady look. "Are you sure about that? That being is the one who tore Lord Josiah's heart out four years ago. Not me."

"How do you know?" asked Lillith Crane, wife of the now deceased Thomas Crane, one of the village tanners. Mercy remembered her son, Robin, playing with Josiah. The boy now clung to his mother's side.

Mercy certainly couldn't tell them about her grandmother, Tessa Blagden, who'd tried to kill the newborn, Josiah.

"Josiah and I visited Old Lizzie before it happened," she told them and looked to Joem for validation. He nodded to the others. "We didn't believe her, or listen to her," Mercy continued. "It all goes along with the prophecy. Raxxix wanted to turn Josiah into a shell and then fulfill the prophecy. Have any of you ever seen or heard of that many Blagdens living in this vicinity? What better way to destroy a man than slaughtering his family before his eyes and then blaming the woman he loved? And why not kill him too? Wasn't it all about him? No. He was kept alive because he's the only one Raxxix cares about. And no matter what some of you think of him, he's managed to resist that force so far."

"And now you're back," Jacob the miller said, still sounding sour. "Are you here to entice him to give in?"

"Why would I do that?" she asked him. "Why wait til now when if your doubts about me are right, I already had him in my clutches that night?"

"Where have you been all these years, while he drifted deeper into madness?" Joem asked her in a tender voice.

"I was taken by a relative and it was very difficult to return." She couldn't tell them anymore.

He nodded and spooned some stew into his mouth. When he remained quiet, she tugged on his sleeve. "Captain Sherwood? Did he make it?"

Joem shook his head. "None of the guards but me made it out alive."

Louise looked at Mercy over her cup. "You were friends with Hester, Emmaline and Alison."

"Yes!" Mercy said. She knew what became of Hester, but the other two girls—

"They were killed." Louise informed him. "Cut down with my dear lady Ava and the other Ashmore wives and their children."

Mercy wiped her eyes but finally cried into her hands. She looked toward the castle. As far as Josiah believed, she was responsible for all those deaths. No wonder he hated her.

※》》》※※※

JOSIAH GLARED AT the blank canvas in front of him. He hated her. Didn't he? Why hadn't he killed her? He'd wanted to. He'd wanted to for four long, torturous years. He knew she'd come back. He'd had her. Why did he let her go when he could have squeezed the life out of her?

He blinked away from the absence of creativity and swallowed. His throat ached and he felt feverish. He swore under his breath. Not again. He'd been free of the fevers for three years, but in the fourth year, they returned and he came close to death each time.

He heard the echo of the knocker being pounded on the door rising up to the studio. Who else could it be but her? No one dared visit the devil of Ashmore. He closed his eyes and willed her to go away. Stubborn wench.

He waited while images of her sitting amidst daffodils, set ablaze by the sun, smiling up at the heavens, and then at him, haunted him.

After a few more moments the knocking returned. He pushed his stool away and rose up to leave the studio. Where was Oswald? This time, Josiah would throw him out. This time, he'd make sure Miss Blagden understood the consequences of coming here.

He stormed down the stairs and as the rapping grew louder, Oswald's punishment grew more severe. "Stop knocking!" he shouted, holding his hand to his head. When he reached the door, he yanked it open. Should he strangle her again? Why did she have to look exactly the same, save for the glint of strength that replaced the shadow of uncertainty in her azure gaze. Killing her would be the end of him because she was a vital part of his life.

"Didn't I tell you to leave? Leave Dorchester. Leave Dorset, England, leave this century!" He looked away when her eyes filled with tears. He told himself they weren't real. "What do you want?"

"I want my life back, the part that Raxxix stole. Four years of happiness with you. Probably children—"

"Enough." He swallowed and licked his dry lips. She'd become even better at beguiling him this time around. He took a step back.

"Those men were not my family, Josiah," she insisted, moving forward. When she reached for him he tried to pull back but he nearly toppled over.

Damn it, she was there trying—and failing to hold him up.

He was torn between pushing her away and laughing as they both went down.

"Josiah!" she cried in his arms when she fell into them. "You're burning up!"

"Use that breath to call for—"

"I'm here, my lord," Oswald said, appearing over him, pulling him up.

"Where the hell were you?" Josiah swore at him.

"Getting food for you to eat." Oswald told him, helping him to his room.

"You eat it," Josiah told him. "Fill your belly because I'm throwing you out in the morning."

"Oh, no, don't throw him out!"

Josiah and Oswald stopped and turned their heads to look at her. Josiah threw his head back and closed his eyes. "Why are you following us?"

"How can I help?" she asked, wide-eyed and eager.

"You can't. Get out."

"Do you need my blood?"

He closed his eyes, hating that he did, indeed, need it. "Oswald?"

"Yes, lord?"

"Don't let her follow us."

Somewhere in the back of Josiah's mind, he felt her presence remaining. Was Oswald outright disobeying him? He wanted to ask but he wanted to go with her more when she came for him in his head.

He opened his eyes several hours later, tucked in his bed, something heavy on his wrist. He looked to find Mercy asleep, her head resting on his arm. He felt better. The fever was gone. She must have used her blood on him. He wanted to gaze at her sleeping face the way he had when she'd fallen asleep in his studio. He suddenly realized that his numb wrist masked the feel of her hand holding his.

He pulled away, waking her from her slumber, and not caring.

"I didn't ask for your help," he accused. "Get out of my sight."

"As thanks, may I sleep in Samuel's barn tonight without getting anyone in trouble? It's cold and I have nowhere to stay."

"Samuel's barn?" She wanted to sleep in Samuel's barn? He clenched his jaw, refusing to be moved by her odd request. If she was here to betray him again, he shouldn't let her anywhere near him. "Don't get involved in anyone else's life, and tomorrow leave Dorchester."

She breathed his name. "Please stop hating me. I don't know what I'll do if you can't stop. You're in my heart, Josiah. But I'm not in yours."

"No, you're not. Not anymore."

Her expression hardened, perhaps finally realizing he wanted nothing to do with her.

"Has Raxxix tried to speak with you?" she asked him.

"No," he replied. "There's been no need. He doesn't have the ruby dagger. Have you brought it back?"

"No."

He scoffed. "Are you lying again?"

She shook her head. "I don't have it."

He pulled the blanket covering him away and got out of bed. "Then there's no reason for you to be here."

"You're here," she answered quietly. "You're the reason I need to be here."

He stared at her, realizing then that he was going to have to be less merciful with her to get rid of her. "You'll never have me back, Miss Blagden."

She looked up at him and a slight smile played across her lips. "We'll see about that."

He laughed but there was no mirth in the sound. "Oh, we will?"

She nodded and went to stand near him. He was unexpectedly bombarded with memories of her size and how it had felt to dip his gaze a little to look at her when he pulled her into his arms. He moved away, then he drew in a deep breath and turned to her. "You're in my room. I don't want you here."

"Fine," she gave in—too easily. She even wore a little smirk on her face. "Then I'll see you downstairs."

"Miss Blagden," he called after her through his teeth. "If you're here when I come down, I'll throw you in the dungeon."

Did she *twirl* around to face him? Josiah blinked and gave his head a slight shake. She looked too happy. Was she mocking him? Did she expect him to believe she was happy to be back? He believed she'd gone to the future. He'd seen her disappear into thin air.

"Then throw me in the dungeon, Josiah. I'll be here with you, so I don't care."

He watched her walk away. A scoff of disbelief sounded from his lips. She was bewitching him again. He could feel it. He was tempted to smile! Well, he'd put an end to her temptations once and for all. He wasn't a fool.

"Oswald!" When he didn't answer, Josiah pulled open the door to his chambers and shouted his name again.

"I'm here," Oswald appeared at the door a moment later. "I was packing my things."

"You can continue later," Josiah told him. "Prepare the dungeon."

"Prepare it?" Oswald gave him a blank look. "How?"

"Plug up the rat holes in one of the cells, "Josiah ordered. "Put new hay in it...and a pillow... and blanket...and a lantern."

"As you wish," the servant said.

Josiah shut his door after Oswald went about his task. Josiah didn't need help washing or dressing. He didn't wear anything fancy. Just a shirt and pants—and if the pants only came to his knees, he'd add hose and shoes. He combed his hair and tied it into a tail at the back of his neck. All his locks stayed in place until he began to descend the stairs. The first strands to come free fell over his eyes.

Reaching the main floor, he started toward the great hall. It wasn't the first place he usually came to in the morning. That would be his studio. But he wanted to see if she was here so he could lock her away.

He searched all the empty rooms and halls but didn't find her. So then, he thought smugly, she wasn't willing to be put into the dungeon just to be near him. But his smug expression faded an instant later and turned into a scowl. He took one last look around. Nothing stirred but the ghostly echoes of his family. They were always here, laughing or arguing in the great hall, drinking in their father's private solar, running through the halls as children, and stirring trouble. His adoring father who ordered six of his men to guard and protect the apple of his eye at all times. All dead because of him. Because of her.

His chest felt heavy, weighted with betrayal and grief as he climbed the stairs to his studio. He didn't hear the light footsteps coming down above him.

"Oh, Josiah, I left a cup of tea on your small table in the studio. I wasn't sure what you like to eat for breakfast."

He took her by the shoulders and spun her around on the stair, perched precariously at the edge, and pushed her back against the wall. "Never go into my studio again."

She teetered. But he had her. So close he could feel the pounding of her heart against his chest.

His mouth went dry. Something rumbled in his chest. He looked down at her parted lips. So close. Too close. He took a step back, pulling her gently to a safe spot on the stair. She still appeared a bit dazed, so he reached for her wrist and led her to the bottom stair. He didn't let her go but kept descending.

She must have remembered where he was bringing her. When she began pleading with him, he gritted his teeth and continued on to the dungeon. He had believed there was nothing worse than what he'd been through, but he was wrong. Her returning and him falling victim to her wiles again was worse...much worse.

"Oswald!" she cried when she saw him. "Don't let him put me here!"

Josiah ignored her and the imploring gaze of his perhaps not so loyal friend. He pulled her into the cell with fresh threshing and mint strewn onto the floor. A folded blanket and pillow, and a cool lantern waited for her use.

"You'll be fed," he told her, passing her to leave the cramped space. "It's more than you deserve."

"Thank you."

He stopped and turned to her. "What? No snide reply? Have you given up your weak defense already?"

"You warned me to leave. I didn't." She looked around the small cell. "I'll probably spend a lot of time here. I should get accustomed to it."

He had no defense for her surrender. He laughed inwardly at himself. Pitiful fool he was.

He left the dungeon with a prayer on his lips. Take her from his life, or take his life from him.

CHAPTER NINETEEN

MERCY WAS THANKFUL for the clean threshing on the floor and the other things left for her, but Josiah was a fool if he thought she wasn't angry at his treatment. At first, she didn't care if everything pointed to her guilt, he should have trusted her and how much she loved him. But as she lay on her pillow and stared at the ceiling, she realized how selfish she was being. She believed she was here to save him, not to be angry and feel slighted by him.

She was thankful to be here, in this time with him. She hadn't lied when she told him she didn't care about being in the dungeon, but she wanted to see him, hear his voice, so when Oswald brought her food, she refused it and sent him back with a message. She wouldn't eat until Josiah delivered her food himself.

She was happy and relieved that it hadn't taken long before Josiah came to her. Granted, he came to her like an angry dragon ready to breathe fire on her and turn her to ash, but he came. And didn't make her wait. She almost wasn't surprised. After what she saw in his studio, she didn't doubt that she haunted him.

"Here's your food. Now eat it." He slipped a bowl of stew through a slot in the cage door.

She took it from him. "Thank you."

He lingered about until she looked up at him.

"Is that all you wanted?" he asked, his voice a husky growl.

"Why?" she countered. "What else will you give me?"

She tried not to weep and show her emotions when it came to feeling pity for him, or guilt.

"There is nothing left," he told her and left the dungeon.

Mercy ate her stew, which wasn't bad, and then rested her head on the pillow. How many paintings had she seen up there in his studio? Two or three dozen. All thrown to the floor as if they were terribly imperfect. To her eye, they were breathtaking, and they were all of her. Her sitting in the daffodils, a portrait of her with the raging ocean for the backdrop, her hair blowing across her face.

"They were like snapshots," she said out loud to herself now. "Why were they all tossed aside? And where's the portrait of me hanging in the castle in the future?"

Was she getting through to Josiah at all? Was she making even a dent in his armor? It was impossible when he never gave them a chance to talk about it. She was tired of defending herself when so far, it hadn't seemed to move or convince him. He would believe what he'd been believing for the past four years. She didn't care. She'd stay here and chip away at his defenses. If Raxxix hadn't taken him over yet, and she believed it hadn't, then she had a good chance of taking Josiah back.

He brought her food three times a day for the next three days. But he didn't speak to her until she asked him a question, and even then, his replies were curt.

"You're so angry," she said in the middle of the third night. She hadn't been able to sleep and woke to find Josiah there, outside the cell watching her. He looked so broken she felt the sting of tears behind her eyes. But he wouldn't have it.

"You lied to me," he accused.

"You lied to me too," she countered.

"When did I lie to you?"

"You promised not to leave my side. You promised to always be within my reach. Have you forgotten?"

Instead of answering her, he turned on his heel and left the dungeon, ignoring her pleas.

She gripped the bars and shook them. "Josiah! You promised! You promised!"

The next morning he didn't return but sent Oswald to release her from the dungeon with orders to escort her out of the castle.

"I'll be back, Oswald. Make sure you tell him that. I won't leave him again. No matter what he does to me, I'll forgive him."

"Oh, Miss, why did you return?" Oswald lamented, pausing his steps. "I believe you when you say you love him, else I wouldn't have helped you. But he seems to be suffering more since you returned. Can't you just return to when you came from?"

She sniffed and wiped her nose. "No, I can't return to where I don't belong. Tell him I'm not leaving no matter how much of a coward he is."

She left the castle and lifted her chin. She'd be back.

She felt a bit bad for Oswald when she returned later with the Lawrences. "They're here to cook for you," she told Josiah bravely, despite the deep frown he aimed at her.

"No," he growled out.

She turned to the older couple with a bright smile. "The kitchen is through there." They looked a bit shocked and a little afraid to continue with Josiah scaring them. Mercy turned to him and gave him a scowl of her own. "You need to eat better. Oswald told me that you skip days! You never make vegetables—"

"Oswald!" he shouted, his voice booming through the corridors.

"You're scaring the Lawrences," Mercy moved closer to him to whisper. He looked as if he wanted to argue with her, or be sick at her nearness. She stepped away. He looked at the distance she created between them and flared his nostrils.

"I don't want people here," he told the Lawrences. It was more than he had spoken to them in four years.

"You need to eat better, Josiah, and they've agreed to cook for you," Mercy told him, then returned her attention to the older couple. "I told you he would behave this way. Just go to the kitchen and do what you want in there. I don't think he's eaten breakfast yet."

She could feel Josiah's eyes on her while the Lawrences headed toward the kitchen. She closed her eyes for a moment. She could do this. He meant too much to her to let a bad temper and misguided hatred stop her from finding her way back into his arms. She'd fought too long, searched for too long to give up and walk away—even though he told her to go away, get out, or go back to her future all the time. Even though he barely looked at her, and when he did, she saw only betrayal, she'd do anything to mend his broken heart.

But she couldn't promise anything about his kneecaps.

"Has flitting around time made you dull witted," he asked, ignoring her narrowing eyes.

"Flitting around?" she asked through clenched teeth.

He ignored her fury and nodded his head.

Had he moved? He hovered over her. Was he always this tall? She wondered. His shoulders were wider than she remembered, as well. "Woman," he said in a smooth, quiet voice. His minty breath fell on her lips, her chin, "What do I have to do to get rid of you?"

His words pierced like barbs. She turned to walk away but he reached out and shackled her wrist with his fingers.

"Hmm?" he murmured.

"Your words hurt."

"And yet you remain."

"You're so cold," she said softly to him. She wasn't sure how much more she could say without bawling like a fool on the floor at his feet. "I thought I couldn't ask you to forgive me for something I didn't do." She didn't bother wiping her tears. "But I'm asking anyway, Josiah. Forgive me. If this is what it takes, then please forgive me. I'm so sorry for your pain, whether I'm responsible for it or not. I would do anything to take it all away. To see you smile again. To see you smile at me."

He stared into her eyes and then shook his head. "I don't see it. No matter how hard I look, I can't find it. I can't paint it."

"What?" she asked on a shaky breath, thinking of all the discarded paintings of her in his studio. "What is it?"

His eyes glittered like lightning in a storm as they filled with tears. "The lies. The deceit behind your eyes and...your smile."

"You can't find them?" she asked. When he shook his head, her heart thudded in her chest. "That's because there are no lies, there's no deceit, Josiah. That's why you don't see it.

He looked as if he were considering her words, but then he turned and walked away.

Instead of letting him go, she hurried forward and closed her arms around his waist from behind. "Please don't go," she breathed into his back.

The warmth of his hand when he lifted it to cover both of hers, made her tremble. She didn't breathe, afraid to move. But then, he pulled her hands away and turned halfway toward her.

"I can't forgive you."

She dropped her hands to her sides and dipped her gaze to the ground. "Then," She paused for a moment, "I'll just have to prove my innocence in this. And then, I want to help you heal. Okay?"

He turned to face her fully. He looked as if he might smile, despite his tears. But then whatever light had just sparked in his soul went out again. "Just leave."

"I won't give up, Josiah. You should know that by now."

JOSIAH KNEW IT. After all, how many times could he throw her out and find her at the castle doors an hour or two later? Now she brought the Lawrences with her to cook for him. Did she care if he ate well or not? Why would she? Didn't the seventh son of the wicked Catherine Ashmore have to die? Instead, she claimed to want to help him heal.

Okay? It was such a simple word and yet it had the power to make him want to smile. Smile at a woman who betrayed his family? He hated himself for being tempted by her. He would never forget, never forgive. And if she didn't leave him alone, he would fling her out of one of the studio windows.

He paused for a moment while it occurred to him that there was a time when such a thought would never have crossed his mind—not only about Mercy, but anyone. Flinging someone out the window to their death—or choking the life from anyone, from...her... were vile, heinous things to do. To even think about. The difference now, at this moment, was that he *cared* that he was having vile thoughts. He turned to look back down the stairs to where Mercy had been standing. Did he care because of her? His heart sank and his sweaty hands shook as he wiped them on his pants.

He turned to hurry to his studio but hit a brick wall on the next step. He almost went tumbling back down the stairs if not for Oswald's quick reflexes grabbing his hand and having the strength to pull Josiah up.

Josiah was almost instantly transported to when he pulled Mercy back from falling down the same stairs and how she felt pressed against him.

"Are you all right, my lord?

Josiah blinked at Oswald, then yanked his hand away. "What are you doing standing right in front of me on the stairs?"

"I was on my way down."

"And you didn't see me on the way up?" Josiah asked him incredulously. Then, before Oswald had time to answer, "Did you know she was bringing the Lawrences here to cook for me?"

Oswald's eyes widened and Josiah thought the strong man's teeth may have chattered. "She doesn't tell me what goes through her head."

"Right," Josiah said, his gaze darkening. "She's good at concealing that."

"My lord," Oswald said, making him pause when Josiah

reached the top stairs. "If my opinion means anything to you at all, I would have you know that I believe her heart was yours. That it is still yours. She knew nothing of what was being planned—"

"Oswald," Josiah said and then remained silent for so long, his servant was about to speak again. "Oswald, has she bewitched you?"

"My lord, no. I simply heard her with an unbiased ear."

Josiah pivoted around to face him, his eyes dark and thunderous. "Unbiased? You're not biased toward me?" He held up his palm when Oswald opened his mouth to speak. "Leave with her!" he shouted, tempted for a mad moment to push him down the long stairs. He shook his head, clearing his thoughts, at least somewhat. "I don't need you. I never asked you to stay. Get out before it's too late."

He heard Oswald say something but his thoughts were clouding over fast, so he hurried up the rest of the stairs to his studio and bolted the door behind him. He looked around, his eyes falling to the last painting in a row of paintings leaning against the wall. It was wrapped in layers of silk, secured in rows of twine the day after the massacre. He couldn't bear to look at her but he also couldn't bring himself to dispose of the painting. He wanted it to always exist to remind him that he'd been betrayed by a heartless witch disguised in beauty and innocence. His gaze roved to the paintings he'd meant to burn. He'd left them in a pile, but now they were set neatly against the wall. She'd been in here, looking through them. He wondered what she thought seeing herself through his damned eyes. Perfect and in love. Did seeing them make her feel guilty for fooling him so completely that he'd gone against his whole family for her? And now, she was back to finish what was started four years ago. She'd already won Oswald over.

He went to the paintings she had stacked and kicked them. His foot went through several paintings. The rest he slashed with the dagger he carried in his belt. When they were all completely destroyed, he sat back against the ruins and wept. This was never going to stop. He was cursed. He'd always known it. Had grown up hearing it. He felt cursed, and he was tired of fighting. Would giving up to Raxxix ease all this pain? The demon was close, almost had Josiah in its clutches. Yes. He'd almost given up his thoughts to Raxxix already.

Someone knocked at the door. "Josiah, can you let me in please?"

He looked up and shook his head through his tears. "What don't you understand about leaving me alone, Miss Blagden?"

"I've never wanted to leave you alone since the day I met you, Josiah. Even when you walked me through the gate that first day. I was praying the entire time that you wouldn't leave. When you kissed me, I felt as if I'd come home. Don't ask me to leave, because I can't."

Josiah had risen up while she spoke and went to the door, but he didn't unbolt it.

"You're going to have to talk with me about this sooner or later," she said through the door. "The sooner you get on with it, the better you'll feel."

He wiped his eyes and slammed the bolt open, then pulled open the door. He looked at her for a moment and thought about how he still didn't see her scar. He could see it if he looked for it. It was still there. But he didn't see it. She was still as breathtaking as she was the first time he'd seen her.

"I'm not asking, Miss Blagden," he told her woodenly. "I'm telling you to leave. I'm commanding it. If you can't tell that I *want* you gone, then you're daft and pathetic."

She took his hard blows on her feet, though he imagined it took all her strength to stay standing.

"I dreamed of my mother. She told me I was here to pave a new path."

"What?" Josiah bent to stare into her eyes.

"Josiah," she said looking up at him. "I'm daft and pathetic because I don't believe you really want me to leave."

He huffed a derisive laugh and ran his hand down his face.

"Well, you're wrong."

"Am I?"

His gaze captured hers and held her still. "Yes." He tried to sound convincing but even to his ears, he knew he failed. Did he want her to stay then? No. His convictions were crumbling before his eyes. He remembered the hurt, the empty days and cold nights she caused. His life had been hell for four years. He'd sworn to himself that if he ever saw her again he'd kill her, but here she was traipsing around his castle as if she had every right to be there, as if she'd done nothing wrong.

"I'll never let you sway me again, Mercy," he told her and disappeared back into his studio, bolting the door when he was inside.

MERCY STARED AT the studio door without saying a word. Her curling lips were accompanied by her thrashing heartbeat.

He didn't call her Blagden witch or Miss Blagden. He called her Mercy. She closed her eyes and let her smile widen. He called her Mercy.

CHAPTER TWENTY

MERCY CAUGHT SIGHT of Oswald hefting bags of his belongings to the front doors of the castle. She hurried down the stairs, calling out his name. Had she caused too much trouble and now he was leaving because of her? "Oswald, what are you doing? Where are you going?"

"I'm leaving."

"I see that, but why? Is it something I've done?"

He shook his head. "He told me to leave. It's not as if it's something I've never heard before, but this time it was different."

"How?" Mercy asked.

"This time he meant it. He told me he didn't need me."

"Oswald, Josiah isn't himself. His heart has been crushed and defeated in the worst way by an enemy that's been out to get him for a long time."

"Raxxix," Josiah's loyal servant and friend said.

"Yes. I told you about him. That demon took everything, and needed to take me too to complete his destruction. He knew I wouldn't leave Josiah on my own, so he figured out a way to make Josiah leave me."

"Yes," Oswald said disheartedly. "I know the prophecy."

"Then you understand that Josiah is saying things he doesn't mean? We're the ones who care about him, Oswald, but what good is it if we run away when he's been so hurt that he's forgotten who he is? I think you've stayed around because you love him, and if you do, then trust that he doesn't want to hurt you and forgive him when he does. He doesn't really want you to go."

"Is that why you don't leave when he tells you to?" he asked her. "You don't think he truly wants you to leave?"

She shook her head, then rethought it and shrugged her shoulders. "He thinks he wants me gone because he thinks I betrayed him. Once he discovers the truth, he'll regret it if I go. Raxxix thought he would win if he got rid of me. But Josiah has been so strong while I found my way back. Now I'm here to help him."

Oswald nodded and moved to return to his chambers.

Josiah was blocking the doorway. He stared over Oswald's shoulder at Mercy while he spoke. "I'm hungry."

Mercy smiled. He hadn't changed all that much. Her heart exalted at the slight trace of the old him.

He dragged his gaze off her and onto his loyal friend. "Let's go eat."

Mercy watched Josiah lead Oswald to the kitchen, and Oswald's joyous relief over being forgiven. She caught Josiah glancing over his shoulder at her. She took a tentative step forward, then hurried after them.

Margaret Lawrence greeted the lord of the castle with a hot sweet bread roll with butter dripping down the sides. He glared at her only for an instant and then his eyes opened wider and he took another bite of the roll. Harry had cut various fruits and vegetables and laid them out on the table. There were two stools and they squeaked painfully when Josiah ordered her to sit in one and Margaret in the other.

Mercy found herself smiling the entire time she ate with them. She silently rejoiced at the slightest traces of Josiah's beautiful heart. Seeing it revealed in his thoughtfulness compelled her to continue to fight to win him back. To protect his heart. Not to be the hilt, but his shield.

She secretly watched him while he ate. He spared the slightest smile to Margaret, but he didn't speak and he didn't laugh with them. Mercy did, however, catch him looking at her while she laughed, or sipped her drink, or swiped her tongue over a drop of butter on her lower lip. She knew from looking at Margaret and the others that Josiah's gaze fell back to her the second she turned away.

When Louise stepped into the kitchen wiping her hands on an apron, Mercy could feel Josiah's gaze on her, and he wasn't happy.

"Now, Josiah, think rationally," she argued, though he hadn't spoken. "You need someone to clean up around here besides me. You also need a laundress and a—"

"What do you mean 'besides you'?" he ground out between clenched teeth.

"What?" she asked, confused for a minute. "Oh, I mean besides me cleaning up around the castle."

"No, you won't be doing that," he told her. Everyone stopped eating and turned to them. "There will be no 'besides you'. If you insist on staying here, you'll serve me. Only me. Only you." He motioned between them. "You won't be helping anyone else."

She sized him up—all six feet, two inches of him. Serve him? At first, she almost laughed. She was raised in the twenty-first century, after all. But on second thought, it would give her plenty of time to be with him. "Fine."

He nodded, looking satisfied with himself, and began to leave the kitchen. He stopped when he reached the doorway and turned back to look at her. "Well?"

Mercy leaped to her feet and shoved her last bite of sliced apple into her mouth. "Coming."

He stared at her for a second and then continued to leave.

"I wonder," she said, hurrying to catch up, "if you were always this bossy and I was too blinded by your charm to notice."

He didn't answer her, but she caught the slightest hint of a smile on his lips. Seeing glimpses of the Josiah who loved her before she left tempted her to fling herself into his arms and beg him to believe her. But the hint of a smile didn't mean he would accept her back into his embrace.

When she saw that he was heading up the stairs, likely to his studio, she was glad. Maybe she could talk to him about him not seeing the lies in her eyes—

He stopped so abruptly on the stairs that she almost hit his back. He looked over his shoulder. "I'm going to my studio. You can go...ehm..."

He was clearly thinking of something for her to do.

"I'll just come with you," she suggested.

"No."

"You said I'm to serve you, and nothing else," she reminded him.

"And you're choosing *now* to do as I say?" he asked in an incredulous tone.

She gave him a cheeky grin. "As long as you don't tell me to leave."

He looked up the stairs; a crease marred his brow as if he were worried about something. He did an about-face and blinked down at her, then motioned for her to move aside.

"Now where are you going?"

"Out."

"Should I come?"

"That would involve you leaving," he said without pausing.

"But I'd be coming back."

Now he turned to smirk at her. She smirked back and put her hands on her hips.

"Should I be worried then?"

"Probably. But I doubt you will be."

"Because I trust you, Josiah." She said it playfully, but judging from the way the blood in his face appeared to drain, leaving him pale, he didn't find it funny. Right. He used to want that from her, didn't he, she remembered. Only that. For her to trust him. "I still trust you to keep your promise to me."

She could almost see his guard go up. He was afraid to care

for her after what he believed she did. She could almost see the disdain in his eyes toward himself for letting her move him. How could she prove to him that she was innocent? It made her want to slump her shoulders and walk off in defeat.

But...he didn't say anything. He didn't demand that she stop trusting him. He sulked and brooded as he stormed out of the castle, but he didn't tell her not to trust him anymore.

So, she wouldn't stop. She followed him out, hurrying to keep up with his long strides while he went to the stable.

"Did you learn how to saddle a horse?" he asked, stopping at the only stall with a horse in it.

"No," she confessed.

"How do you intend to serve me if you can't saddle my horse?"

Looking at him, she could think of a dozen different ways right off the bat. She didn't speak any of them out loud. She wasn't *that* twenty-first century. "Teach me," she said.

He huffed and shook his head at her while he saddled his horse as if he couldn't believe her audacity, but he didn't refuse her request and showed her each step slowly and with patience.

She watched him do the work and then fit his booted foot in the stirrup and lift himself up. She lifted her hand in the air.

"What?" He peered down at her.

"Take me with you."

He appeared as if he might laugh in her face, so instead of waiting for him to refuse, she slipped her foot into the same stirrup he'd used and hoisted herself up. She meant to toss her leg over the saddle and straddle the horse like any woman with a brain cell in her head would do, but she hadn't practiced horseback riding in the four years she'd been away, and lost her balance. She would have fallen backward to the ground if not for Josiah's hands closing around her waist. She took an instant to stare into his eyes just before he pulled her up the rest of the way. She landed hard between his thighs. He grunted and painfully moved her, then closed his arms around her and flicked the reins.

"I'm sorry," she told him softly, covering his hands on her waist with hers.

He immediately pulled his hands away. "I don't want you to fall. Don't add anything to it."

She nodded in front of him. "But seeing how you tried to choke me to death a few days ago, I'd say not wanting me to fall is a pretty huge improvement."

"Perhaps. Depending on which side you're looking at it from."

They rode to the gate and stopped when they reached it so that Josiah could dismount and open it, rather than wait for Joem Macey to do it.

Mercy waved to the self-appointed gate guard as they rode out of Ashmore. She picked up the tension in Josiah's arms when he put them around her again and took the reins.

"Is something wrong, Josiah?" she teased.

"Besides the fact that I haven't thrown you off my horse? No."

She exhaled with a sigh and remained quiet. She tried to keep her tears from falling, but a few escaped and fell to his hand. He held it up to see what it was, then bent over her to get a better look at her.

"Are you crying? Is it because—? Mercy, I wouldn't throw you from the horse."

"I'm crying because I know that," she told him. "I know you wouldn't actually kill me. You proved it. I'm sorry that I had anything at all to do with that day, even if my involvement was all a lie, Raxxix involved me. My love for you was tarnished and tainted. I'm crying over that and because I wasn't here to comfort you at the worst time of your life."

"You told me you were taken away," he reminded her in a husky tone behind her. She nodded. "Then you didn't have a choice. It's better that you weren't here."

She wiped her eyes, "No. I should have been here, Josiah."

His body relaxed around hers. He slumped over her for a

moment, lingering there, breathing on her neck. She was afraid to move, in case he shattered like a mirror...or a heart.

He didn't say anything. What was there to say? That her love for him was still honest and pure? That his was for her?

They rode to the cliffs, where, with Oswald's help, they had disposed of the ruby dagger.

"How did you get it back?" he asked her, helping her dismount.

Good, it was a start. Forget that her heart was pounding like a battering ram. "Hester...Tessa had it. I don't know how she got it."

"Tessa?" he asked, looking as stunned as he sounded. "As in the woman who tried to kill me when I was a baby?"

She bit her lip. She hadn't meant to give that away yet. He wasn't ready for that.

"Josiah," she said in a quiet voice. He looked like he might run. She had one chance to tell him everything. "What Old Lizzie told you was true. Your mother murdered six families in an effort to find me. Because I'm the one prophesied to kill you. But I'd been whisked away to a place...or time, where I couldn't be found. I was taken to the future with my mother. I was never supposed to find or touch the dagger before it brought me to you. But I did touch it. I bled on it and my blood mixed with yours and healed you, and tied me to you. They all think I was born to kill you, but they're wrong, Josiah. I was born to love you, to have mercy on you. I've been dreaming of my mother and she keeps telling me to make a new path, and that's what I'm going to do with you."

He remained quiet, staring at her as his eyes filled with tears. But he fought them away and his gaze darkened as if a veil just dropped over his heart. "You're very convincing."

"What?"

His flinty eyes narrowed on her. "Who told you that you're the child born to kill me? Hester? Or rather Tessa? The witch who killed my mother and then stabbed me moments after coming from her? She lived in my home as a trusted nurse until only moments after being alone with her, my mother died. Moments after being alone with her, I was stabbed with a poison-tipped dagger. She then had the bold audacity to return as Hester and live here again as a servant until she gave the ruby dagger to you so you could kill me with it!" He sounded as thunderous as the waves below. His eyes darkened like the sky before the storm. "Did you come back to see it done, Mercy?"

She shook her head emphatically. "No. I came back because I love you. Because I love the way you loved me. I can't live without it."

He didn't come back at her with a cold reply. In fact, he looked so pitifully sad and broken, he tempted her to go to him. Oh, the very idea of her being responsible for destroying that playful, sheltered young man who found her, claimed her, and then smiled with her every day they were together felt crippling.

"I would never—" the wind snatched her breath and her tears from her cheeks. "Josiah, I would never hurt you the way you were hurt. I don't want to live knowing you believe I betrayed you."

The wind didn't have a chance to snatch the tears about to fall from his eyes. His fingers caught them first. He held them to look at them, then looked at her. "They knew you."

Patience, Mercy. She told herself. *At least he's listening.* "Who knew me?" she asked calmly.

"The Blagdens, who..." he paused and closed his eyes, forcing his tears to fall. "...the murderers. They knew you."

"Right. They were Raxxix's men...I mean, whatever they were. They knew me because that monster showed them who I was."

He let out a mocking chuckle. "Or, my father was right about you, and you were planted here by your relatives to take us down."

"And the whole point of that was to kill you like Tessa Blagden tried to do, right?"

"Right," he agreed. "You even had the ruby dagger. I saw it."

"I did. And I tossed it away. I could never ever stab you with that thing! I tried to toss it away but I went with it, back to the twenty-first century. So no matter what else you believe, believe that I would rather leave you again than stab you, Josiah."

He stood before her brooding and breathing white smoke from his nostrils like some dragon from one of the fantasy books she loved reading. He took a step closer to her and grasped her hand to lead her away to his horse.

Mercy didn't care where he was taking her. Nestled between his strong thighs, with his arms closed around her and his chin resting in the crook of her shoulder, she was most content. She was home. She didn't even care if she froze to death in his arms. They reached Ashmore Castle before that happened. He walked his horse before putting him in. Mercy walked on the other side of him. He didn't try to touch her again or even look at her.

"What is Hes—Tessa to you?" he asked.

"My grandmother," Mercy told him, closing her eyes to prepare herself for his reaction. "I didn't know," she continued, peeking at him when he remained calm and quiet. "She was also one of the sisters at the orphanage. I have a cousin named Bernadette. I never knew she existed. Tessa allowed me to grow up alone in order to save me from Raxxix."

He tossed back his head and let out a deep breath ending with a groan. "Because you were born to kill me."

"I didn't know who I was, Josiah. My mother left me messages in my dreams. She said I should pave a new path in mercy. I guess I wouldn't have known what she meant if I hadn't lived this life. I know my name was given to me as a reminder of that. I'll never hurt you. I would die first."

He opened his mouth just as his horse, that had stopped with him, pulled him hard, propelling him into Mercy's arms.

Hanging over her, he lingered there, his shoulders draping hers, his lips against her ear for just an instant or two, but it was long enough to turn Mercy's world upside-down.

"Forgive me," he said, straightening, then scolded his horse. He walked the beast into the stable and removed the saddle.

Mercy waited while he did everything a stable hand would do. While secretly watching him go about each task, she tried to think of someone from the village who could work as a stable hand here. Perhaps Jacob the miller.

When the work was done, he took her hand as if he'd never let it go, and led her into the quiet castle, to his chambers.

"Wait while I wash up," he ordered. She nodded, wondering what she was waiting for exactly. And what had changed his mind about being around her? What did he want to talk about? What else did he want to know? She'd tell him everything. Was she reaching him?

She didn't wait long before she heard his voice again—like music in her ears. "It's changed in four years, hmm?"

She turned to face him. He donned a fresh white shirt with an open collar and sleeves, buttoned at the wrists, with suede looking knee-high pants with beige hose and brown shoes.

"What's changed?"

"The chambers," he explained.

She shook her head. "The castle has, but not in here or...upstairs." She caught the glint of anger and anxiousness in his eyes about her going to the studio. She quickly changed the subject. "Why are you allowing the castle to fall into disrepair?"

When he didn't answer, she answered for him. "Does it symbolize you, Josiah?"

"Perhaps," he let her know. "In the end it will fall."

"But it doesn't fall," she told him. "It's just been fully repaired by a castle trust. It's quite imposing and majestic."

He cut her an amused glance and sat at the edge of his bed. "I'd like to believe all that you're telling me, but I did that once before."

"I never turned on you. My goodness!" she slapped her knees. "You're stubborn. I mean, I get that you were traumatized and you probably have PTSD, but really, Josiah, did you change your mind about having me around so you could continuously remind me what you think I did to you? Don't you know how much I love you? Why would I betray a man who didn't see my scar? I saw the painting, the first portrait of me, in the future. It was hanging in your chambers opposite your bed. I had no scar. That's how you saw me, Josiah. No other man ever saw me that way."

"Fools." She thought she heard him swear under his breath while he rose to put more wood on the fire.

As he poked the embers, she watched the nuance of muscles dance in his back, along shoulders that had become broad and able to carry the heaviest of sorrows. She smiled when he rolled up his sleeves. His arms pulsed with long, lean sinew. She loved the look of him. She wanted to be in his arms again. What would it take? How could she prove her innocence?

"Mercy." He began to turn and stand—or did he stand first, then turn? She was too captivated by the sight of him, the sound of her name on his lips, to notice. "I thought I knew how much you loved me, but then—"

"There are no buts," she cut him off, shaking her head and breaking whatever spell she was under. "Goodness, I'm tired. I'm going to find a place to be alone and rest my mind."

She moved to head for the door. Everything had finally caught up with her. All the struggle, every day for four years being haunted by his smile, his adoring gaze, his encouraging words, the kindness and generosity he showed to his people. It was hard finally returning and finding him so cold and careless. She was tired and frustrated.

"That's another thing." She paused and turned back to him. "Help your villagers! They're starving right under your nose. You better do something about it!"

He took two long strides to her and stopped in front of her, his expression foreboding, his gaze unyielding. "Are you threatening me?"

She took a step back. "Yes," she managed without looking at

him.

He scoffed. "What do you have to threaten me with?"

She lifted her chin. She had what he needed, whether he knew it yet or not. She met his powerful gaze. "I have me." She turned for the door.

His fingers around her wrist stopped her and pulled her back into his arms. She stared into his eyes, wet with tears. "Mercy," he said as though her name were being torn from him. "Don't go."

CHAPTER TWENTY-ONE

Josiah's thrashing heart, awakening from its long slumber, made him feel dizzy as he bent his head to kiss her. Was he dreaming? He'd dreamed this scene dozens of times, holding Mercy in his arms, bending to kiss her. What would wake him up this time? The memory of what she did to him? He commanded those thoughts to leave him.

Mercy. In his arms once again. Even as alarms went off in his head, warning him not to fall to her wiles again, he dipped his head lower. His heart pounded in his ears. She tilted her mouth to his. That was all the temptation he needed. He pressed his lips to hers with a moan and dragged her closer, deepening their kiss. How he'd missed her! He'd missed her even when he cursed her and swore to kill her. And he hated himself for it. But not now. Now, he only wanted to live in this moment. He melted against her when she reached up and closed her arms around his neck, matching the passion in his kiss. He tasted her, teased her, branded her, possessed her, and was possessed by her until he leaned down and scooped her up to cradle her in his arms while he continued kissing her.

He carried her to his bed and set her down gently. "Do you wish to sleep?" he asked close to her lips.

"No," she whispered, then pulled him close.

He climbed over her, then laid down to face her. "Every moment I spend with you reminds me how much I needed you back then."

"As much as I needed you," she said softly, close to his lips. "You saved me."

She saved him, as well. He wanted to tell her. She'd believed in him, trusted him to be the best he could be and never let any force change him. It was that remnant of belief that remained that kept him from Raxxix all these years. "Mercy—"

"Josiah," she told him, looking into his eyes. "I'm the only one who can kill you, and I never will. I'll never do anything unforgivable that could make you leave me for good, because then I would die too. And I'll never leave you again. I'll make sure of it."

He cupped her cheek in his hand and leaned in. He liked how she looked at his lips before she kissed them. He smiled and made sure his mouth pleased her. When she rolled him back and moved on top of him, he felt his body harden. He almost couldn't believe he was here with her. Was he forgiving her too easily? What if she wasn't guilty? The more he thought about her, the more he remembered how she'd loved him, how she'd healed him. Had he been wrong about her all these years? Had Raxxix been behind it all, and she'd known nothing? It made him want to cry out. He opened his eyes and looked at her instead. She had lifted her head to gaze at him, her hair falling around them, curtaining them.

"What is it?" she asked.

Should he tell her? Dare he be tender with her? He exhaled. He wasn't a coward, he would march on and see where it led. "When I'm not with you time seems to move at a snail's pace, but despite our years apart, when we're together, it feels like no time has passed at all."

She smiled and nodded. "Yes." She leaned down, intoxicating him with the nearness of her, of her lips. "Let's spend some of it finding happiness again," she whispered against him.

He leaned up on his elbows, covering her mouth with his, unable to wait another instant to kiss her. When she parted her lips, he slipped his tongue over hers, reveling in the taste of her. Without breaking their kiss, he curled one arm around her waist, holding her closer before he pulled her down gently on top of him, molding to his angles and tight muscles. He felt his eyes burn and though he continued kissing her, tears escaped through his lashes.

"Josiah," she said gently, in her sorely missed voice. "Did you miss me?"

"I missed you even when I hated you," he told her, then kissed her again. This time, she didn't part her lips to him, so he licked the seam of her mouth with his tongue like a brand. She matched his hungry kiss for a maddening moment, then withdrew again.

"Did you really hate me?"

"It felt as if I did," he answered honestly. "But how can you hate someone you'd give up the sunrise or sunset to see just one more time?"

She smiled, satisfied with his reply and closed her eyes when he continued kissing her. Kissing her was better than giving his attention to the haunting images of his father and brothers dying before his feet. But even without succumbing to the memories of the night the walls were stained with blood, he felt anger begin to bubble up. He looked down at the woman in his bed, the only one who'd ever been there. He didn't want to be gentle with her. He wanted to tear off her clothes with his teeth, hold her down, pin her to the bed while he took her to the other side of reason— where he'd been living.

He was hard enough to feel pain and rose up on his knees to release himself from the confinement of his pants. Set loose, his cock sprang forward, tight and stiff.

With a cool gleam in his hooded eyes, he pulled the hem of her skirts above her thighs and with one tug, ripped her underwear from her body. Without a word, he lowered himself to her and pushed against her opening with the head of his cock. She was tight, unbroken still. He wanted to cry out. He wanted to be rough, a monster…but he didn't hate her.

He pulled away after a moment and spilled his seed over her opening to wet it. This time when he pushed, she received him. When she lifted her hips and wrapped her legs around his waist, he came again. It didn't stop him, but made it easier to slip and thrust his way into her.

"Mercy," he whispered her name like a guttural cry for the same. "Tell me if I hurt you." He pushed harder, deeper, breaking her barrier. She clung to him, his hair, his shoulders, as he surrendered this part of himself with his enemy.

He spread his fingertips thoughtfully over her throat, remembering it trapped in his clamped hand. He leaned down and spread kisses and quiet apologies over her neck.

She forgave him as easily as he had believed her story of time travel the first time he'd heard it.

He smiled into the folds of her hair. It felt good. He hadn't smiled at anything in so long. He heard her sniffle and lifted his head to look at her. Would a woman sent to betray and destroy him weep while she became one with him? He drove himself deeper, slower and with more meaningful thrusts, kissing her, her ear, her face, her hungry mouth.

"Josiah." Her labored breath over his ears when she tilted her face for air set the heart he thought long dead to racing. She widened her thighs and ground against him. With his breath coming almost as hard as hers, he pulled at a certain lace in her stays and loosened all of them. Pulling them off like a wolf hungry for his kill, he set her free from the stays and tugged her shirt over her head. He did the same with the chemise someone had loaned her. An instant after they were free, he lowered himself to her creamy breasts, and closed his lips over taut nipples that awaited him.

She moved her hips with him and found her release while gazing into his eyes.

No matter how he'd felt for her in the past, he touched his fingers to her cheek now and kissed everywhere on her face with slow, heartfelt kisses.

He held her while she told him, between sobs, what he meant to her. "I'm not angry with anyone for putting me in your way, Josiah. I'm happy it was me and no one else."

"Were you always so transparent?" he asked as they both fell exhausted against each other.

"Yes, I think so," she answered.

He smiled, gazing down at her. "No wonder I fell in love with you."

They held each other until late in the night, talking about grandmothers and great aunts, and cousins Mercy never knew she had. He knew the truth before she told him about Hester. He had to admit though, Old Lizzie being Mercy's great aunt was a surprise.

How could he trust Mercy with women like that around her? He understood a little more why she hadn't told him the truth of who she was. He would never have let her get close.

Did he wish she would have told him?

MERCY DREAMED WHILE she slept in Josiah's bed. She didn't move about or cry out at the images flooding her mind. She felt...uncomfortably charged. As if she'd stuck her finger into an electrical outlet. It was enough to pull her from her slumber and sit her up in his bed.

He wasn't in it.

She swung her legs over the side of the high mattress, then slid the rest of her off the bed. "Josiah?" she called out softly.

She could see a little, thanks to the hearth fire. Josiah wasn't in the bedchamber. She took a step toward the door, and then another. She opened it and peeked her head out. She checked either side and stepped out into the empty corridor.

Remembering what Sister Tess taught the girls when their

group hamster escaped its cage;. instead of searching in every nook and cranny, stop and listen. So, that's what she did. After a moment, she thought she heard something coming from down the hall. She followed the sound and as it grew louder, her heart shattered into pieces.

She came to the door of a vacant room—her old room where she'd been taken after he cut himself with a poison dagger. Was he inside? Her skin tightened and pushed any hair she had away from her flesh. He was there, hunched over on the floor weeping and sobbing out wailful moans, clenching his hands at his chest.

Mercy had never seen a man cry before—and never like that. She was sure his heart was bleeding within. Why wasn't there anything she could do—even to prove her loyalty to him?

She stepped away unseen, giving him privacy and peace while he cried. On her way back to his rooms, she met Oswald.

"Is it almost dawn?" she asked, stopping him. She hated not knowing what time it was here. It's dawn, it's morning, it's noon, it's midday. Etc. Etc. She sighed and looked up to heaven.

"In about two hours," he advised her. "Where's Lord Winterborne?

"He'll be along," she assured him. "What are you doing awake?"

"I came to see to him," he explained. "He usually wakes up at this time."

"Ahh," she nodded and looked down the hall to her old room. "I'll see to him, Oswald."

"You, my lady?"

She nodded. "Yes. I'll take care of him. You may go."

Oswald gave her a look of pure gratefulness, and then glanced over her shoulder at her old chamber door, as if he knew exactly what was going on.

"Yes, my lady." He stepped away and was gone.

Mercy looked over her shoulder at the door and then returned to it. She'd leave Josiah alone for now and let him heal while she waited outside the door. She was elated that he'd accepted her back—if he had—he'd made love to her as if he had. She hugged her knees to her chest thinking of them sharing their bodies, their breath, their sweat. She sighed. She'd waited so long. She'd missed him more than her heart could endure. She listened to his cries, and then, when she could no longer bear it, she entered the chambers and bent to him. She didn't speak. She simply held him, patting him as he wept for everything he'd lost.

He wiped his eyes and finally looked at her through his tears. "I'll be alright," he reassured her and moved out of her reach.

She watched him slide away. But she wouldn't let him go. She lifted her finger to her mouth and bit her skin until she bled.

"What are you doing? Josiah scolded but then seemed to melt all over his bones when she held the blood to his palm.

"Maybe it can heal your heart too," she told him.

The slow, heartfelt smile he offered her moved her more than anything in her life ever had or ever would. It was beautiful, touched with traces of the playful Josiah from whom she'd been taken, and mixed with something more akin to sorrow. It engulfed her.

"I've missed you so much," she breathed out.

He nodded and reached out his hand to pull her to face him, knee to knee on the floor. He said nothing but stared into her eyes and smoothed her hair off her brow.

"Tell me," she said softly when he remained quiet, seemingly content to look at her.

"Tell you what?"

"What you're thinking."

He shifted his gaze off her and sighed. "So much time has passed. So much has happened."

The velvet richness of his voice seeped into her, warming her blood, even her bones. "Yes," she managed. "So much has changed."

He nodded, then looked around. "I hear them. My brothers laughing and running through the halls, sounding like a stampede of cattle, my father always defending me when I caused trouble, my little nieces and nephews asking me endless questions. Even Captain Sherwood haunts me, following me around, believing I don't know he's there. I hear them all, alive, vibrant. I'm the one who's invisible. I'm the one they can't see or hear. I'm the one who's dead."

Mercy let her tears fall for him and shook her head. "No. I know what the world is like without you. I lived in it for four years. Right now, you're alive, Josiah. Alive and vital. The sound of your voice is as comforting as my own sanity being returned to me. The meaningful way you consider me is as cherished and needed by me as my heart is to live. Right now, you're like one broken and battered and left in the cold night to die. But the force trying to destroy you doesn't know that I prayed for you. It doesn't know my path or that I'll carve the way right through it, so—" she rose up on her knees, put her hands on his shoulders, and leaned her face close to his, "it had better get out of the way."

A new smile appeared on his beloved face, one painted in smoky veils of seduction that lit her blood on fire and made her forget the pain of losing her virginity.

"I love you, Josiah," she said, climbing into his lap. "Shhh." She held a finger to his lips when he opened them to speak. "You don't have to say it back. I understand."

She watched as if in slow-motion, those full, shapely lips of his purse and press against her finger. "I was going to say," he smirked at her while he coiled his arms around her waist, "that when the wind beat against me and tore me to tatters, snatching away what I remembered of you, I still loved you."

Oh, he was so worth the four years of searching and living to be with him again. She wanted to hold onto him forever. "Take me to your bed."

"What's wrong with the bed in this room?" he growled against her ear.

"It's dusty," she told him, breaking free and standing up. "If you're not interested in going back to your bed—"

He reached out to grab her, but she lifted her skirts above her ankles and ran laughing out of the room. He chased her and caught her, and then laughed with her as he scooped her up in his arms and carried her the rest of the way.

"You tempt me beyond reason," he told her, tossing her onto his bed and climbing in over her.

"I think you have a good command over your reason, Lord Winterborne," she told him, staring up into his eyes, "You didn't give in to Raxxix."

"I wanted to."

"But you didn't."

He nodded, finally agreeing that he wasn't a weak-willed fool. At least when she wasn't involved. When it came to her, his will wasn't so strong. They didn't care. Not now while their whispers of love filled the air and their hearts.

"You were a virgin," he remarked, holding her in his bed after they changed the sheet.

"Of course," she whispered, then kissed his chest. "I belong to you. I'd never give myself to anyone else."

He kissed her shoulder and pulled her closer.

"How about you?" she asked him. "Were you a virgin too?"

"My brother, Edward, snuck a prostitute into the castle when I was eighteen. I was awkward and she was impatient. She left when it was over, which took less than five minutes."

Mercy laughed. "Fool!" she cried out, and then he laughed too.

Soon, they exchanged their laughter for kisses. They undressed each other slowly, with curious fingers, savoring everything they missed before. Mercy wept and giggled while he kissed every part of her. She trembled in his arms, knowing that even discovering family in the future, right here was where she belonged—and she'd fight to the death to remain here.

He moved over her and held himself up on his palms. "You're doing it again," he told her, running the backs of his knuckles down her face.

"What am I doing?" She offered him an inviting smile while

he lowered himself to her.

"You're healing me."

He entered her in one slow, smooth thrust, then stopped to kiss her and tell her how beautiful she was to him—and to let the pain ebb away.

"Mercy," he whispered her name while he began to move on top of her slowly. "Don't leave me."

"Never," she promised, and held on when his thrusts grew deeper, harder. But he wasn't one for quickness. He took his time thrilling her, smiling decadently when she cried out, stealing her breath and making her pant.

He lifted himself on one palm, bringing her up with him with his other arm curled around her waist. He ground his hips against hers, driving himself deeper into her until she arched her back, swinging her head back. When he took her tight nipple between his lips, a thought flashed across her mind that his sensual lips were crafted for this. Shudders of ecstasy washed over her again and again, convulsing her muscles around his long shaft as his body found a steady rhythm of pushing in, then slowly out, in then out, again, and again, and again. She clung to him, wanting to claw at him as some primal, almost feral ecstasy washed over her. He brought her to her climatic release and went there with her in his arms.

Before Oswald knocked at the bolted door with a tray of Margaret Lawrence's breakfast an hour later, they made love three more times. He was a strong, virile man, hard and ready for her every moment his eyes were open. They laughed about it a few times, but Josiah made no apologies for wanting her.

"You're no longer worried you'll get pulled back and be a single mother in the future?"

She shook her head. "I'm never going back. I'm never touching that stupid dagger again."

"I'm glad to hear it," he told her and pulled her closer.

"Where's the first portrait of me," she asked him while they lay in bed tangled in each other's arms and legs.

"In the studio. You said you saw it in the future?"

"Yes. It's hanging right there." She pointed to the spot across from his bed.

"I'll bring it down from the studio later and hang it there. Don't tell me anymore what you thought of it. I want to see your reaction myself."

"Okay," she promised, leaning up to stare at him. She smiled. He responded with a smile of his own. She had him back. She prayed for strength and courage to deal with Raxxix when he showed up and then she pulled Josiah out of bed.

CHAPTER TWENTY-TWO

J OSIAH LOOKED UP at the clear sky and felt the urge to smile. He didn't now, but he had last night until early in the morning. It was Mercy Blagden's doing. His father would curse him and his brothers would spit at him if they knew. He still loved her. He believed her and trusted her without any proof—just as he had before. He wanted her in his bed forever, but he needed sleep and he found it difficult with her in his arms.

He didn't bring his horse for his daily ride, but strode to the nearest tree and sat under it. All around him resilient little white flowers grew. He didn't know what they were. He'd never bothered to ask Oswald, but this afternoon they were his bed. He plucked one and put the thin stem in his mouth with the flower dangling from his lips and fell asleep.

He was awakened two hours later by Mercy conversing with Oswald over him.

"I'm always so stricken by the sight of him," she told his friend. "I can't believe he's real, and that it's me he loves."

Josiah opened his eyes and lifted his fingers to his lips. He swiped the stem with the flower out of his mouth and smiled at her. When she giggled at him, his blood bubbled in his veins. He glanced at Oswald. How could he have doubted her? "Go, find a priest."

His loyal servant blinked at him. "Pardon?"

"A priest," Josiah sighed. He stood up, cracked his back, and took Mercy by both hands. "You know—a man of God."

It took *Muscle* another moment to get it.

Josiah was already smiling down at Mercy. "Stay by my side forever and be my wife, Mercy. I promise to always love you. I promise to cherish you and treasure you, protect and provide for you, and never leave you for a demon."

They both smiled. Mercy said yes and was whisked into the air in his arms.

"Oswald, what are you still doing here?" Josiah asked him when he noticed him just standing there, slack-jawed.

"Just taking it all in, my lord. It's been a long while."

Josiah nodded and looked down. Oswald hadn't left his side even when Josiah was at his angriest and most lonely. Josiah knew his friend had seen him through it all. He'd have a celebration for him. He'd ask Mercy for her help, and the Lawrences, as well. For now though, he feigned impatience. "Go on then and stop gaping."

Oswald hurried off, Mercy returned her full attention to Josiah, dipping her gaze to his lips.

"Does this make me your betrothed?" she asked him when they were alone.

"Yes," he answered, pulling her into his arms.

She laughed at his belly rumbling. "Come on, Margaret has prepared food."

"All right, but then I want to go to the studio with you." He was still amazed at the change in him. It was as if he'd never stopped loving her. He knew he never had. When she came back into his life, her sincerity that she had nothing to do with the attack on his family had chipped away at his thick defense as if it were made of paper. And here he was, promised to her.

He let her lead him back to the castle, to the kitchen, where Margaret Lawrence and two other women from the village greeted him cautiously. He still didn't like having all the people in the castle. So much life and laughter chased away the dead.

He did like Margaret Lawrence's cooking though. He complimented her on it twice. "Oh, and we'll be needing a lot of food tonight," Josiah told Margaret. "Enough for the whole village. Think you can do it?"

She blinked, then nodded. "What's the occasion?"

He cut his glance to Mercy and smiled. "Our wedding announcement."

At the mention of the word wedding, the women sprang to their feet and almost leaped at Mercy. She laughed in excitement with them. Watching her, Josiah felt a wave of happiness wash over him that he hadn't felt in a long time. It gave him hope that all would be well. She brought hope back to him. Again.

When they finished eating, Josiah took Mercy to the studio. He'd gotten rid of the paintings of her that he'd smashed and decided not to mention them. He was thankful that she caught on and didn't ask. He didn't want to tell her what he'd done to the paintings. She seemed not to care about anything but the portrait wrapped in silk and twine. He unwrapped it with a thumping heart. He hadn't seen it in four years. He knew it was his best work because his whole heart was in it.

She waited while he pulled the silk away. At the last moment, she reached for his hand and took it. And then the silk fell away like liquid to the floor and the portrait he'd waited four years to show her was revealed.

He'd almost forgotten how it looked. How could he? Seeing it again made his knees feel weak. He should have looked at it sooner. It would have helped him remember that her feelings for him were genuine. She hadn't betrayed him. He was happy he destroyed the others. Although there had been no lies in her eyes or in her smiles, there hadn't been any joy or life in them either. Not like this one.

He'd painted her hair away from her face and falling in rich, chestnut curls over one shoulder. Tiny yellow colored petals were scattered throughout her hair. He'd added them after their day among the daffodils. Her cheeks were creamy with a hint of color. A soft smile curled her full, painted lips. Her beautiful eyes were huge and the color of the sea, and within them Josiah could see her love for him revealed. "What do you think?" he asked.

She smiled despite the tears streaming down her face. "It's beautiful...but she isn't me."

"Of course she is," he told her softly. She made him want to smile all the time. "You're beautiful."

"There's no scar."

"It's how you look in my eyes, my heart," he told her, taking her in his arms.

She wiped her eyes and kissed him. "Let's go hang it in your room."

While they were at the task, he asked her more about the future painting. How did anyone know that particular painting hung across the bed? Had it been there all along? She told him what the tour guide had said. "The placement of everything has been the same for the last four hundred years." Her smile warmed him. "I've always been here watching over you, Josiah."

He finished hanging the portrait and took her face in his hands. "I've always felt you. I tried to chase you away, but you were persistent and stubborn." He kissed her mouth and smiled. "Exactly how you've been since you returned."

When she gave him a hard stare, his smile widened. She didn't appear amused. His smile turned more playful until the mischievous impish grin shone in all its glory and made her laugh.

"Are you happy I returned?" she asked as his arms came around her.

"Yes." He was now. Now that he could see a little bit of light again. But how long would it last until Raxxix or Tessa Blagden came for him? Would he lose Mercy again? He knew this time he'd never be able to bear it. "But it won't stay peaceful."

"I know," she whispered against him.

"Look what Raxxix did the first time. I'll be honest, Mercy, it scares me."

"Me too. But I love you, and that's enough to defeat any monster."

If this was his defeat, ah, then let it come! he thought as his smile deepened. "And I'll keep my promise to never leave your side."

"My lord?" Oswald called through the bedchamber door.

"Yes?"

"Is Miss Bl..er...Miss Smi..?

"Yes, she is." Josiah called back and his smile turned into a laugh at Oswald's awkwardness.

She went to the door and opened it with a smile, then took Oswald by the sleeve and pulled him inside to see her portrait.

She waited by Josiah's side while his friend took in the art and pulled a napkin from his pocket to hold to his nose.

They waited another moment until he turned to them, wiping his nose. His watery gaze slipped to Mercy first. "It makes me happy that I trusted you, Miss," and then to Josiah, "I'm glad you finally uncovered the truth, my lord."

Josiah nodded his head in agreement and swung his arm around him. "And I'm glad I didn't beat or kill you all those times I wanted to. You're very wise and good to have around." He laughed when Oswald wiped his tears and offered Mercy an innocent look when she tried to glare at him. He wanted to kiss her. "What of the priest? Have you found one already?"

"Yes," Muscle chuckled at himself. "I forgot everything I came to tell you both. The priest will be here after supper, and Louise and Lillith are looking for you. Miss. They said they sewed you some dresses."

"Oh, how kind of them!"

She started to walk out of the chamber when Josiah took her hand, stopping her. He turned to Oswald. "Tell them the soon-to-be Lady Ashmore will see them later. And now that you've seen the portrait, we'll see you at supper." He practically pushed the more muscular man out the door. When Oswald was gone, Josiah bolted the door behind him and cast her a hungry smile.

"Even with a deserted castle, it's difficult to be alone with you."

She covered her mouth with her hands as she laughed and let out a little squeak when he took a step nearer.

"You would run from me?"

She nodded and scooted out of the way, avoiding his grasp with a loud laugh. He'd always loved playing with her. He hadn't played in a long time. He chased her around the room, and when he finally caught her, he pushed her back against the wall and pressed his body to hers. "Mercy," he said in a rough whisper in her ear, "even if a thousand demons take me over, I'll never hurt you."

"I'll never let even one take you over," she promised.

He leaned in and kissed her with achingly sensual slowness. His lips molded to hers. When they parted, he slipped his tongue into her mouth. When she did the same, he grew harder and pushed off her to unlace his pants and free himself.

With one fluid move, he bent down, took two handfuls of her skirts, lifted them over her waist, and lifted her off her feet. He looked into her eyes. She let out what sounded like a purr and smiled at him. That was all the provocation he needed. He pulled her legs around him and pushed his hard cock against her wet opening.

She yielded to him with enough resistance to drive him wild without him worrying about hurting her. He ran his fingers over her hair, down her temple, over her nose while he thrust into her. She was his and he poured himself into her.

He let her throw him down on the bed and pull off his clothes while she pulled off hers. She kept him down on his back and straddled him. "Tell me you love me."

He smirked at her. "Or what?"

"Or I'll leave."

He scoffed. "Preposterous. I'd never let you make it to the door. But to avoid more empty threats...I love you, Mercy."

She moved on him, pressing her hot niche to his shaft. He closed his eyes and felt lightheaded. "I love you," he told her again. When she impaled herself on him, slowly, cautiously, he had to clench his jaw to hold onto his control. But just a few instants later, she cried out, drenching him, moving up and down on him faster, taking him deeper until she emptied him and left him weak in his bed.

"Mercy?" he said into her hair while he held her.

"Yes?"

"I love you enough to set the world to ruin for you."

She leaned up and gave him a worried look. "No, Josiah, I don't want that."

He gazed into her eyes. What she saw there brought tears to her eyes. "Please," he whispered, "don't leave me again."

TESSA BLAGDEN STOOD back in the shadows of Ashmore Castle's small chapel waiting for her granddaughter to arrive and be married to the cursed seventh son.

Was Tessa wrong for letting it go on this long? Her granddaughter was such a dear, but stubborn, girl. Tessa wanted more for her than a bleak future more alone than she'd been in the past. Her Mercy would never be the same if she killed the man she loved. Was there really another way? Had Mercy's mother, Claire, known about another path that even Lizzie hadn't been aware of? Had Claire called her baby Mercy knowing her daughter would wield forgiveness like a hopeful light? A light that would shine in a lonely monster's darkness? Tessa closed her eyes to stop her tears when she remembered Claire. Her beautiful daughter who'd had no obvious powers—or so they had believed at first. Claire had never spoken of being clairvoyant, but she had to have seen her daughter's life and named her Mercy to remind her what her purpose was. Was Mercy working? The seventh son had, after all, lasted four years in misery without succumbing to Raxxix. Had the young earl been waiting for Mercy to find her way back?

Tessa remembered speaking with him as Hester. Back then she had thought it a shame that he had to die. She'd liked him, and he'd seemed to genuinely care for her granddaughter. But there wasn't any place for the heart in this business. As long as the dagger existed, the seventh son belonged to Raxxix. One day soon, the demon would claim him.

What would happen to the vessel's wife then?

Oh, how Tessa wished there was a way to destroy Raxxix without killing the earl. But the heart blood of the seventh son was the only way to destroy the ruby dagger, and destroying the ruby dagger was the only way to destroy Raxxix. It had to be done.

And it had to be done soon. Raxxix was close on Mercy's trail. It was only a matter of days before she was found.

Tessa spread her gaze over the dozen people in the chapel. She remembered all the villagers from four years ago. Had they all deserted him then? Tessa understood her granddaughter pitying him. It had been a dark day, and Raxxix had been behind it all.

It didn't escape Tessa that Mercy had no way to prove her innocence to her new husband, but Josiah Ashmore didn't need it to let his heart surrender to her again. He could have been good for Mercy if he wasn't cursed.

Had Claire known? Had she seen Josiah Ashmore cursed by his own mother and healed by her daughter? Tessa wanted to smile at the thought of it. When she saw her granddaughter at the entrance of the chapel, she closed her eyes and thanked God, and then asked Him to protect her dear girl.

WHEN JOSIAH FIRST saw her coming toward him down the aisle, he covered his mouth with his hands and pulled in a deep breath. This was how he wanted to paint her, arrayed in tissue-thin layers of coral-colored chiffon, gathered at the waist by thin cords of silver. Her long hair was gathered at the temples and set loose over her delicate shoulders. Around her brow was a circlet of tiny, peach-colored roses. Judging by her red-tipped nose and puffy eyes, she'd been crying. For a moment, he considered that her tears hadn't been happy ones. But he knew better. He knew the way her eyes, the color of sparkling seas in the sun, settled on him and filled to the brims with pure, unadulterated love, that she had never faltered. And she was about to become his wife, though he felt as if they had always been destined to be together.

He didn't care about the life in the deepest shadows of his being. It was no longer important to him. Only she was. It was time he let go of all the ghosts of his family. Mercy helped him by filling their place with laughter. She was all he needed.

Their eyes met as she walked slowly toward him. He smiled and told himself that he meant it.

CHAPTER TWENTY-THREE

MERCY RESTED ON top of her naked husband while he slept. It was their first night together as a married couple. She lifted her chin to look at him and grinned. She still couldn't believe she was married. Her! She kissed his bare chest and went back to staring at him in the candlelight while he slept. "You're so handsome," she whispered.

Suddenly he smiled. "You're so in love with me."

She scowled. "Were you dreaming of looking in a mirror again?"

"No," he let her know amidst tickles that made her laugh and squeal. "I dreamed of you and laughed while you captivated me."

They kissed and wrapped themselves in each other's arms and legs and stared into each other's eyes.

"I'm memorizing you," he told her, running the pad of his thumb down her nose, lightly over her lips.

"Why?" she asked, leaning in to kiss him. "I'm not going anywhere."

"I'm going to paint you."

She grinned at him. He grinned back and they both burst into laughter.

"I love you," he told her while he pushed himself against her opening.

"I love you too," she whispered, then spread her legs wider.

From then on, their days were filled with laughter, their

nights with passion. But it didn't escape Mercy that Josiah had a wound that wouldn't heal. Despite him welcoming more villagers to the castle, sharing his contagious laughter with them and his intimate smiles with only her, she often caught him looking off, as if he was watching a memory play out. When he wasn't putting on a smile to greet a vassal, as he had once done, he seemed distracted and melancholy.

Tonight, she found him sitting in his large chair by the window in their bedchamber. He assured her that his troubles had nothing to do with her. In fact, she brought happiness back into his life. But he was still suffering.

"I lost everyone I knew," he told her in a low, husky voice. "My family, friends, guardsmen, servants, the only faces I knew growing up. Ashmore was my world and I lost it all in one fell swoop."

She went to him and sat at his feet. She took his hand and pressed it to her cheek.

"Before you returned," he went on, "I lived with their ghosts, but now the sunshine streaming through the castle again has vanquished them—and It's like losing them again."

There was nothing she could say to comfort him, so she leaned up and closed her arms around him. He clung to her in the silence, then rose up and took her back to bed.

Mercy would have done anything she could for him, that's why when her grandmother showed up the next night while everyone slept, Mercy left her bed and padded up the stairs to the northeast tower. She'd received Tessa's note and did as she was bid. No one followed her.

"Have you come to accept what you need to do, Mercy?" her grandmother asked her.

Mercy shook her head. "No, because I'm not doing it. But I need to know if I can bring back his family."

Her grandmother didn't answer right away, and then, "And what happens when another catastrophe befalls him and you lose him to the darkness again-but this time, it's Raxxix?"

"I won't lose him to Raxxix. No matter what that demon thought Josiah was prone to do, my blood now flows through his veins. He'll resist until the monster leaves him alone."

"No." Her grandmother shook her head. "You will lose him to complete heartbreak. As he was, only worse, and for as long as Raxxix decides to play with him. How much do you think he can bear before he gives in? Raxxix is coming, Child. What will you do?"

Mercy wrung her hands together. No! How could she allow Josiah to suffer any more heartbreak? To live like a zombie under Raxxix's control? Was the only way to save him to plunge a dagger into his heart? Oh, the chilling horror of it was too much! Just how close was the demon?

She took a step forward and reached for her grandmother's hand. "Help me, Grandmother. Help me and Josiah. What can I do to stop Raxxix without killing the man I adore? There must be a way."

"The end of Raxxix will only come when the lifeblood of the seventh son is shed on the ruby dagger."

"Okay, and Raxxix needs the dagger, right?" Mercy asked her grandmother. "How will the demon get it?"

"There's only one way, Child," her grandmother told her, looking her in the eyes. "To take it from your fingers when you choose not to kill the vessel."

"Oh! Oh my! He's not *a vessel*. He's a person, Grandma!"

"Mercy?"

She spun around at the sound of Josiah's voice.

"Who is that?' he called out, coming forward. "Who are you talking to?"

Mercy's heart thrashed wildly, making her feel dizzy. No! He mustn't see her grandmother. She had to stop him. She held up her hands and stepped in front of Tessa. "Josiah, don't come any further! She's from the village. She has... has a contagious fever." When he completely ignored her warning and rushed to her, she tried to convince him. "Thousands are dying in London from a plague—"

"If she has it, you've been exposed. We'll leave here together."

"Josiah," she said, staring into his dreamy eyes. "If I had the plague, you would die with me?" Thank God, they didn't have it, but he didn't know that.

"Of course," he said as if she should already know the answer.

"No. I would never let you."

He seemed to remember the other person with them. He turned, but Tessa was gone.

"Who was that?" he asked as Mercy coiled her arms around his neck. "We should quarantine her."

"Josiah?"

"Hmm?"

She smiled when he set his adoring eyes on her. "No one has ever loved me the way you do. Thank you."

His smile lit on her before he closed his arms around her waist and molded his lips to hers. "Mercy," he whispered, withdrawing for a moment.

"Yes?"

"Do we have the plague?"

She laughed and basked in being alive and in the same time with him. She wouldn't let some lowly demon take another thing from him.

MERCY LOOKED AROUND the small kitchen, her cartoon character kiddie fork paused in delivering an impaled a SpaghettiO to her mouth. She watched the woman, the love of her three-year-old life, fill her cup and then come sit with her at the table.

"Mercy, you're here to pave a new path."

"New path," she echoed, adding a raspberry to the end of the word so that her SpaghettiOs flew from her mouth. She laughed with her mother and did it again until her mother had to take away her food.

The scene of Mercy's dream changed and she appeared in her pink bedroom, fresh from a bath and dressed in her soft pajamas. She climbed into a pink bed in the shape of a castle and smiled while her mother tucked her in. "Mercy, you won't forget this will you?"

Mercy giggled and shook her head.

"The answer to everything will soon be within you, Daughter. Look within and start again."

Look within and start again.

Mercy opened her eyes in the morning with those words on her lips. Look within. When she did, there was one thing that stood out—one thing her mother had to do with. One thing that was within her. Josiah's blood. There was a way to end this without killing him. Her mother had given it to her. A way to make a new path. A way to start again.

"Are you smiling because you dreamed of me?" Josiah asked playfully, pulling her spine against him and spooning her. He brushed her hair aside and dipped his mouth to her neck. "What is it? Is something wrong?"

She smiled and closed her eyes in front of him. "I woke up smiling and you're asking me if something's wrong?"

"Yes."

She laughed and then sighed at herself. "Raxxix is always just beyond all my good thoughts to try to darken them."

He nodded and held her tighter. "I'll never give in to Raxxix. That old beast will never have my heart. It belongs to you."

She ran her palm over his knuckles while he held her. "Do you promise?"

"I promise," he whispered into her hair, then moved her under him.

He vanquished every thought that was not about him, conquering them with his decadently carved lips, his curious tongue, his bold knees spreading her wider, his hand lifting her hips, positioning her better to take him fully. The weight of him and every nuance of movement she felt above her made her moan for him. Pinning her gently, he took her from behind and kissed the back of her neck when she came in his hand.

They remained in bed for most of that day and the next, as newlyweds were wont to do. But one night, a different kind of cold covered Ashmore.

"Child," her grandmother said on the steps of the northern tower. "Your enemy has found you. You must do what you're meant to do now. Do it while he sleeps. The dagger will resist. If he awakens, he'll stop you and you might not get another chance. Get him drunk. Ensure that he doesn't wake up if there's movement around him."

Mercy tried to swallow. Was this really happening right now?

"You think you can defeat it, but you can't, Child. Before you know it, you will be dying, Raxxix will have the dagger, and your beloved will be…worse."

A howling gust of frigid air swept through tower windows. Somewhere in the distance laughter echoed through the hills.

Mercy closed her eyes and said a prayer. When she opened her eyes again, she set her gaze on her grandmother. "Bring me the dagger."

MERCY SAT ACROSS the table from Josiah and took a sip of wine from a jug Harry had given them as a gift. She watched Josiah drink and smile at something Oswald said as he set down a bowl of rabbit stew before him. She wondered why Harry had given them the wine tonight of all nights, and why Josiah seemed extra tired, yawning and stretching in his chair. Did her grandmother poison him? Was it something worse? What powers did Tessa Blagden actually possess? Mercy had never asked for a list. She went to their chambers first and checked in a few trunks for the dagger, then she thought about where her grandmother may have put it. She went to the bed and checked under the mattress. It was there, crimson and malevolent, cushioned under millions of feathers.

It was close enough to the edge for her to just reach for it—

The bedroom door opened. Josiah stepped inside, unlacing his shirt. "I think I'm coming down with something." he told her, dragging himself to the bed. "I feel like there's something I need to tell you, to warn you about—" He stopped and seemed to be listening to something she couldn't hear.

"My love," he said softly to her, "if there's a way...a way for you to leave. You should go."

"Go where? You're the love of my life. Do you think I would abandon you?"

He rubbed his forehead and ran his hand down his face. "Something isn't right." He appeared worried but then he slid his flinty gaze to her. "Is the dagger here, Mercy?"

Her lips parted and she stepped back in surprise. How could he know? "What? Josiah—"

He began looking around the chambers. "Why would you bring it here?" He disturbed everything, knocking over whatever was in his way. "Tell me where it is."

"Josiah," she said, trying to remain calm. She didn't expect him to react this way. "Why do you want it?"

He stopped searching and became still, staring at her.

"Are you okay?" she asked him, taking note of the glint in his eyes. He was angry.

"Why are you playing games?" he ground out. "Just tell me where it is. You brought it back again. Are you going to use it this time?"

Was she seeing things or were the irises of his eyes turning yellow? He ground his teeth and snarled at her. "Bring it to me."

It was Raxxix! Had the demon taken over Josiah? No! No! "Where is he? Where's Josiah? I want to speak to him now!"

"It's too late. Give me the dagger."

How could she resist him when he looked and sounded like her love? She had to. She ran to him. "Josiah!"

He caught her in his hands and pushed her away. She landed

on the bed…or at the edge of it.

It was time. Her heart nearly stopped on its own from her thinking of what she had to do. She had to. He'd been drunk tonight, unguarded, and she'd led Raxxix right to her on a platter. She knew what her mother meant now. She knew how to pave her path. Once the dagger and Raxxix were destroyed, every evil wrought by the dagger would be reset and restored.

"Josiah, everything is going to be okay," she promised him and tore the dagger from its hiding place. "Raxxix, there are two things you didn't account for. One: I love him. Two: his blood flows through my veins. Killing me is like killing him."

He nearly leaped on her, eyes blazing, and snatched at the dagger. She evaded his touch and he missed. She brought the dagger down, and a moment before it plunged into her chest, his eyes went gray and filled with horror too inconceivable to take in.

"Mercy!" he screamed out as the bloodstain on her gown grew bigger. The castle walls began to crumble and Raxxix wailed from somewhere within him, and then outside him, undefined.

"Mercy! No! Please! Please!" Josiah took her up in his arms while her blood poured from her body and puddled at his feet.

"My love," she breathed out. "I'm fixing things."

She stared at him and coughed up blood and then took her last breath. Josiah threw back his head and opened his mouth, and then was gone.

Everything was gone.

Dorchester, England
1661

JOSIAH ASHMORE, THE young earl of Winterborne and seventh son of the duke of Dorset strolled through the marketplace smiling at everyone who greeted him, not just the pretty girls batting their lashes and turning all sorts of different red.

"When will you choose a wife, Josiah?"

He offered his father a grin he knew would soften the duke's heart to him. "I'm only twenty. I'm still young, Father. I haven't found her yet."

"Who?" his brother Edward asked.

"Who what?" asked another of his six brothers coming to walk between them.

"Josiah is looking for a girl," Edward let the eldest know.

Thomas arched his eyebrows in surprise. "I didn't know you had a woman."

Josiah looked down and laughed. "I don't."

"Josiah is saving himself for someone," Nicholas let them all know, despite Josiah's murderous glare.

"Who are you saving yourself for, little brother?" Gil asked him. "Is she real or an ideal?"

"I hope she's real," Josiah told him, thereby telling them all. "I'll know her when I find her."

They laughed, and all but Josiah hurried after Captain Sherwood, their father's most valued soldier when he entered a small shop to buy something for his wife.

Josiah looked up at the cloudless sky and smiled—and walked straight into a soft body, which he almost sent into the mud.

After an apology to the fair lady he almost mowed down, his gaze and his smile lingered on her. "Do I know you?" he asked, staring into her huge blue-green eyes. She had long, chestnut hair pulled up at the temples with pins and tiny yellow flowers, and set free in the back. She smiled shyly and shook her head and then stepped around him to leave.

With her was an older woman who resembled her, likely her mother. Around her, a small flock of younger, giggling girls. Her sisters? He let her pass, but the instant she did he felt as if something had been pulled away from him. He hurried back to her, stopping her with a hand on her wrist. He didn't know what came over him. He didn't care. He looked back at his father once.

She's the one I've been waiting for, his eyes seem to say.

The duke smiled at him and nodded, understanding. They'd heard of odder things.

"I'm afraid I may have hurt you," Josiah told the young woman. "Please allow me to spend the day with you and make certain you're well."

"Oh," said the older woman. "Handsome *and* thoughtful."

"Mother!"

The mother smiled at him as if she knew something he didn't. "He's a good one, Mercy."

"Mercy," he repeated her name, finding it rather beautiful to his ears. In fact, he found her more than just beautiful. It was as if his heart and soul knew her, had waited for her. She was perfect, without spot or blemish, but he was sure he would have felt mesmerized by her even if she were scarred and disfigured.

He spent the afternoon with her and her family and invited them to Ashmore Castle as soon as they could visit. Her mother accepted and left them alone for the next hour.

He was in the middle of telling her about his love for painting and how he would like to paint her, when they heard pigs squealing for all they were worth. Josiah knew what it meant. Old Samuel had slaughtered enough pigs outside his barn for Josiah to recognize the sound.

He looked at Mercy covering her ears beside him as if she couldn't bear the pitiful soul. No one ever looked more appealing to him. "Do you want to help me free them?"

"Yes!" she answered without hesitation.

"You might get dirty," he warned with a grin fashioned for trouble.

"I'll live if I do. They won't if I don't." She started off toward the sound, holding her skirts above her ankles, and leaving Josiah to smile after her.

He wondered if it was too soon to ask her to marry him.

The End

About the Author

Paula Quinn is a New York Times bestselling author and a sappy romantic moved by music, beautiful words, and the sight of a really nice pen. She lives in New York with her three beautiful children, six over-protective chihuahuas, and three adorable parrots. She loves to read romance and science fiction and has been writing since she was eleven. She's a faithful believer in God and thanks Him daily for all the blessings in her life. She loves all things medieval, but it is her love for Scotland that pulls at her heartstrings.

To date, four of her books have garnered Starred reviews from Publishers Weekly. She has been nominated as Historical Storyteller of the Year by RT Book Reviews, and all the books in her MacGregor and Children of the Mist series have received Top Picks from RT Book Reviews. Her work has also been honored as Amazons Best of the Year in Romance, and in 2008 she won the Gayle Wilson Award of Excellence for Historical Romance.

Website:
pa0854.wixsite.com/paulaquinn